# PULSE

# MLR PRESS AUTHORS

Featuring a roll call of some of the best writers of gay erotica and mysteries today!

| | |
|---|---|
| Maura Anderson | Wayne Gunn |
| Victor J. Banis | J. L. Langley |
| Laura Baumbach | Josh Lanyon |
| Sarah Black | William Maltese |
| Ally Blue | Gary Martine |
| J. P. Bowie | Jet Mykles |
| James Buchanan | Luisa Prieto |
| Dick D | Jardonn Smith |
| Jason Edding | Richard Stevenson |
| Angela Fiddler | Claire Thompson |
| Kimberly Gardner | |

*Check out titles, both available and forthcoming, at*
*www.mlrpress.com*

# PULSE

ANGELA FIDDLER

mlrpress

Copyright 2008 by Angela Fiddler

Published by
MLR Press, LLC
3052 Gaines Waterport Rd.
Albion, NY 14411

Cover Art by Deana C. Jamroz
Editing by Judith David
Printed in the United States of America.

ISBN# 978-1-934531-41-9

First Edition
2008

To see all our available titles and learn more about our authors, visit our website.
http://www.mlrpress.com

# CHAPTER ONE

The dream started out any number of ways, from a nightmare of a test not studied for to running through fields. The threat always remained the same. Something heavy wanted him, and Chris never needed to know what it was. He'd seen enough darkness in his life that he didn't have to name it.

Then, the rain came. Not real rain, cold and unforgiving, but dream rain. Chris felt it on his skin, but the wetness didn't chill him. A fog followed, and rather than being threatening, it enveloped him. Anticipation replaced breathless fear.

And, eventually, he came. The young man was naked, as always, except for the knife belt around his waist. The blade was almost the full length of his thigh, more of a machete than a knife, and the leg strap was down by his knee. There were things in this dream that clawed and bit, but the young man kept them away.

Chris had been having these dreams for over a year, and he'd seen the young man's body fill out. He had lost the last bit of coltish length to his arms and legs. He'd broadened considerably across the shoulders, and today he appeared without a single scar marring his perfect skin. Chris had seen such horrible scars crossing his chest and belly, marks so deep they didn't seem as though anyone would be able to survive them, and then the next night, a week or a month later, there'd be only a ghost of a scar.

His black hair was slicked down from the rain. His green eyes were bright, despite the apparent lack of sun. His lips were full – that had never changed – and when they kissed, those lips always felt bruised. Chris's cock stirred as the young man emerged from the mist, but he kept his arms by his side and didn't stare too long. There had been more times than not that he'd come this far and then something had spooked him. He'd withdraw as quickly as he appeared, leaving Chris with a raging hard-on and the feeling of rain on his skin.

In Phoenix.

They never spoke, either. Not that Chris could. He would open his mouth, ready to ask a million questions, but in the logic of this dream, in this place, no words would come. Or could come. That would ruin the whole thing. In the beginning, the young man played along, giving him a smile and pressing a finger against Chris's lips. The smile seemed forced somehow.

They circled around each other. That much was allowed. The knife should have been a threat to Chris. As a police officer, being unarmed in front of the young man with the huge knife strapped to his thigh, naked though he was, should have raised every bit of instinct for self-preservation Chris had, but it never did. When he was on his knees in front of the young man, his hands on the narrow hips as though he could pull him deeper down his throat, Chris would occasionally hook his fingers into the belt.

The young man would always, without flinching, remove Chris's hand, moving it up or down, and Chris would let it be. It was only a dream, even if he could taste the salty residue of semen on his lips for hours after he'd woken.

Tonight, this night, the young man was especially skittish. Chris knew he wouldn't stay. They circled around each other one more time. Chris held out his hands, beseeching. The young man glanced over his shoulder as though someone were speaking to him. A moment passed, then two, and the young man nodded, taking a step closer to Chris.

The young man's skin was the temperature of the rain. Again, in fuzzy dream logic, one moment Chris was wearing his uniform, the next he was naked as well, naked and on his back in the loam. It shouldn't have been comfortable. It should have been wet and cold and crawling with insects, but it was soft and dry, despite the rain. It seemed the most natural thing in the world, dream logic or not, to spread his legs, grip his knees, and let the young man push inside him.

There was no burn and no discomfort. The rain was still falling – now Chris felt it running over his shoulders as he was pushed back into the ground – but it fell silently. All he heard was his own breath, and a part of him realized that he was alone in his bed, and not flat on his back, that the hand gathering up his cock was his own. The constant pressure, exact and perfect on his prostate, was nothing more than a distant memory spliced into the dream.

The young man shifted, pulling Chris's hips to him. He grabbed Chris's thigh, leaning forward, and his arm came down beside Chris's cheek. The muscles were tight and sinewy, and Chris, for the first time, saw how callused his hands were. He'd used the knife for more than just show. Chris grabbed onto it, digging his nails in. The young man hissed – making the only sound Chris had ever heard from him.

Chris ran his hand down his own belly. His cock was so hard that at even the brush of his – dry! – fingers against his length couldn't stop his shudder. The young man pushed him, riding him hard. But as much as Chris felt their bodies moving together and, the sting against the back of his thighs as their wet skin slapped together, he could still feel the sheets wrap around his legs and tangle hopelessly, sweat the only slickness on his skin.

"No," he said. Actually forming the word woke him up. The young man's face was sad, even as the ghost of his weight over Chris's body followed him back to the sound of the ringing phone.

Ringing phone. The dry heat of the bedroom, the sounds from the street outside his window, and the soft whomp from the ceiling fan brought him the rest of the way out of his dream. Phone. He groped for it, bringing it to his ear even as his other hand was still desperately moving against the hot, sticky sheet over his cock. He stopped, shame-faced, and pushed the talk button.

"What?" he demanded.

There was a pause on the other line, and Chris immediately regretted his outburst. He rubbed his face. "Hello?" he asked, instead.

"Did we catch you at a bad time, lieutenant?"

Chris recognized Jamie's voice even through the static. It *was* a bad time – the only night off he'd had in three weeks. He was bone tired and his body suddenly reminded him of all the neglect he'd been forcing on it. But there was only one way to answer the question. "Of course not," he said. He was the officer on call during the night until the other lieutenant, Niles, returned from his sabbatical, and as much as Chris hated being woken up for wild goose chases most nights, it was nice not to have to hear Niles's thinly veiled dislike for Chris's particular tastes. "What is it?"

"The Owl's struck again, sir. Betty's Kitchen on Fourteenth."

Chris shook his head. "How many?" he asked. The Night Owl had been holding up late night diners for weeks, herding the staff and what few customers remained into the deep freeze or storage area and killing them all. Deserted restaurants kept the number of deaths down, but they hadn't a single shred of physical evidence against the guy. Cameras, panic buttons, it was as though he knew what was there, disabled it, and was out before the cups of coffee on the tables lost their warmth.

"None, sir."

"What?"

"No one died. Well, besides him."

Chris sat up in bed. "He's dead?"

"We assume it's him, yes, sir."

"What brought him down?" Chris asked. Sometimes it came down to that. An off-duty cop who was still packing, an irate owner with a sawed-off shotgun, it wasn't as though the Owl had tried to keep a low profile.

"One of the staff. He's here with us now."

Chris threw his blanket off. "Don't let him go. I'll be there as soon as I can."

"Of course, sir."

Getting dressed when he felt as though he were moving through mercury wasn't easy. He had to unbutton and rebutton his shirt twice to ensure that both ends met evenly, and even with the last bit of stone-cold coffee from the pot in his system, he was still groggy. Luckily the wind was cool, bordering on brisk, and the green lights ahead of him spanned as far as the eye could see. By the time he pulled into the small parking lot, full of emergency vehicles and a lone ambulance with its lights turned off, he felt human again.

The diner had originally been painted in pale yellows and pinks, but now was so grimy it looked more like darker and lighter patches of dirt. The neon light, announcing it was open twenty-four hours, gave off the same snapping sound as the average bug zapper. The bricks of the small walkway were broken and uneven, and the abandoned lots on both sides said that this had been a bad neighborhood for a very long time.

Stepping into the diner, Chris was surprised by the difference. Inside the diner, every surface was clean. The floor was polished and even, and the tables that hadn't been occupied were spotless. In the past few months, Chris had resigned himself to see the abandoned seats where the dead had sat, little bits of their life, a key ring here, a cell phone or a purse still waiting for its owner to come collect it. There were no remains here. The dishes had the familiar hardened food on them, the coffee cups were still cold, but the people who'd been sitting at the tables were wrapped the requisite gray blankets kept on hand by the paramedics. They sat at one of the empty, clean tables, the night's trauma making them all suddenly closer.

Chris looked toward the customers first. Four would-be victims. They'd been sitting apart, it looked like, one just in for coffee and a piece of pie, but the old man had the old woman's hand in his, and the young man had his arm over the younger woman's shoulder. Chris didn't doubt for a second they knew how lucky they were. All were studiously not looking at the draped body by the cash register. The white sheet was still white; it hadn't been a bloody death.

The cook stood with two officers by the rotating dessert display. That it was still on and still spinning was an affront, but Chris said nothing. The cook was a big guy, easily a head taller than either officer interviewing him, but he was muscular and thin. His white shirt was spotless, unlike any of the stereotypical cooks at a greasy spoon, and there was something about the muscles of his arm that made Chris think ex-con, except for the relaxed way he was talking to the officers. Still, if there was one person in the entire diner who could have taken out the Owl, Chris would have put his money on the big cook.

But Harrison, a cop Chris had worked with since coming to Arizona, looked up from thanking the cook for his time and shook his head. Not him. *Who then*, he wanted to ask, and Harrison glanced over his shoulder. Chris nodded and walked past the small group.

And stopped.

At first glance, he saw Jamie, his partner, the lone female officer at the scene, her hair plaited back in a thick French braid, her light coffee-colored skin bleached almost white by the florescent lights. Then his glance took in the figure beside her. He was seated and wearing loose T-shirt and jeans so it was impossible to see if his build resembled the young man in Chris's dream. But there was no mistaking the dark hair and eyelashes or the bruised look to those green eyes. "Lieutenant," Jamie said, and she stood.

Chris couldn't stop staring. The young man noticed the look and turned slowly on his stool. But when their eyes met, there wasn't a second of recognition in his guileless face.

Jamie stood up. "Lieutenant, this is Gregory. He stopped Richard Heath from committing this robbery."

Chris nodded. He had to lock his jaw so he didn't ask if Heath was stabbed. Despite the surreal aspect of the moment, he wasn't going to be accused of leading a witness. This Gregory did not have the calluses that were so familiar in the dream. His hands were smooth. Still, Chris could see the long knife in his hands as easily as he saw the watch on Gregory's wrist.

"What happened?" he asked instead.

Gregory glanced to Jamie. "Do I have to repeat it?"

"You're going to have to get used to it, Mr. Edwards."

For the first time Gregory's expression changed. It was barely noticeable and if Chris hadn't spent hours studying his face, he would have missed it. Chris had intended to repeat his question, but he knew that it would spook Gregory back into the mist. So Chris waited, patient as always, and let Gregory come to him.

"The man came into the diner," Gregory began, hesitantly. Chris tried to keep his face blank, but he couldn't stop the encouraging sound from the back of his throat. He shouldn't have done it. Pure panic flared in Gregory's eyes. "He tripped, hit his head on the counter, and fell."

Jamie's smile faded. "That's not what you told me," she began.

Gregory didn't look away from Chris's face. "I must have been mistaken," he said.

Chris didn't let himself react in any way now that the horse had left the barn. He wanted to let a long string of curses out; they hadn't sequestered the witnesses, and the only other eye witnesses had heard Gregory recant. Chris turned to the cook. "Is that what you saw?"

Nothing passed between the cook and Gregory. If anything, Gregory was staring out the window, but couldn't have seen anything but his own reflection staring back. "He fell," the cook said without hesitation. Gregory's shoulders relaxed.

"And them?" Chris demanded, motioning to the group at the single table.

"They were already in the freezer, sir," Jamie said quietly. That was the Owl's standard MO, but she didn't say that. They had nothing that said the man on the floor was the same perp as in the other crimes. Chris still felt something was off, and it wasn't just Gregory.

"Can you leave us alone?" Chris asked Jamie. Jamie nodded, touched Gregory on the shoulder over his gray blanket, and left them.

"Walk with me," Chris said. Gregory nodded and stood up. They walked far enough away that they were standing directly in front of the door. With their voices low, no one would hear them. Chris stared at him, expecting some sign that Gregory recognized him, too, but Gregory wouldn't look past his shoes.

"You look like a good kid," Chris began. The "kid" got him a frown, one that was achingly familiar. The young man in his dream would look at him like that at the beginning. He wanted to take Gregory by the shoulder and shake him, but he refrained himself. He continued. "If you are in trouble, or were in trouble, and it's a small thing, we can overlook that. We're more interested in the truth."

Gregory met his eyes for the first time, and the remembered dream all but slapped Chris across the face. He almost stumbled. "I'm not in any trouble," Gregory said, speaking in a whisper. "But you can't take me in."

"I beg to differ," Chris said. "We certainly can."

Gregory frowned again, obviously angry at being toyed with. *Problem with authority*, Chris decided. "The man you –" he stopped himself. "The man who died may have been responsible for previous attacks. We just want to make sure we have the right guy."

Gregory's face went blank. "You have the right guy," he said, and his voice sounded older than both of them. "Can I go now?" Gregory shrugged the blanket farther up his shoulders. "Officer?"

The word was only slightly ironic, as though Gregory knew Chris had spent the entire time they were together remembering what he looked like naked.

"He fell." Chris repeated.

"He fell," Gregory agreed, but he looked pained again. Chris wanted to touch him, to comfort him, but didn't dare.

"I'm going to ask you not to leave town, Gregory."

Gregory laughed, but barely made a sound. "You can ask."

Chris stepped between him and the diners behind them. "I don't think you realize how serious this is."

Gregory looked at him again. And without a word, Chris knew that Gregory had had a gun to his temple. He'd been on his knees, on the clean, tiled floor. He'd grabbed Heath's pant leg, yanking him off his feet, and the sound of his skull striking the counter had been surprisingly loud. And suddenly, Chris wanted to apologize for being so insensitive. "Come on."

Jamie was by the table. She was taking notes from the witnesses, diligently, but Chris knew from experience she wasn't enthused by what she was writing. "Are we done here?" he asked.

Jamie waited for the old woman to stop talking, and nodded. "I think we are."

Chris dutifully gave everyone one of his cards, in case they remembered anything more. "Thank you so much for your cooperation." Chris raised his voice so they all could hear. "And if you're willing, I'd like an officer to escort you all home."

He was looking at Gregory, expecting him to refuse the ride home. Instead, he went quietly to the car. Jamie stood by his side until the last of the black-and-whites pulled onto the street. "Coroner?" Chris asked.

"On his way." Chris nodded. They waited for the black wagon to pull up before moving to the body.

"What do you think happened here?" Jamie asked.

"You took the witness statements."

"None of them saw him approach. He was just in the middle of the diner. After that, it was all so quick. The cook was struck over the head first, and left on the floor. The rest –"

"All comes down to what Gregory saw. Before I showed up, what was he saying?"

"Not much," Jamie said. She opened her mouth again, but didn't speak. Chris waited. "He seemed very frightened."

"But…" he prompted. There was a very big *but* in her voice.

She hesitated. The coroner's wagon was pulling up. "He didn't seem to me to wonder, even once, why him. He looked like he knew why he was being targeted."

"Run him."

"Of course, sir."

Chris knelt down beside the body and flipped back the sheet.

The most noticeable thing about Heath was the fact he was dead. It was the only thing that differentiated him from anyone else on the morning commute. His clothes were average, brown suit, brown tie, brown shoes with scuffs polished over, the bald spot on the back of his head just beginning to be combed over. On his face was a beatific smile.

"You don't see that every day," Jamie said.

"What do we know?" Chris asked.

"He's a former security guard."

"Last known place of work?"

"Brantley Jones Ministry. They let him go almost two months ago."

"Right when the killings began."

"Yes, sir," Jamie said. "Near perfectly."

Chris signed off the necessary paperwork and was back in his bed an hour before his alarm was to go off. Tomorrow would be a busy day.

# CHAPTER TWO

The two officers in the front seat were tired. Gregory felt it pouring off them like the cold air from an open fridge. It pooled around him at his feet where he sat in the backseat.

It was thick in the air. They'd both pulled double shifts, and the call had come in at the end of their second shift. They'd found the Owl. He felt their remembered excitement. One more beast off the street. One more sicko.

But that sicko had been his friend. They had had breakfast together a thousand times, and had hung out with each other when the big man himself was on camera. He'd only had two people in the world who were there for him, and Brantley had taken them both. Richard tonight and…David. Brantley had split David in two, taking his soul from the body. *Ghost* was the wrong word for what remained. It could just be that Gregory only imagined he saw his spirit, but that was enough.

Gregory shook his head. And then there was the dream. But he hadn't known the man was a cop. A filthy, whore-dog cop. It made Gregory feel dirty that he'd let Officer Cunningham inside him. It was just a dream, he knew that, but he'd needed the protection. It wasn't right. He'd felt so safe with him.

"It probably wasn't him," Gregory said. One of the officers stirred when he spoke, but neither of them turned. "They just looked alike. That was all."

"Settle down back there."

Gregory didn't want to settle down. They didn't actually rattle the cage between them with one of their nightsticks, but Gregory could tell that was the other part of the threat. He sat back deep into the seat, and touched his lips, remembering how they'd felt when he'd been kissed. He was a cop, that wasn't something Gregory could change. "I loved him."

The officers didn't respond. Gregory continued. "My master splits people in half, their bodies from their souls, and their bodies keep living."

Still nothing. Gregory wouldn't have been able to say the words in front of them if they weren't under Brantley's control. "He's a bastard," Gregory continued. "The extra energy he uses to suck people into following him."

"Settle," one of the cops hissed, sounding like something reptilian.

Life was full of disappointment. When Richard came into the diner, Gregory had actually smiled. He'd been so glad to see Richard's familiar face. Even better, Richard's face wasn't see-through, like what remained of David.

Only it hadn't been smiling. It hadn't been Richard at all, Gregory quickly realized, but something else that wore Richard's face. It took Gregory an extra second to see Brantley's cold blue eyes. By then, Richard had taken out his gun.

And then, time seemed to slow down. And not just slow down, but detach from him. He observed with no more involvement than if he'd been watching a rerun of a show he didn't like on a wall of televisions at a department store. It showed him in perfect clarity the fear and dread on the diners' faces as they were herded into the freezer. Mike, the cook, exploding with blood as the gun's grip smashed his lips into his teeth. The way Mike crumbled when the return blow tried to crack open his skull.

Gregory saw it all, down to the soft hair on the back of Mike's arms rising up from the adrenaline in his system. He smelled the blood. It paralyzed him. Worse, Brantley knew that he wouldn't fight.

"Why are you doing this?" Gregory had asked. He couldn't make himself understand. Brantley had learned how to split people, but to use the body as a puppet…he didn't want to think about how much stronger that made him.

Richard's lips pulled back in a snarl, but it was Brantley inside him. He held Gregory in place with one finger. It rooted him to the ground. "Down," Brantley said in a strange, rusted voice.

Gregory felt like his legs had been kicked out from under him. He hit hard, the pain from his knees absolute for an instant. Richard's face smiled. Richard, who stepped around ants and didn't like any kind of suffering, enjoyed his pain.

Gregory looked away.

Brantley stepped past him. He wore loose-fitting trousers. Boot cut, Gregory saw, because that was the only thing in his line of sight. He didn't want to go back. Nothing in life was ever fair. Gregory had learned that early enough in his life, but at least he should have had the right to fight against it.

He lifted his hand, carefully, though it was like trying to move through an icy current of water. He reached up as Brantley passed him, about to press the muzzle of the gun in his hand against his temple, but Gregory had grabbed hold of the dirt brown material of Brantley's pants-leg.

For a heartbeat, it was too little, too late, and then Brantley was brought up short. He lost his balance, and Gregory pulled as hard as he could.

Brantley fell into the counter, the sound of his fall a crack like something going supersonic.

Whether it was enough to kill a man was immaterial. Richard's body fell down dead. His body hugged the cracked red stool as though it were a life preserver, and then slid bonelessly to the ground.

Richard had been dead awhile, but his body twitched once and was still.

Gregory shuddered at the memory. The back of the police car had seemed safe in comparison to the rest of his evening, but the officers missed the turn into Gregory's neighborhood.

Suddenly Gregory became very aware of the radio. It was faint, but Gregory would have recognized it anywhere. Brantley recorded his day show for late night broadcast. It was too quiet for Gregory to hear the words, but that didn't matter. The sound itself was lulling him to sleep, to give in and just let the officers take him wherever.

*"What are you doing?"*

Gregory opened his eyes, unaware even that he had closed them. Less than a minute had passed by the clock on the dashboard, but his entire body felt as though he'd been woken from a deep, full sleep. He was exhausted.

"What," he mumbled. The orange display lights made the officer behind the wheel look evil. Gregory shivered.

David sat across from him. He wore the same light blue shirt Gregory had last seen him in. Through the years it had gradually adjusted its shade to match the paler blue of David's eyes. Gregory hadn't seen David in months, and the amount of energy it took for him to appear made the air in the car crackle. David had been the first person Brantley had separated body from soul, and he'd been fading ever since.

Gregory rubbed his eyes. "Let me sleep," he said. But David shook him. He didn't actually feel the touch, but when they had been Brantley's boy toys together he'd been shaken enough times that he had the muscle memory of the gesture.

"You don't want me to let you go back to sleep, and we both know that. He turned Richard into one like me; do you think he will ever trust you enough to welcome you back into his fold with open arms?"

Gregory shook his head. "Richard is dead," he said.

David was quiet for a moment. He even gave up the illusion of breathing, something he did solely for Gregory's benefit. Gregory found it disconcerting that David's chest did not rise or fall. Everything David had done since they met was designed to make Gregory more comfortable.

He had loved David like a brother, but that had meant nothing to Brantley when it came time to try his new power from the dark room in which he prayed. David's living, breathing corpse had been released back into the wild like a house cat that had lost its owner's favor.

Gregory sighed. His eyes were so heavy that he could barely keep them open. He lifted his feet up and kicked the metal divide with both feet.

The first effort was sadly lacking. But it was shocking enough that the officer in the passenger seat turned off the radio. And that was all Gregory needed. He rattled the cage again, harder this time, and that shook both men from their stupor.

"You missed the turn," Gregory said, keeping his voice calm. "Maybe you should turn around."

"Bloody hell," the older of the two said. He was obviously annoyed at Gregory. He glared at him through the mirror. "You could have just said something."

Gregory lowered his eyes.

"I'm sorry. But you did miss the turn. Look. I'm really tired. Can you just drop me off here? Please?"

The cops glanced at each other. They were still exhausted. Gregory felt that in both of them. Perhaps if they hadn't just been...

Gregory didn't even know what to call it. Seduced? No, that was the wrong word. Hypnotized, maybe, but he hadn't known it was possible just through the radio's voice.

Regardless, the car rolled to a stop in front of a small park just beside an interstate exchange.

Gregory got out, the heat of the evening a shock to the system after the air-conditioned car. He could feel David's silent presence beside him, and Gregory willed the men to go. One of them looked to be coming back to his senses, but by then the car was already in motion.

The patrol car drove away silently and took the only source of light with it. Gregory waited for it to be completely gone. He was being watched from behind. He turned, and only then did he hear the sound of the swing behind him rocking back and forth. There was no wind.

Richard sat on the swing. Rather than actually swinging, he was dragging his feet. He looked sad – broken, actually – and it was Gregory who had broken him.

Gregory sat down on the other seat. He swallowed and cleared his throat. "I'm sorry."

Richard said nothing. Gregory could see through Richard's gray hands to the blackened chain of the swing.

However Brantley had separated Richard from his body, it was different from the way he'd separated David. Gregory knew Brantley had...fed from Richard. Not only fed from him, but somehow had controlled him after his death. If Gregory lived to be a hundred, he would never forget the way Richard's corpse had looked at him.

They swung together for a minute, then two. Gregory didn't want to speak. Richard had no voice. His eyes were unfocused and full of horror, and Gregory knew that, unlike David, Richard had been aware of what his body was doing. Every waking moment, he'd known. Gregory wanted to take Richard's hands, tell him that at least it was over now and...to go on,

Gregory supposed, but the unspoken words were ashes in his mouth.

"He knows how you feel," David said over his shoulder. "You shouldn't be out here."

"I can't leave him here," Gregory protested.

"You can and will. He's not here anymore. You have to let him go."

"How am I going to do that?" Gregory demanded. He couldn't rid himself of the salty taste of tears in the back of his throat. He was tired, and still more than a little scared, and wanted everything to go back to the way it was before.

"Of course you do," David said. "But even if you don't know it, you're getting stronger. Let him go, and he'll go."

Gregory looked up, but David was almost gone. He couldn't appear for long, and this had been the longest he'd stayed with Gregory in one appearance.

David was right, of course. The darkness brought with it the sound of little claws and teeth chittering. He didn't see them on this side unless he caught a glimpse from the corner of his eye, but he felt them crawling out of the dream world to find him. He'd killed many of them in the dream world, but with so many doors open, like Richard, like David, it was hard to keep them away. Once the dream world had been as safe as playing in a sandbox on a warm July evening, but lately there'd been more and more...things. When he was with...Officer Cunningham – when they were together – nothing could possibly find them.

A line of red appeared on his wrist, and only then came pain. Something with furry wings swept past him, and it laughed like a hyena at the smell of his blood. Gregory shook his head, but Richard was already mostly gone. When Gregory reached the street, he turned, and Richard was gone, though the swing kept swinging in the still air. Gregory ran the rest of the way to his house and spent the remainder of the night in the cellar. The dirt floor protected him more than the walls could.

Gregory woke before the sun was all the way up. Brantley had dominion during the day, but in the morning he was not quite strong enough to take complete control. It was the main reason he moved his show to later in the day despite the better ratings first thing. All that adulation gave him more power than he'd ever known, and Gregory had been the one who had opened that door for him. It made Gregory sick just to think about it, so he didn't. He went upstairs and showered off the dirt.

David waited for him at the kitchen table. The body of David, that was. It ate and drank and slept, soulessly. David's ghost had been on his best behavior last night. A lot of the time he was bitter and sarcastic and furious over what Brantley had done to him. And it wasn't that Gregory blamed him. If he thought about it too long he wandered into that same trap.

But, worse, if David *was* a soul, Gregory was terribly disappointed by how miserable it would be to be dead.

Still, he forced himself to smile. "I didn't hear you come in last night."

He locked the door, of course he did, but David had his ways. He looked up at Gregory and smiled broadly. His blue eyes were flawless and open, his hair trimmed back to the best of Gregory's abilities. He was still beautiful, but beautiful in the way an empty vase was – lacking something. David wasn't missing something; he was missing everything.

"You probably want breakfast." Gregory kept his voice light. He went to the cupboard and brought down a bowl. He wasn't hungry, but he had boxes of high-sugar cereal he kept for David. It was the only thing David really liked to eat, and Gregory didn't feel like entering into a battle to get him to eat something a little healthier.

David grinned like a child and held out his hands expectantly. Gregory poured the milk and gave it to him but left the carton on the counter for his coffee.

It had taken Gregory weeks to find David. It had been a foolish quest, but one that he was sure of. He thought that when he found David – never *if* – *when* he found David, that was all he had to do. Find him, look him in the eye, and he would have his David back.

It hadn't happened that way. He'd found David in a bus station, like David had found him, but nothing had brought his David back.

Gregory had been seventeen. Just turned, if he remembered correctly. That was, what…five years ago? It seemed like forever. He'd still had his ugly bruises from…from…the accident, and those, if nothing else, had kept him safe from most of the predators on the street. And when he met David, it seemed like he'd known him for ever, though they barely had time for a coffee.

David had given Gregory his number. Then that night, Gregory was picked up for soliciting.

He hadn't been. It had all had been a huge misunderstanding. He hadn't been surprised that the man who threw him against the bathroom wall and demanded that Gregory suck him off was a cop. The very last thing Gregory had wanted to do when his jaw still ached from meeting the steering wheel so rudely the week before was suck a stranger off in some public washroom. So he'd said no. And that was when his real troubles began. It was a blur. He tasted blood in his mouth, but didn't know if it was because he had been struck or slammed against the filthy mirror of the public washroom. He had the distant memory of both.

Blood dripped down his shirt. He wanted to wipe his mouth, but his hands were cuffed behind his back. The cop was behind him, guiding him by his hips to the cop car. *Nothing here to see. Just another dirt bag.* It was clear that the cop had no intention of taking him to the station.

Another officer passed them. He was talking to his female partner, and he didn't really look at him. Not at first. Still, Gregory shook his head, not actually expecting help. But the cop stopped and looked at him for real, and saw the obvious stress. "You taking this one in?" he asked.

The hand on Gregory's hip tightened. "Solicitation and resisting, sir."

The word had no respect in it, but the officer ignored the insult. "Let me take him in. You must be tired from your shift."

"I can't let you do that for me, lieutenant."

Gregory studied the memory. The officer – the lieutenant – was the same officer who had interrogated him at the diner. The same man as in his dreams.

David smiled at him, the empty bowl licked clean. "It was him," Gregory said. "But why now?"

# CHAPTER THREE

Brantley disliked tents. That was an understatement. He despised everything about tents. He hated the canvas smell of them, the heavy feeling of the air in them and the way the sweat stuck to his forehead. He'd spent his childhood in tents, in the front row of cheap folding chairs that hurt the small of his back, and he hated them.

Still, it was what the rubes expected, with their round faces and their polyester. Looking down on them from the pulpit made his stomach turn most times, but he was their own private miracle baby, rescued from a terrible accident when he'd fallen into a cave. The accident had been about the best thing that had ever happened to him. Though that wasn't exactly right. He certainly hadn't been a baby, but a full teenager, and he hadn't even fallen alone. The fall hadn't even been all that horrible; he'd broken his leg, but he hadn't been in the hole for more than an hour. And, of course, it hadn't exactly been an accident.

He forced himself not to think about what else had been in the dark, so instead he stared at the side of the tent. He doubted any of the rubes realized that each of the tents that they sat in for the summer tour cost as much as any one of his cars. The reflective yet breathable skin kept the sun's heat out. Two semis parked outside the tent pumped in fresh, climate-controlled air and kept the public cool and the human smell down. They also mixed in wonderful, calming pheromones Brantley had had spent many years perfecting.

And oh, had Brantley perfected them.

His driver opened the door for him, and he slid inside the car's cool, dry interior. Even the twenty yards from the tent to the car left him uncomfortably hot.

Billy waited for him, settled on the seat like a parrot on his perch. Beautiful, stupid Billy. So eager to please once Gregory had buggered off. Such impossible shoes to fill and Brantley felt a ripple of anger disturb his otherwise vaguely amused day. He lashed out only because he could.

"Drink," he snarled.

Billy leapt at it like he'd been electrocuted. Crystal glass, polished until it shone. Two perfect ice cubes, not a crack in sight, and three fingers of Lagavulin, from his special whisky stock, swirled three times around the glass, never getting higher than half way up. Billy did it all flawlessly.

Thus saving himself from a tongue lashing, and perhaps worse, later.

Sinfully, Bentley's cock thickened at the thought of Billy naked, sprawled – tied – to his bed. Billy's body stretched out so that each muscle group was distinct against his skin and his dirty blond hair finally dark enough for Brantley's tastes. He'd start by sucking on Billy's toes and working his way up. Unlike Gregory, who fought him tooth and nail before accepting his punishment, Billy seemed to crave the attention, positive and negative.

Rather than finding it appealing, Brantley only wanted to punish him more for it.

Without being told – and Brantley would never say the words – Billy dropped to his knees, and unbuttoned Brantley's cool, crisp slacks. His mouth was as hot and as moist as the old-fashioned tents, but for once it was welcoming.

*Sins of the flesh*, Brantley thought, closing his eyes. That thought aroused him almost more than Billy's ministrations did. His very special horse-hair flogger waited for him in his dark room. It helped to imagine the sound of the horse hair sailing through the air. The slow burn of its impact worked deeper and deeper into his muscles until every stroke was like touching a live wire to his skin.

He grabbed the back of Billy's head and, forcing him all the way down his length, kept him there even as Billy struggled for breath. The orgasm, so wrong, so filthy, wanted to break free and the sudden desire to slap Billy's face for just taking it was almost overwhelming.

And Billy always did take it, but it wasn't enough. It was almost never enough anymore. Brantley pushed Billy away in disgust and zipped his pants back up. Billy wiped his mouth off, and sat back across from him.

Brantley finished the scotch and opened the intercom. "Stop by the studio. I believe I left something there," he said, He switched off the intercom again before his driver had time to acknowledge his request. There was no question it would be done. People just did what Brantley wanted them to. Gregory had shown him that, and even without Gregory at his side he still had the ability to pull.

Billy said nothing for the rest of the drive but got out of the car and preceded Brantley into the television studio without being told to. The lobby, full of signed photographs of the man and former guests on the show, was outdated. He wanted to redo the wall treatments, to pull out the linoleum and replace it with something that would not show the wear and tear the beige tiles did, but his focus groups told him that the slight disrepair was good for the television audience to see before being asked to donate in the pretty blue envelopes Brantley kept behind the chairs.

He kept three security guards at the studio at all times, but without being told Billy found them all and shooed them away. His ministry kept three coffee shops in business so there was always some place for them to go. Billy locked the door behind the last man and joined Brantley on the stage.

Brantley's hard-on hadn't subsided, and Billy knew exactly what to do. He walked over to the desk – the desk from which Brantley had spent so much time preaching about family values and moral decay – and dropped his pants. He didn't step out of them; when they were out in the open he knew Brantley didn't like him completely naked. But he spread his legs as wide as he could.

Brantley flicked the switch, and light flooded the room. Warm, yellow light he'd spent a fortune on so that it made even his homeliest guest look beautiful and trustworthy. It made Billy, bent over his desk like a whore, look welcoming. Like it was good and proper that they should rut here, of all places.

And Billy let himself be taken, all but crawling across the desk to make it better for Brantley. As was his place. As was Brantley's right.

□ □ □ □ □

The compound was huge, all hidden behind the ten feet high fence around the property. Behind it was a full forest of dry sage and prickly bushes. The main house was half built into one of the dunes, and the private church and small building they used as the token admin site were a dozen or so paces away. The call center, the huge administration wing, and the private vaults were all underground. Even his house had a private floor, accessible only through the pantry. It was his own personal sanctuary.

Billy jumped out of the car first and held the door open for him. Brantley nodded. "Wait for me downstairs."

Billy's smile faded. "Downstairs, sir?"

"Do you have a problem with that?"

Billy fought to keep a smile on his face. He hated the old bomb shelter. But it was the only place safe enough for what Brantley wanted. Billy would wait, like a good boy, and Brantley would take his time joining him, as punishment. As the start of his punishment.

Brantley forced himself to go to the administration wing first. The artificial lights mimicked sunlight almost perfectly, which made the oppressive stone walls and beige carpets seem less harsh. Anything out of the public eye was not a priority to him at all.

"Oh, Brantley," Donna, his PA, said, coming around the desk. "You didn't hear the news." She was middle-aged, and her soft features were a brilliant cover for her ruthless mind. She'd been his father's secretary when they worked in the back of a trailer that broiled in the summer and froze in the winter, and he doubted he would have built half as much as he had without her. She was also one of the very few people who he didn't mind using his first name, although that was standard on the grounds. It grated on his teeth, but it made a show of equality between him and the peons.

"What is it?" he asked. He hid the stab of annoyance. He'd only come to the administration side to punish Billy. Any actual distraction was neither welcome nor wanted.

She took his hand. "It's Richard, sir. He's dead."

"Richard?" Brantley said, playing it cool. He'd sent Richard Heath out himself to find Gregory, but Richard Heath had failed. Still, as far as staff knew, he'd been nothing but a failed security guard, let go for incompetence, just one of a thousand men and women who constantly rotated in and out of the ministry.

"Our security guard," Donna said. She touched a strand of her salt-and-pepper hair. "He'd only been gone, what was it, three months. I can't believe he'd fallen so far, so quickly."

Brantley took her hand. "I'll pray for him," he said earnestly. "But for now, I'll be in my room. No disturbances, please."

"Of course."

Brantley wasn't stupid. He knew Donna knew what he was doing in his private rooms with Billy, and with Gregory before and with David before that. She cleaned the rooms afterward, mopping up whatever blood had spilled, among other fluids.

And she never asked questions. He paid her more money than the ministry used to see in a year in the beginning. She was his fiercest guard dog, and there was no price he could put on that.

The air conditioning was strongest in the underground rooms that Brantley had staked out for himself. As he stepped down the stairs one by one, letting the anticipation grow, he felt the temperature drop for every step he descended.

This had been the bunker. The rest of the house, specifically his "real" rooms upstairs, were opulent and comfortable from the plush carpet thick enough to dig his toes into to the imported marble in the en suite bathroom. The walls were specifically designed to keep the rooms as cool as possible, and the curved banister going up to the second and third floors had been imported from Italy. Every room was done to the nines in comfort and style.

Brantley put his hand on the cement wall, feeling the dampness that always seemed to permeate the surface. Billy was waiting for him, in the innermost chamber, and he was afraid.

Brantley smiled. *Good.* Billy should be afraid. Stalking his way past the rooms that still held outdated cans of food and murky bottles of water, he could taste the fear. He could see it, carried to him on the cold currents, and it colored the air in stark and naked shades of red and orange. The alarm was obvious to him.

It was an invitation to any predator in the area to put the prey animal out of its misery.

He hadn't been able to taste the fear before, not before Gregory, at least. What Gregory had given him was a greater gift than Gregory would ever know. Brantley had been strong before, able to push his own desires on others, but he'd never been able to completely suppress their will. The longer he was without Gregory, the weaker he was becoming.

Brantley pushed open the bunker door. Despite its years, it didn't offer a whisper of protest. Billy didn't move from the bed, but his shoulders relaxed. The waiting was over, and Brantley supposed that, at least, was a relief.

It hadn't taken long to train Billy to crave the attention; it never did. Donna was so much better than he was at finding those young men who would take willingly what Brantley gave.

Although, he did learn his lesson through poor David, the first young man he'd taken. Brantley had stripped him of his fear, of his pain, of his sense of self-preservation. It had left him completely open, turning every emotion Brantley could pour into him into straight pleasure, leaving him completely useless.

Brantley hadn't killed him. It wasn't an act of compassion so much as cowardice. He'd released David back onto the street where he'd found him. Brantley supposed it had been his fault. He'd told Gregory what had happened to his predecessor. Because when Gregory had pulled the rabbit out of his hat, going so completely catatonic that he'd even fooled Brantley's doctor into thinking he was no longer there, Brantley had believed him.

He let Gregory go. And why the hell not? It had worked once before. He had felt Gregory coming back to himself like blood rushing into a limb long since gone asleep. And after that, he'd felt nothing.

Until last night, when Heath had been so close. He'd been in the same room. Gregory had touched his ankle.

And then, nothing. Again. Brantley supposed he was fortunate not to have felt the counter striking his temple, though that was little comfort.

Billy had stopped trembling on the bed. And that wasn't good. Brantley needed the one he chose to be more aware of him than anyone on the planet. He crossed the few feet between him and the king-size bed and locked his fingers into Billy's hair. He yanked back Billy's head, and smiled. The only reaction Billy gave was to relax into the pain, though it still obviously hurt him.

"I told you to wait for me," Brantley snarled. He kept Billy at that impossible angle for a second longer, then released him and obviously wiped his hand on his shirt. "Did I tell you you could nap?"

"No, sir," Billy said. In truth, Brantley really hadn't said anything. But that wasn't the point.

"Knees," Brantley snapped.

Billy raced to obey, and in that instant, Brantley knew why he despised Billy so much. It wasn't that he craved the abuse; with enough time even proud Gregory had taken it. It was that Billy thought he deserved it.

But, he was beautiful on his knees. He was naked – he'd never enter Brantley's chamber any other way – and his hands ran up and down his inner thigh as though they were a substitute for Brantley's cock. His mouth was open, his tongue already covering his bottom teeth like a good whore. He leaned into Brantley's space, yearning for it.

And that was exactly what Brantley wanted. He unzipped his slacks and grabbed the back of Billy's head. He wasn't quite ready, and Billy wasn't going to push it. He remained on his knees, mouth open, and Brantley entertained himself by running the tip of his cock over Billy's lips.

"Tell me you want this," Brantley said.

Billy was beyond words, but Brantley wouldn't be where he was if he needed to hear the words. He felt them, inside Billy's skull.

Billy moved his hands to Brantley's thighs. That was allowed. So was lifting himself up so that he could cup Brantley's testicles. Still, he kept his mouth open and let Brantley roll his cock over his face.

Anticipation filled Brantley. This is what he'd been waiting for. His hold on Heath had grown progressively weaker. He needed Billy tonight more than any other time. Gregory would have taken the static in his brain. Just being this close to him would start to put everything right.

Billy pulled away and wiped his mouth, and rocked back on his heels. "I'm not him."

"What did you say to me?" Brantley demanded.

Billy wouldn't look at him. "I'm not Gregory."

Brantley stared down at him, the fury at being addressed – being questioned – by Billy, of all people, almost more insult than he could stand. He didn't know if he should punch Billy first or kick him.

But then Billy ran his hand up and down Brantley's thighs.

His anger at Billy for talking to him was entirely out of proportion, but knowing that didn't help control the fury. The desire to backhand Billy across the face, to knock him onto the bed and fuck him with his legs spread, was almost too much to bear. And it was entirely Billy's fault.

Billy smiled, and pushed back. He slid onto the bed on his back, and spread his legs like Brantley wanted, as lewdly as a whore. "Come on," he whispered. He must've lubed himself up, because he could push one finger easily inside himself. Brantley couldn't look away. "I'm not Gregory," Billy repeated. "But I could be better. If you let me."

Brantley got onto the bed and grabbed Billy's legs. Billy gripped his own cock, his knuckles white from the pressure, but he was smiling. "Use me, Brantley. Stick your dick into me. You want to make me your bitch, don't you? You want to make me yours."

Billy's voice sounded different. Darker. Brantley was pulled to it. His dick was so hard. Sliding into Billy was unlike any other fuck he'd ever had. It seemed for a second that there was no resistance whatsoever. For an incredibly long moment, the image in Brantley's head was of sliding into something organically rotten, like fruit.

Billy smiled at him, licking his impossibly sharp teeth.

Brantley shook his head and the tight ring of muscle around his cock was suddenly very obvious. Billy's eyes were closed although Brantley swore he still felt his gaze on him. "Please, sir," Billy whispered taking a better grip on his thighs to hold himself open. "Fuck me."

Brantley reached down and grabbed Billy's throat. He didn't squeeze, or at least not as much as he wanted to. Billy arched his back off the bed and offered himself.

Brantley came right there. Waves and waves of intense pleasure surged over him. As cliché as that sounded, there was no other way to describe the electric shocks his body felt. In that moment, between the building of the orgasm and the self-hatred that would inevitably follow, Brantley wished he could lose himself. He never could, and he came back to himself revolted. Billy had jerked himself off in the meantime, and the smell of his semen joined Brantley's. Just for a heartbeat, rapid and trembling in the back of Brantley's throat, he smelled the rot again.

Billy collapsed bonelessly onto the bed. "You can go," Brantley gasped, as though it had been his own throat he'd held. Billy turned on his side. The room was cold, and felt colder with a thin sheen of sweat over his skin. Billy just rolled over, naked on top the blankets. He went to sleep, not a single goose bump marring his perfect skin.

Brantley stumbled away into the private room he had built off the bedroom. With the door closed behind him, the room was absolutely dark, and the only sound was that of running water. He knelt in the dirt, finding his flogger by touch. The first blow on his bare skin stole his breath. The second, across already reddening skin, burned. The third and fourth, far too close together, would have narrowed his vision if he wasn't already in pitch black. After that, he swung the whip with the precision of a robot.

By the time he pushed the door open again, he felt clean. Purified. He could watch Billy sleep once again feeling just repulsion. The sheets looked as though he'd used them to hogtie a pig that had since escaped, but Billy's blond hair was unruffled and perfect. It wasn't right. Even though they spent the evening fucking, he no longer wanted to thrust Billy down on his knees and grab on tight to his pretty hair.

Brantley felt his lips curl into a snarl. He'd spent his life disciplining every muscle on his face for complete and utter control; it felt good to show his displeasure. He must be getting stronger. Billy whimpered and curled up away from him as though he could sense Brantley's displeasure. And then the phone rang, something that was never supposed to happen. It didn't wake Billy, and Brantley took his time to answer it.

Of course it was Donna. She spoke in a hushed, rushed voice. He turned on the closed-circuit cameras in the office. She wasn't alone. Two officers stood behind her. The woman, blonde, was a foot shorter than the man, making even Donna look tall. But Brantley was more interested in the man. He wasn't pretty, not like Gregory. Not even like poor stupid Billy, who was so far into his nightmare he twitched like a dreaming puppy. The man's nose had been broken at some point and was slightly crooked, not unattractively so, and his eyes were some light shade. It was noticeable even on the grainy gray camera. Green, Brantley guessed. Or blue. Not that it mattered. Brantley wanted him.

Donna lowered her voice to a bare whisper. "They want to see you about Richard."

Richard. The very name was a stab to his guts and he felt the poisonous hatred spilling out of him. He hated the power that anything even remotely related to Gregory still had over him. "Tell them I'll be right up."

The officer looked familiar. Some days it seemed as though he shook a thousand hands before breakfast, but he was sure the officer was important. He touched his nose, felt the bump from when it was broken, and realized with a start that the cop was the boy he'd fallen down the hole with. Call it morbid curiosity, but Brantley had been covertly following his career for a number of years.

"If this isn't fortuitous, I don't know what is," Brantley said. The timing couldn't have been better. Billy wasn't what he needed, and the strength of someone who had been down there, who'd seen the shadows moving like he had…

"What's fortuitous?" Billy asked. He sounded sleepy, and whether Billy was asking about the situation or what the word itself meant, Brantley didn't care.

"Fetch me water from the spring," Brantley said. "And bring it up as soon as you do."

Billy got out of bed, but remained by the edge of it. "Yes, sir."

"Good."

# Chapter Four

The fan on the reception desk did very little to cool the room. Despite its industrial-size blades, it only created rivers of hot air flowing sluggishly over smaller currents of slower moving air. The woman behind the desk had every aspect of a mild church lady, even down to the proper pink shade of her cardigan. Her hair was pulled back, natural curl tamed by the tightness of her bun. Her eyeglasses had rhinestones, which didn't make up for the chill in her eyes. She still smiled at them, as warm as anything, but Chris felt cold looking at her.

It was almost as good as air conditioning.

"He'll be right with you," she said and replaced the handset. Chris smiled back at her, and knew she knew his smile was as disingenuous as her own.

When Brantley Jones arrived, he did so with a swirl of energy. He shook both their hands, firmly clasped between his and pumped up and down. His smile was genuine, or at least looked close enough that Chris couldn't tell the difference. He was not unattractive, and his cheeks and chin were both strong. He gave off waves of trust. And Chris *wanted* to distrust him. Despite his instincts, he honestly found himself liking the man. "You're here about Richard Heath," Brantley said sadly.

"You heard," Chris said.

"Of course. Richard was a dear friend. It was a tragedy compounding the tragedy." When Brantley spoke, his voice was soft – heartbreakingly so – but when he looked up, his eyes were calculating. A young, blond man came into the room carrying a tray of water, and the crystal glasses were far too pretty to be used simply for water. "It's a hot day. Would you like something to drink?"

Jamie refused. Chris took one, just to be polite. Brantley smiled the moment he did, but it wasn't a very nice smile. He looked down to the water. The glass was cold in his hand, and the water sparkled. "From our own private oasis, right here on the property. Makes the surrounding area a bit dangerous, sinkholes and all, but it's worth it for the purity."

His words were carefully calculated. Chris stared and then remembered.

Brantley's face had gotten heavier; it was equally obvious that he worked out religiously and still loved rich food. But his eyes were the same. Just looking at them reminded Chris of the metallic taste of terror in the back of his throat.

Chris had been thirteen, butting on fourteen, and it had been the last summer he'd known that seemed endless. His parents had shipped him off to his grandmother's house before their last major fight, and Chris had loved the calm, away from the screaming and the breaking of plates.

His grandmother lived just on the outskirts of the city, and hers was the last house that had pavement. She thrived on order, and always had lunch on the table at noon on the dot, and every day she went to visit her husband in the hospital. Chris went with her every second day and he was secretly glad that that day had been an off day. He barely remembered his grandfather being healthy, and the way his grandmother was around his grandfather, feeding him like a child and wiping off his chin, made Chris uncomfortable in ways he didn't completely understand yet.

There'd been some debate as to whether he should come again; there had been an altercation at the closest convenience store, and Chris had come home with a scuffed knee. He hadn't started it, but a few of the local boys had taken a dislike to his east coast accent and how fast he spoke.

But he'd begged, and she'd gone off without him. He hung around the backyard of the house for a while, but the old swing didn't hold his attention for very long, and Gran had just bought him a new bike. For the sake of avoiding trouble and further upsetting his Gran, he headed away from the store and farther down the dirt road.

The bike had been too big for him at the start of the summer, but now fit him like a glove. It was hot, far hotter than New York was, but without the steam and the smell of people it didn't feel quite so oppressive. He didn't know the word back then, but he understood what it meant. While most adults would have collapsed from heat exhaustion, he felt as though the heat charged him.

He pedaled down the gravel road, a lazy pace for a lazy day. Only when he was right beside the crickets hiding away in the long grass beside the road did they stop singing, and their song had been deafening in the otherwise quiet afternoon.

He didn't hear the group of boys behind him until he saw the rock as big as his fist skitter past him on the wheel track he was following. He hit the brakes, the bike sliding sideways a foot, and he supposed that was his second mistake. He wasn't supposed to leave the pavement; sinkholes had been a major issue all summer.

The gang of young men biking toward him were the same ones from the convenience store. They were still dressed in their Sunday best, even though it was Tuesday, and their bikes gleamed as much as their hair did. They looked like they all belonged in the shows that Gran's old TV picked up from his parents' generation, not from the '80s at all.

A sick feeling, like being punched in the gut, spread over Chris's belly, even without them saying a word. They were all older than he was and were in the last spurt of their teenage years. There was a mean, hungry look to them. If Chris had been surrounded by a pack of starving wolves, he would have had the same level of discomfort.

Every bit of him wanted to turn tail and run, but as strong as the urge was, he understood with a cold precision of logic that was new to him that running would just provoke a chase. So, for a second, they all stared at each other, and if they were expecting Chris to beg, that just wasn't going to happen.

"So, if it isn't the little fag who lives down the lane," the first boy called. He wasn't the oldest or the strongest, but there was something about him that seemed to tie the group of them together. Or at least those boys around him didn't move until they knew where he was standing.

Another one of them snickered, though it wasn't that funny. "Good one, Brantley," a second said. Brantley waved them off.

Chris swallowed. They were just insulting him, and they had chosen the most obvious rock to throw. "Is there anything I can help you with?"

"You can suck this," Brantley said, grabbing his crotch. "Do you think we just let fags use our road?"

The laughter that followed was an ugly thing. Still, Chris tried to diffuse the situation one more time. "I'll leave," he said. "You can have it back."

He put his feet back on the bike, about to push off again, when the hair on the back of his neck stood up. There was something different in the boys, and he leaned over the handlebars of the bike. Another rock grazed the back of his head, and hot blood splashed down his neck. The boys were silent for a full second, and then someone hooted. "Get him," another shouted, and Chris said the very worst word he knew and started pumping the pedals.

They bayed like hunting dogs at his heels, and he didn't have to be told he was going to wrong way. They were driving him into the desert, and he knew how bad that would be. The rational part of his brain told him to just turn and take his beating, but this just felt different.

The boys were bigger than he was and on better bikes, but they weren't able to catch him. His legs would probably be ruined the next day (and, if Chris remembered correctly, they had been), but they were true to him when he needed them to be. He made it to the end of the road first, but his bike sank into the sand and was next to useless. He tried it for a couple feet, and almost went up and over his handlebars when the bike's front tire got swallowed. He hit the ground running, just as the boys reached him.

"Stop running, and we'll make this quick." It was the leader, Brantley. He'd lost his jacket and tie, and huge wet patches had spread under his arms. He smelled of anger and the sour odor of sweating adults. He was the only one among all Chris's pursuers who still looked angry.

Chris ran a dozen more steps into the sand. There was a hiking trail with firmer ground another dozen steps away, but it was closed off with huge warning signs. "Don't run, cutie," Brantley called. "You're just going to make it worse. Come here, take your beating, and we'll tell someone where you are."

Chris looked behind him. Half the dirt path leading into the desert had collapsed over the summer. It had even been in the news. It was stupid to even try it.

"Don't," Brantley called. The others were doing this as a lark, but Chris saw the need in Brantley's eyes. It was the same look his father got sometimes; it was the need to hurt people. He took another step back toward the sinkholes.

"What the hell are you doing? Are you trying to get yourself killed?" Brantley shouted.

"Just the opposite," Chris called back.

Clods of dirt flew past him. One struck his ankle. It stung horribly for a second, bad enough that Chris thought maybe the bone was broken, but the pain quickly subsided. He turned around again and ran. He leapt over the chain at a dead sprint, something he'd never had the coordination to do in gym class. Brantley took it a bit slower, but Chris's mad sprint couldn't last forever. He didn't need it to be forever, just longer than Brantley's second wind, but he was suddenly completely exhausted. Brantley had stopped, so he stopped as well.

"If you don't stop, I'm going to hurt you," Brantley said. "You know I will."

"You're going to hurt me anyway," Chris said.

"You know there'll be a difference." Brantley smiled, and his pleasure came from the idea of hurting Chris. Chris felt it like a bruise. He took another step back. The dirt here was firmer than the sand encroaching on the path, but he swore he felt it shift deeper below the ground.

"Don't come any closer," he called. "It's not safe."

Brantley sneered, and started walking again. "Do you think I'm chicken?"

They were too old for *chicken* to be the worst thing to call someone, but to Brantley, it obviously was. The ground shifted, but Chris didn't warn him again. The ground gave off a low rumble, like a disturbed house cat.

Brantley's fists were tight and his fingers bloodless. The ground beneath them shook. The ground shifted harder, and Chris had to run to keep his feet. Brantley ignored the warning. Chris kept backing up, holding his hands out, but knew the ground was going to give way seconds before it did. Brantley was almost on him; Chris could see the acne marks on his face. The ground started to move, pulling Chris back to Brantley. Chris wind-milled his arms trying to break the forward movement, but the hole that had opened up was growing to engulf them both.

Brantley smiled, heedless of the danger, and waited for the ground to bring Chris to him. Fear spiked inside Chris as sharp as an ice pick. This was bad; this was very, very bad. He fell on his ass, but his wrist found firmer ground behind him. Brantley was on his hands and knees, still not fighting the downward motion. Chris had his forearms on the solid ground, but it wasn't enough. He couldn't get the momentum to get all the way onto the shelf, but with Brantley right behind him he didn't want to kick out with his legs. He had to, though, and the moment he did he felt Brantley's hand on his ankle, as though he had been waiting for it. He pulled himself up to his hip on the solid ground, but was now supporting both their weights. "Let go of me," he howled, and got pulled back half a foot. He scrambled for any purchase, resisting the fear that tightened his bladder and made his throat hurt, but he didn't know how long he could hold out from it.

His nails found purchase, one of them bending back and the shard of pain was blinding. He kicked out again, and his free foot caught Brantley on the nose. He heard the bone break, felt it against the thin sole of his tennis shoe. His elbows caught solid ground, but there was no way he could pull the both of them up.

"I go, you go," Brantley growled.

"I can't, you're too heavy," Chris said. "Please, let me go."

"Please," Brantley said mockingly. "I go, you go, you little shit."

The ground burned his elbows. "You have to let me go," Chris said. The hole was now more than six feet across, and gaped like a hungry mouth. They were its next meal. From behind him, Brantley was obviously trying to scramble up the rock face. From the amount of pain from Chris's ankle, it felt as though Brantley was trying to twist it off as he went.

"Pull me up now!"

"I can't!" Chris howled back. His fingers were about to give way. Even if Brantley let go, he didn't think he could pull himself up any more. His whole body hurt, and only the fear of falling kept him fighting. "Please, you're hurting me. Let me go. We'll both fall."

"Then we both fall." Brantley must have found purchase, because the grip on Chris's ankle slacked off slightly. But only for a second. Just as he tried to use the relief to find a better hold, Brantley yanked him back. Chris flailed, but there was nothing to stop them both from falling. They fell forever, and Chris's fear of striking his head against the wall overtook the fear of landing. He was falling into hell.

He hit the ground, or rather, he hit Brantley, who had landed first. Brantley probably saved Chris from broken bones, at least. He rolled off Brantley as fast as he could. The cave, if that was what they were in, was dark but for the beam of light from the hole through which they'd fallen, and Brantley was in the dead centre of it. Motes of dust filled the air, making the edges of the light as sharp as a knife. For a moment, Brantley looked like he was dead. At the very least, he'd landed wrong on his left leg, and it was at a rough angle.

Chris backed away until he was against the wall of the cave. The air was stale, but he expected something else. Sulfur, perhaps. He heard something behind him, and it sounded like a rattle. Not a rattle, something rattling. He leapt forward, his throat so tight he couldn't swallow.

He jumped away. It didn't help. The thought he heard bones rattling around him, like how he imagined graveyards were arranged. He took a huge step back, closer to Brantley. "Hey," he said, wanting to warn Brantley that they weren't alone in the hole, but when he turned to look down at where Brantley lay, Brantley sat up, the breath he took seemed to last forever, and then he started to scream.

Chris jerked back, but there was nothing more alarming from the wall than the sound. The rattling sound from the wall was alarming, but not terrifying. There was almost a song to it. He pressed his hands against the wall and felt whatever it was just behind his fingers.

Brantley's screams reached a fevered pitch. He held up his hands to ward his face against nothing Chris could see.

The firemen came with a ladder within twenty minutes, but it seemed so much longer. Chris climbed out unassisted, though his foot twinged. He walked away, leaving his bike still half buried in the sand. The firemen were occupied with Brantley and didn't seem to miss him.

It made the news, and he was summarily called back to New York. That was the last time he was allowed to visit his grandmother until he went out west to go to school.

Brantley, of course, remembered him. His nose was still a little crooked from where Chris had broken it. He met Chris's eyes, and they both knew the other knew, but they both pretended they'd just met. Brantley had tried to kill him, and yet he couldn't quite shake the smile off his face.

Jamie grabbed his arm and shook him. Chris shook his head, like he was trying to wake up, but he just couldn't break free from the fog. The glass in his hand was so heavy, and cut crystal created dozens and dozens of prisms within the water. *It doesn't work that way*, Chris told himself, *there isn't enough light*, and the prisms were…dancing. "Sir," Jamie said. "I don't think…" She didn't finish but took the glass from his hand and put it down. The swimming in his head lifted enough for him to speak.

"Can you tell me anything about Richard?" Chris tried again, and fought for every word to be clear.

Brantley turned to Donna and the look they exchanged seemed much practiced. Donna shrugged and Brantley turned back to them. "There isn't much to say," Brantley said. "We are quite a large organization, as you probably know. I would like to say that we're one big family, but realistically people are hired and fired all the time. I remember Richard being polite, and in the beginning, very good at his job. But his demons were stronger than I was. The bottle got to him. I don't know what else to tell you."

Chris turned to look at Jamie, almost pantomiming Brantley's expression. She shook her head as well, and he nodded. "I don't think we have any more questions," Chris said.

Brantley reached into his pocket. Even with Chris's years of experience, he still didn't feel an ounce of self-preservation. Of course it wasn't a gun; Brantley pulled out a card holder. It was gold embossed leather, and Chris found himself just wanting to stroke the leather with his finger. Jamie took the card from Brantley's fingers, even though it had clearly been meant for Chris. For a moment Chris wanted to grab it from her, to press her up against the wall and hold her by her throat until she gave it up. Instead, he thanked Brantley, nodded to Donna, and followed Jamie outside.

Once outside, even though the air was hotter and he could feel the sun beat on the back of his neck, it was still a relief to be out.

"Chris?" Jamie asked.

"Yes?" Chris asked. Her voice sounded far away, but she was becoming more into focus. "What?"

"What the hell got into you?"

"What?" Chris asked. The time in the tiny reception area was becoming dreamlike.

"You are grinning like an idiot."

Chris touched his face. It explained why the muscles on his face were sore. "Was I?"

"You still are."

He nodded. "Find me Gregory."

"I'll call the officers who dropped him off at home."

Chris turned around once they reached the car. The sun was merciless at its highest point of the day, and this place was oddly familiar. Gregory – it smelled like him. In the dreams, he'd licked off the taste of the buildings from Gregory's exposed throat. "He wouldn't have let the officer drop him off at a house. Or at least at his own house. But get him on the horn."

But, of course, the officers were off for the day. Chris returned to the station, and then really wished he hadn't.

The boxes and files that had accumulated on Niles's desk were gone. And there was a fresh cup of coffee on his desk day planner, and a brand new bible plaque. It was innocuous; Chris had had to go to the highest level last year to get the charming Leviticus quote off the desk across from him. Niles wasn't supposed to be back for at least a few more days, but all good things came to an end eventually. Andrews, the captain, saw him come in and immediately offered him a cup of black coffee. "You had a pretty late night last night and were here pretty early in the morning. Maybe you should go home."

Chris was going to argue. There was still a lot to do, and no one really who could do it but himself. But the door to the break room upstairs was open, and he could hear Niles's voice floating back. The last place he wanted to be was at work. There was a time when Andrews was committed to making them all work together. But that was a long time ago. It was obvious to all involved that there wasn't going to be reconciliation. And Chris was fine with that. "I'll take you up on that."

Andrews nodded. Chris drove his car home, parked it, made a beeline to his bed and went to sleep.

He was dreaming. That much was obvious. The sun beating down on him should have been too hot, but he only felt it on the surface of his skin. His head was in Gregory's lap, and Gregory was running his fingers through his hair. "It's not raining."

"It doesn't have to be," Gregory said, and it was the same gravelly voice. Rough, like raw silk.

"Are you going to tell me what's going on?"

Gregory was quiet. "You didn't tell me you were a cop."

"I'm a cop. Was that you at the diner or not?"

"No," Gregory said. His voice was distant. The alarm was sounding off in the distance, and Chris fought against waking up. "And yes. Maybe a little."

"Don't go," Chris said, but he said it out loud, and of course he was alone in the room. The buzzer switched off, and the calm, soothing voice of the radio news reader came on. The city was going to be hot again, no surprise, and the Owl had been caught. All in all, a good news day. Chris got dressed to the traffic report and avoided both of the traffic hiccoughs on his way to work.

Day shift meant more paperwork. The press conference was in time for morning coffee. They gathered around the television in the break room, and Chris turned up the volume.

The official story was very carefully worded, giving all the credit to the responding officers rather than the young diner waiter who took the killer down. Not that Heath was actually a killer, not officially. The Owl had left no physical evidence behind, and all they really had on him was one attempted robbery.

But Gregory had been convinced, and against every ounce of professional skepticism that he had, Chris believed him.

The cook, Mike Nicolson, had originally attacked Heath, knocking him to the ground. How Heath had gotten up incapacitated Nicolson was unclear. No one saw how it happened. But Mike went down, and Heath had managed to herd the diners into the fridge before putting Gregory down on his knees.

And then…

Then Chris knew what had happened. He could almost feel the cheap polyester pant leg in his own fist. He needed to see the crime scene again. Jamie was still filing reports when he stuck his head into the records room. "Come for a drive?" he asked.

"To the diner?" she asked.

"Am I that obvious?"

"It's bothering me, too."

Betty's Kitchen looked different in the day. The other night, he'd been struck by the interior, but in the daytime it had lost some of its luster. Mike, the cook, was still there, but looked tired. Gregory wasn't there, but an older woman was, her too-yellow hair sprayed into more of a helmet than anything natural. Her face was lined, and her pink blush and blue eyeshadow was garishly bright.

"Good afternoon, officers," the woman called. "Sit anywhere you like."

Half the tables were occupied, even though it wasn't quite noon. Chris picked the table closest to the door, and a moment later, she joined them.

"I'm Betty Nicolson."

"Nicolson," Chris repeated.

"Mike's my boy. He's a good kid," she said. Defensively. He had been in trouble before. His rap sheet was a page long, but all of it minor and nothing in the past year or so.

"All the witnesses reported he nearly took Heath down himself," Chris said as gently as he could.

Betty looked back to where Mike was working in the kitchen. "He never told me that."

Chris waited. When she didn't say anything else, he cleared his throat. "I'm more interested in Gregory."

Betty's face changed. The guarded openness closed down, and her face was stone. "Gregory had nothing to do with this."

"I'm not even implying otherwise," Chris said. "I'd just like more information, if possible."

Betty glanced to her son. Something passed between them; it was almost electric. "He quit," she said, voice dull. "This morning. He left a voice message."

"What's his address?"

Another glance. "I don't have it."

"Ms. Nicolson, don't do this. I can and will get a warrant if I have to."

"That won't help you," Betty said. "I won't have it then, either."

"Ms. Nicolson, if you're planning on destroying evidence…"

Mike came out of the kitchen, watching them with hooded eyes. "There isn't any evidence to destroy. Gregory came to us, needing our help, and we didn't need no paperwork to help him. He was a good kid who made this place better. There ain't nothing in the back room with his name on it, and no search warrant will find what ain't there," Betty said.

Chris exhaled. He could, if he wanted to, involve the IRS for payments made under the table, but that wouldn't help. Betty hadn't chosen her diner to be the crime scene, and he didn't want to make any more trouble for her. More people came in. Betty smiled, and motioned them to sit down. "Is there anything else I can help you with, officers?"

Chris paid for the two untouched drinks with a five. "That's everything. Thank you for your assistance."

As they left, another couple entered. Jamie followed Chris out of the restaurant. "That's it? You aren't going to…" Jamie didn't finish.

"Try again to get in touch with the officer who drove him home," Chris said. "Find out where he was dropped off. It's not much, but it's a start."

Of course Gregory hadn't been dropped off at a house, but at a playground, in the shadow of an interstate exchange. It had taken him most of the afternoon to find the location, so Chris dropped Jamie at home and found the park himself with the poorly written instructions. The interstate's streets in the sky, held in place at impossible angles, looped overhead, and beleaguered grass around rusty equipment had to fight with litter for space. Even before the sun went down, the sky darkened.

It was hard to say what changed. Sunset came so quickly, the sky was only blood red for what seemed like a moment, but Chris, alone and sitting on one of the swings, felt as though someone was right behind him. He turned to check, but he was alone.

The day had been effortlessly clear, but now clouds whipped across the sky. Then came the wind on which the clouds had ridden. The air temperature dropped drastically, and the wind tugged on his clothes. Chris did his jacket up, tugging on the rarely used zipper. A part of his brain tried to calmly tell him that it was only the difference between the heat of the day and the sudden storm, but to him, the air suddenly felt arctic.

Someone grabbed his arm, pulling him around. Even through the leather, the hand felt hot.

Of course it was Gregory. It had to be, and the look on his face was pure fury. "What the hell are you trying to accomplish?"

That was not exactly what Chris had been expecting. Gregory didn't wait for a response, however, but hauled Chris behind him and across the street. The block was an average residential area, between an industrial area and the interstate. The houses were uniform, the only difference the color of their siding – even that blurred by the particulate in the air.

The wind was icy. Chris's breath came out in billowy clouds. Something struck his head, hard enough to leave a welt on his forehead. Something else, the size of a golf ball, hit the car beside them. It sounded like a gun shot. Chris covered his head and another piece of hail stung his fingers.

He ran faster; Gregory no longer had to pull him behind. Gregory guided him between two of the houses and down into a storm cellar behind one of them. It took him a moment to pull the slats aside, and Chris was stung a dozen times before Gregory managed to close the door. The cellar was dark but not dank. Chris could have walked from one side to the other in ten paces. But it was dry, warm, and out of the storm.

Outside, the hail struck the slats with a fury that Chris couldn't believe. "The weather forecast said warm and sunny."

"Go ahead. Use logic. See how far that gets you," Gregory said but didn't look away from between the slats. "What were you doing out there?"

"Waiting for you."

"At sunset?"

"Is that somehow relevant?"

"Yes, officer, it is. Sunset's a dangerous time. Doors open that you don't want to be open, and you're quite the little filet right now."

"I don't know what you mean," Chris said coldly.

Gregory held out his hand, and Chris, despite his best efforts, stopped talking.

Gregory paced from dirt wall to dirt wall, his fury barely contained. Once out of the rain, Chris could allow himself to feel the sting of each of the welts the hailstones had caused. He felt like a drowned rat. Gregory should have as well, but the rain just made him look even sleeker.

"You reek of him," Gregory said finally. "Even through the rain. Did you drink the water? Did you let him touch you after?"

Chris tried to think back, but his only solid memories of yesterday morning were slamming the car door shut and then pressing his palm against the burning car hood right before they left the compound. He vaguely remembered the feeling of

Brantley taking his hand and the way the rainbows seemed to move inside the glass. Chris held out his hand in front of him. "We shook."

Gregory stopped. "Of course you did."

"I take it that's a bad thing."

Gregory opened his mouth to say something but then didn't. The harshness to his face melted away as if it were just too much work to keep up the façade. "Did it hurt?"

Chris shook his head.

Gregory took his hands. The touch shocked Chris like static, though as sopping wet as they both were, he knew that was impossible. He knew was going to happen next; Gregory was supposed to take his face into his hands, and they were supposed to kiss. All the pretence that Gregory didn't know who he was, that they hadn't been fucking in Chris's dreams since Chris had been transferred to Phoenix was supposed to crumble at their feet.

Instead, Gregory released his hands and shook his head. It was anticlimactic in every sense of the word. "He's marking you," he said. "He'll be coming for you, next."

When reality slapped Chris upside the head, it did so with a reminder that he was still a cop, and this…kid…in front of him was a key witness to something that Chris didn't believe for a second was actually over. "How do you know Jones?" he asked.

"Off the record, officer?" Gregory asked with a twist to his lips that could never be called a smile.

Chris said nothing. There was no such thing as off or on the record in a murder investigation, and although others may have possibly fallen for that omission of truth, he somehow knew Gregory wouldn't be that stupid.

"You're an honest one, I'll give you that," Gregory said. He went to the futon that had obviously been dragged from somewhere else. It had been "fixed" with a dozen different mends. Gregory threw himself back onto it, and while Chris expected to see a cloud of dust envelope Gregory's dark hair, the mattress was too clean for that.

"You didn't answer the question," Chris said.

Gregory rested his head on the back of the futon, exposing his long, clean neck. "Nor did you, officer."

"I didn't think I needed to."

"I just like tit for tat."

"I'm more of a tat man, myself," Chris said before he could stop himself. If he could've clapped his hands over his mouth and still retained an ounce of professional dignity he would have. Instead he kept his face impassive and hoped the gloom of the basement hid how red his ears were no doubt becoming. He couldn't turn on his filter around Gregory. He felt too comfortable. *This is just a witness*, he told himself, for the hundredth time. One that looked as though he'd known Chris for a thousand years one second and was as alien as a stranger in the next.

"I've been known to prefer that myself," Gregory said but didn't move his head. He touched his fingers to his throat, running them down the length of his trachea, and Chris was very glad Gregory hadn't looked up to see Chris staring like he was. "But what can I tell you about Brantley that you could actually believe?"

Chris didn't answer. He was silent for a minute, then cleared his throat. "You have a way of not answering a question," he said.

Gregory smiled. "I suppose that's true enough. It's a bad habit I picked up from the very best."

"Brantley."

Gregory didn't answer, just touched the side of his nose. "See, there I go again. Yes. Brantley taught me. I mean it wasn't like there were flashcards or tests at the end of each lesson, but that's where I learned it."

"You were a member of his congregation?" That made sense. The entire compound had a whiff of Waco to it.

"That's an oversimplification." Gregory laughed, and humorously. "So I'm doing it again. No, I wasn't a member. I was more of an employee, I guess."

"A security guard?"

"Is that what he told you Heath was doing? I suppose that's the title that comes closest. So yeah, okay. But no. I wasn't a security guard."

Chris waited. This at least was familiar territory, and he could extract information from the most reluctant witness. Gregory was silent, but Chris was patient. Finally, Gregory gave in with a sigh.

"Ah, you clearly want to know what I did do for him. Brantley is rich, you know that, right? I mean filthy rich. The money pours in, and he's officially a religious organization. Wealthy guys have a slew of people on retainer. He keeps three masseuses, two nail artistes—that's what he calls them – and the occasional pretty boy around to suck his cock. A legal-aged pretty boy, easier to protest if he ever gets caught, but yeah. I was his pro cocksucker."

"You're lying to me," Chris said. He didn't know how he knew, but he did.

Gregory looked out for the first time, eyes wide, too wide with innocence, and it was Chris's turn to keep his face impassive. "Not a whole lot," Gregory allowed. "But maybe yes. Just a little."

"Why?"

"Well, clearly because I don't want to tell you the whole truth."

"And why is that?"

"That's part of the whole truth I don't want to tell you, see," Gregory explained.

And just like that, the rain stopped. The sun had set during the storm, but Chris still felt the clouds breaking up as though he could feel the sun on his skin. "Whose house is this?" Chris asked, instead of pressing Gregory for more information he clearly had no desire to share.

"No one's."

"Houses belong to people," Chris told him, keeping his voice level.

"And corporations are technically people under the law, but I don't think I'd use the personal pronoun when discussing them."

"This is Jones's property? "

"Not technically. Corporation, remember? He bought it to give to a struggling family. They got a house to live in in grand style while the kids were going to school, Brantley got a Christmas special. Even with today's value, he got the better of the deal."

"You're hiding from Jones on his own property?"

"Believe me when I tell you it's the very last place he checked. Wait. I never told you I was hiding from him."

"Are you hiding from him?"

"Yes."

"Why?"

"Because he wants to find me."

"And you don't want to go back to sucking his cock."

"Believe me, sucking his cock was not the worst part of my day. I'm sure he's found someone to take over that one aspect of my job description."

"Come in," Chris said. "We can protect you from whatever trouble you think you're in."

"I don't *think* I'm in trouble, officer. And if you truly knew what touched you today, you wouldn't just think so either."

"Did he teach you to be this cryptic?" Chris asked.

Gregory bowed his head. "If you only knew. I've been practically forthcoming with you, officer. You can go. He's shot his metaphoric wad for the night; you should be safe for the rest of the evening."

"Safe from what, Gregory?" Chris asked.

"Him," Gregory said.

"And that's all you're going to give me?"

"Trust me, that's all you're going to need."

□ □ □ □ □

"And you didn't charge him with obstruction?" Jamie asked Chris over coffee the next morning. They were standing, leaning over the banister, which overlooked the second floor bullpen. Behind them were the drab gray walls of the interview rooms, and even farther down the hall was the break room.

In part, officially, Chris was waiting for ten o'clock to use the break room. It was the only television in the station, and he wanted to watch the good reverend's morning show. Unofficially, and he knew he wasn't fooling Jamie for a second, was the fact that Niles was down in the bullpen. Niles's thin blond hair was even thinner from the distance. And from their height, Chris saw no amount of combing could possibly hide how large the shiny bald spot had become on the back of Niles's head.

"You really hate him, don't you?" Jamie said, looking down to Niles's desk.

Niles was by the water cooler. He and his cronies were discussing something, but their words were drowned out by the station's ventilation fans.

"Hate's not the word." Truthfully, he never gave Niles much thought outside of work. He wished that Niles could give him the same lack of thought. It was bad enough that the homophobic asshole knew chapter and verse and the letter of the law to keep their animosity just on the right side of an HR issue. His cloying attempts to love the sinner truly made Chris want to drill his fist down the man's throat. And since Chris viewed himself as being predominantly nonviolent, it presented a honking big conflict.

"Ten o'clock," Jamie said. At that exact second, Niles looked up. Their eyes met and there was no hiding the abject hatred in Niles's. Chris felt the hair on the back of his neck rise. The disgust was so exposed there was no way he could have hidden it if anyone had glanced over.

But the captain's door remained shut. Niles returned to his conversation, and the mood passed. Chris crumpled his paper coffee cup and followed Jamie into the break room. Jones's show was an hour-long mishmash up of right-leaning rhetoric and variety show acts. The man, both on and off stage, favored the same comb-over sported by Niles. The ladies all wore dress-up dresses and hose. It was a time capsule of a bygone era that never existed in the first place. Still, when Brantley leapt onto the stage, Chris found himself smiling. He wanted to scrape it off his face, but he couldn't.

Brantley had shaken Jamie's hand as well, and yet she was unaffected. It didn't seem fair.

"There's something going on here," Chris said.

"You can't charge someone with possession of polyester, sir."

The camera panned the audience. Donna sat beside a young fair-haired man who didn't seem to suffer from the same fashion travesties as the rest of the male audience. In comparison, the black suit he was wearing was practically stylish. What wasn't appealing was the panic on his face whenever Brantley looked his way. Chris had no doubt that Jones had found Gregory's replacement.

"What are you looking for?" Jamie asked, after the last singer had taken off her guitar and applauded Brantley for allowing her to be on the show. "It's atrocious, but hardly illegal."

"If I knew, I'd tell you," he said, and the lie didn't stick in his craw like he thought it would.

"Would you really?" Jamie asked.

"Do you really need me to answer that?"

"That's not answering the question, sir."

"Isn't it?" Chris asked. "Then it must be contagious."

"Must be," Jamie said, but she obviously had no idea what he was talking about.

"If I knew, I'd tell you," he repeated.

She looked at him.

"I swear, Jamie. But I don't know what's going on myself."

"Whatever you say."

She left him at his desk to finish up on her paperwork. Chris had hoped to end the shift without running afoul of either the captain or Niles, but his luck ran out just after four, when he rounded the corner and saw both of them talking outside the captain's office.

"Good afternoon, sir," Chris said, studiously ignoring Niles.

"Niles knows Brantley Jones," the captain said. Chris waited for the obvious. "I want you to brief him about any involvement Brantley Jones may have in the case."

"There isn't much, sir. Jones was just a previous employer. He apparently let Heath go for alcohol abuse."

Niles's smile was smarmy. "I asked for a full debriefing," he said, moderating his tone so that it was just this side of insulting. Chris's fist curled up, and he had to deliberately release the fingers so that his open hand rested on his thigh.

The captain said nothing until Niles looked at him. If Chris didn't know better, he'd swear the captain was half asleep. "Why don't the two of you just work together on this?" he asked.

"Because we would likely kill each other rather than get anything productive done," Chris said, not believing the captain's words. Everyone knew he and Niles had been at each other's throats for years.

"Excellent," the captain said, and he patted Niles on the shoulder. "If there's anything else I can do, be sure to let me know."

"I already have a partner," Chris called to the captain's retreating back.

"I wouldn't worry about that," Niles said, his smile dying the moment the captain turned his back on them. "She'll be reassigned."

"I have no desire to work with you," Chris said. It was obvious he didn't have much choice, not until he got the captain alone.

Niles made a clicking sound of the back of his throat. "Be here early tomorrow. I like getting an early start."

"On what?" Chris asked. "The perpetrator died, remember? The case is closed."

Niles just smiled at him.

□ □ □ □ □

The captain must have put in a few long nights lately. His eyelids were swollen from lack of sleep and he brought his head up and down in a strange pattern. He was staring out the window when Chris entered his office. And for a moment, despite a long-standing open door policy, Chris wished he had knocked. "Sir?" Chris finally had to ask, long after the man should have realized that Chris was standing right there.

Andrews still didn't turn. There was white in his hair than Chris had seen before, and when he crossed his hands in his lap, they shook.

"I'm not changing my mind. It's good for both of you to get over your differences." Andrews didn't turn around.

The words sounded rehearsed. Just last month, he assured Chris that Niles would be transferred out of the department. The differences had been insurmountable, and yet four weeks later, Chris was supposed to surmount them.

Chris said nothing. There was no point. He left, closing the door, and could swear he tasted the heat of the desert in the back of his throat.

Something was definitely wrong.

Chris knew if he went home, he would sleep and dream. But that wasn't enough. Instead, he drove to the park. His new sense of what was correct, the part of him that told him there was something wrong with the captain and with Jones, told him to park several blocks away. No one was around as he got out of the car, but still he locked it without setting the alarm. The noise would disturb something that Chris did not want disturbed.

Rather than being cautious in the growing darkness – so many alleyways and sage patches that could provide the perfect cover – Chris felt safe. This darkness welcomed him, and hid him from view, protecting him.

There was a light on in the upstairs, above the storm cellar. It seemed particularly foolhardy on Gregory's part, yet Chris still climbed the front porch. He didn't ring the doorbell, for the same reason that he hadn't set the car alarm. He didn't knock either, but he didn't have to. The door opened before he got three steps from it.

There was no storm coming. The orange sky turned deep indigo as they stood there, but Chris could smell the ozone hanging heavy in the sky.

"You know who I am, don't you?" he asked. Any other time, he knew Gregory could have lied, but Chris kept Gregory's gaze. Gregory's mouth opened and closed, as though attempting to obfuscate, but the naked truth came out.

"Of course I know you," Gregory said. "But you're a cop."

"I am."

For a moment, his hatred caused Gregory's entire body to shake, but he couldn't sustain it. When it broke, he almost collapsed, but Chris was there. Stepping over the threshold raised the hair on the back of his arms and neck, just like the few seconds before a lightning strike. They kissed, Chris tangling his fingers into Gregory's hair. Chris needed to taste Gregory, to feel his fingers deftly pull his shirt free, to feel their bodies together. Gregory tasted of rain, or more exactly of thundershowers, and his skin was cool despite the heat of the day.

They broke free at the same time. This was where Chris was supposed to apologize for whatever it was that had come over him. He said nothing, and waited for Gregory to come back to him. Gregory wiped his mouth with the back of his hand. "Have you ever thought about changing careers?"

"Can't say that I have," Chris said. "Is it that much of a deal breaker?"

Gregory still stared at him. "Have you ever busted up street kids?"

"If by bust up, you mean removing children from dangerous situations and the predators that feed on their misery, yes. If you are asking if I've ever once caused them physical harm, then no."

Gregory still hesitated. "I should go," Chris said. Nothing inside him said that it had been a bad idea to come, but Gregory's face was still conflicted.

"No," Gregory said. "I can do this, but not out here," He took Chris's hand. "Don't strain yourself," Chris said, uncomfortable that Gregory was still upset.

"I'm trying," Gregory said.

"You shouldn't have to."

Gregory took a deep breath and closed his eyes. "Okay. I'm good with it."

"You're good with it," Chris repeated. "Are you sure?"

Gregory narrowed his eyes. "I don't like cops, but I like you. I'm willing to work on the first part if you'll stick around for the second."

Chris nodded, and looked around for the first time. The family had obviously left with nothing. The entire household contents were wrapped in plastic. The office/spare room was unwrapped. The single bed was barely more than a cot, and the 486 computer looked new.

Asking *why this room* could wait. Gregory pulled his T-shirt over his head, tossing it into a corner with all the other clothes. He stripped off his jeans and kicked them away as well. He stood naked in front of Chris.

Chris felt his breath catch in his throat. It wasn't that Gregory was beautiful. He was, of course, young and handsome and perfectly proportioned. There was something else. Chris had seen him naked hundred times in his dreams. Even the small moles on his inner thigh that Chris loved running his fingertips over were still there.

Gregory looked down, just to see what Chris was staring at. "Oh," he said. He was going to cover them up, as though they were more scandalous that full nudity, but didn't.

"You want to keep all those clothes on?" Gregory asked. Chris dropped to his knees instead of answering him. Gregory tasted of soap, and was slippery with pre-cum. Chris ran the tip of Gregory's slender cock over his lips, just to revel in the real sensation. He was here, on his knees, and could just reach up and feel Gregory's hip bones, too close to the surface. He dug his nails into the skin, light enough to create crescent moon shapes but not enough to really hurt. Gregory hissed, but rather than push Chris's hands away, he pressed them tighter into his skin. Hard enough that it had to hurt Gregory. It trapped Chris on his knees. He was afraid that the moment he took Gregory into his mouth, the spell would break. But for now, the position kept him grounded to the fact that he was really here.

"Do it," Gregory said, breaking first. He let go of Chris's hands and grabbed the back of Chris's head. The desperation in the way he grabbed Chris and thrust into his mouth was heartbreaking. Truthfully, outside of his dreams, it was rare for Chris to take anyone down the back of his throat. He had to put his hands flat on Gregory stomach to regulate the thrusts. He was okay, as long as he didn't even think about breathing. And when it was a matter of choking or passing out, Gregory pulled away, his own fist taking the place of Chris's mouth. It wasn't the sweet, touching first time Chris had expected, but nonetheless he nodded as soon as he was ready, and Gregory was less forceful this time.

"Are you going to let me fuck you?" Gregory asked. He wasn't looking at Chris. He could have been asking to take liberties with the wall in front of him. Speaking involved breathing, so instead Chris nodded as best he could. Gregory was shivering even though the room was warm, and Chris waited. His erection was hard against his belly.

"Up," Gregory ordered.

Chris nodded. And Gregory let him climb off his knees, and then backed him into the wall. Chris could have broken his hold in any of a dozen ways, but he let Gregory pin him.

"Are you going to let me take off my clothes, or you going to do it for me?" Chris asked, voice only a little raw. He kept his tone reasonable, like he used when he was talking to someone altered in some capacity. And when he looked into Gregory's eyes, he wasn't much wrong.

Gregory let go. Chris pulled off his shirt, letting it fall from his wrists. "My pants now, okay?"

Gregory nodded. Chris undid them, holding Gregory back with his fingertips long enough to kick them away. "You've got to tell me how you want me," Chris continued, easily. Gregory flared his nostrils. It was a possessive thing, like he was trying to drink in Chris's scent. "The bed? Right here on the floor?"

Gregory didn't appear to hear him until Chris pressed his palm against Gregory's chest. "Right here."

"Okay," Chris said. He reached down to his slacks, and pulled out a condom. "You don't mind, do you?"

Gregory shook his head. He was coming more back into himself, but Chris wanted to know where he had gone. He put the condom on Gregory, and then took his chin. He let Gregory space out for another kiss. "Don't leave me," he said. "Stay with me, okay?"

Gregory nodded.

"We good?"

"Yeah, good."

One last hurtle. "Good. You got to take it easy there, big boy. It's been awhile for me." It had been almost a year for Chris, probably longer, since the last time an old ex showed up on his doorstep. He got down, and Chris kissed his shoulder before slowly pushing back. There was enough lube to make it almost painless, but Gregory waited for him to relax, and ran as fingers up and down Chris's back.

Chris's neglected cock woke up. He reached down his belly, gathering it up. He liked it slow. Gregory knew that, and with a start he realized that Gregory was going to let him choose his own speed.

After the violence of the blow job, this was surreal. Chris went down to his elbows, and buried his face into his forearms.

When Gregory grabbed his hips, taking over the fucking again, Chris was ready for him. Gregory was hard, not completely out of control, but if it had been even longer since the last time Chris had really given himself over to just being taken.

Gregory's breathing came in quick staccato bursts, in time with his fucking, and he was obviously a lot stronger than Chris thought. It was fast; the sound of flesh striking flesh quickly filled the room.

Gregory grabbed the back of Chris's neck, pinning him down. It was like his dreams. Yet all the little details that eluded him were completely different, from the roughness to Gregory's fingertips on his hips to the way his hair stuck to his sweaty forehead. That wasn't a bad thing. In his dreams, every orgasm was the sum of every other orgasm he'd ever had. This was new, it was fresh, and it was happening right now. He wished he could just keep going.

Gregory sounded animalistic and desperate. Chris wanted to slow him down, not to make it last but to make it feel better. But by then it was too late. Gregory finished with a strangled cry, his nails digging so far into Chris's hips the marks would last at least a day. But Chris didn't care. Gregory got off him, allowing Chris to flip over to his back. He took care of the rest himself. Gregory didn't look away; his eyes were too bright and his too cheeks flushed. Again, it was a cliché, but their eyes locked and Gregory wouldn't let him look away until Chris arched his back off the carpet, his thumb finding the exact perfect spot at the head of his cock, and he was coming. He squeezed his eyes shut, but instead of total darkness, the white behind his eyes was blinding.

# CHAPTER FIVE

Afterward, when they both somehow managed to fit on the small bed, Chris stayed awake and listened to Gregory's breathing. His back, shoulders, and ass were pressed against the landlord-white wall, and it never warmed up despite how long he rested against it.

Being trapped didn't bothered him. And trapped with his gun all the way across the room in a pile of clothes that would have taken at least thirty seconds to find hardly caused a heart palpitation. He was right where he was supposed to be. He nuzzled the back of Gregory's neck, because he could, and Gregory made a contented little sigh and leaned back farther into him.

And then he slept. And when he did, the dream came.

Gregory waited for him on a flat rock sticking out of the sand. Chris didn't normally dream in color. He often didn't need to when he captured the gray clouds and Gregory's shockingly pale skin. But he dreamt now in color. He saw the coming storm in exquisite Technicolor. The gentle slopes were sand, and Chris could see himself trying to scramble up their angle and sliding back as much as he made it up.

"We should move," he said, surprising himself. It was not the first thing he wanted to say.

Gregory pulled himself from the rock. "Why?" He was naked. The residual heat from the rock should have scorched him. But he was still pale.

Chris wanted to motion toward the storm, but it was already over them, the ground around them already marked with oversized raindrops the size of silver dollars.

"It's too late for that," Gregory said. "You're going to wake up in a second."

"But I just got here. I have so many questions. Who are you?"

Gregory smiled. "I'm not Gregory."

Chris shook his head. "You look like him."

Gregory smiled, an ancient smile. "He spent so many hours in my presence, I suppose I find it easier to take his shape. But he is not me."

"You both have the same talent of almost answering questions."

"We come by it after hard earned fashion, believe me." Gregory's skin began to shine. Chris had yet to feel a single drop, but Gregory was soaked. He smiled, a bittersweet thing. "There is another, angrier than I am. You will see him, soon. Don't blame Gregory. It's not that he doesn't want to tell you; he cannot."

"What did he do?"

"That's a cop question," Gregory said. Water, ankle-deep, began to pour down the channel. Chris felt it. He felt the chill. But he remained perfectly dry. "Brantley tried to make him like Richard, split him body from soul, to give him more power over the people he controls. He was only successful to a point." He touched his wrist as though he were taking his own pulse. "Gregory's in here, but he's disconnected from this and dreaming his own dream, so I can speak."

"How can I protect him?" Chris tried again.

Gregory kissed him on the cheek, lips blue with cold. "You've got it completely wrong. He's supposed to protect you."

And Chris opened his eyes to see this Gregory…his Gregory, though he'd known the dream version for years longer, staring down at him. Same green eyes, same black, black hair, but this one was wholly alive. And the other?

Wasn't.

Despite the heat of the room, and nothing to do with the cold wall still against his skin, Chris shivered.

Gregory said nothing, even pressed his finger against his lips, and got off the cot. When the two of them had tried to fit themselves before on the cot, it had sounded as though they just stepped on the tails of a dozen cats. But Chris didn't hear a whisper of complaint this time. He got up as well, expecting the springs to protest his motion, but they were silent. Even his heartbeat sounded muffled as he followed Gregory silently to the next room.

There were no lights on in the living room, not even the glow of an LCD light. It was completely dark. Even the lamppost in the front yard was burnt out. The glass was so clean it was like they were standing in front of an open window.

And to say something about it would be wrong. The new instincts growing in Chris were strange, foreign things, but were becoming as automatic as any he'd earned the hard way.

He glanced at Gregory, to say something, but Gregory shook his head. It was not the time for words. Instead, Gregory motioned to the window, and to wait.

In the darkness, a light appeared and began to grow. Gregory tensed, slipping his hand into Chris's, and Chris held it. But the warning feeling came back, and he wondered if it was for him or for Gregory. Gregory squeezed his hand, once, and Chris knew that it was for both of them.

The light did not take long to reach the house, or rather the road in front of it. Chris was suddenly very glad he had the foresight not to park anywhere near the house.

The light started and stopped, started and stopped, and the hair on the back of his neck rose. Whoever they were, they looked into each of the houses. The pink cardigan came into focus first and then the tight hair that was just now starting to come free from the bun. Donna, the cold-eyed receptionist. She walked down the middle of the street, flashing her spotlight flashlight into each of the houses. But Gregory didn't seem concerned. The light would shine right to the window, exposing them both, naked.

When it did, the light completely illuminated Gregory's chest.

But Donna didn't stop. She continued on her path, throwing a beam of light into each of the small houses, and irrationally Chris wanted to charge her with something. Gregory waited until Donna had turned down a side street before letting go of Chris's hand.

"She was looking right at you," Chris said. "Are you telling me she didn't see you?"

"I told you. They don't remember this house exists."

Chris looked at Gregory. He hadn't just deleted it from any computer inventory, he just…deleted it. "But there can't be any lights on inside."

Gregory shrugged. "It has something to do with light on the cornea. I can…bend what she sends in, but not what we send out."

Gregory walked to the window, placing both palms on the glass, at shoulder height.

"This – did you have to same dream as me?" Chris asked. "The flood plain in the rain?"

"No," Gregory said. He stood still, hands behind his back, and for some reason – for the same reason Gregory could make houses disappear and dreams mean something – Chris saw that he had been chained in that position enough times that he'd started to take comfort in it. "I dream about you. I mean, we can't talk, you and I. He would have heard that."

Chris came up behind him and touched his shoulder. Gregory's skin twitched, trying to get rid of him, but Gregory still leaned against him. "We fuck. It keeps the beasts away."

"What did Brantley do?" Chris asked.

Gregory shook his head. "I can't…tell you," he said. "But during…the worst of it, I would sleep, pass out – whatever you want to call it – and you would be there. When I saw you at the diner I didn't think…you held me. Okay? You held me until the hurting stopped."

"Gregory, what did he do to you?" Chris repeated. And he wasn't being a cop. He needed to understand, and for once, Gregory got that.

Still, he didn't have the answer. He opened his mouth, and despite his flawless white skin, Chris saw all the marks and cuts and bruises with which Gregory had come to him. And Jones himself probably didn't truly understand why, either.

"Oh, that he understood," Gregory said, voice pure bitterness.

"Why then?" Chris asked.

"Money," Gregory said. "When tricks of the trade didn't increase his donations, he turned to science. Pheromones, voice modulation, focus groups, and when that didn't work, or least when that the income leveled off, he…" Again, Gregory couldn't finish. "You can't say no to him, Chris. He just won't let you. And I helped that."

Chris put his hand over Gregory's chest. "He feeds on pain," Chris said.

Gregory smiled. "And he has call centers in three different states. All of them are feeding him. And when that wasn't enough, he took David."

Chris took his hand and led him back to the bedroom. The lube and a condom were buried under the tangle of clothes. Gregory lay down on the bed, burying his face into the pillows. As Chris approached the bed, Gregory pulled his hands behind his back. The sight of his hands, opening and closing over the small of his back, was far more erotic than it should have been.

Chris found himself gathering up Gregory's wrists. They fit into his hands too easily, even though they were the same height. Chris probably held the wrists tighter than he had to, and he felt Gregory respond by moving against the mattress for any bit of friction.

"Are you sure?" Chris asked, settling his weight carefully on the bed. Gregory relaxed, letting Chris take all his weight and for a moment, neither of them moved.

Gregory shifted, which brought his arms up tight. Chris was going to let go, to adjust himself so he wasn't pushing hard up against Gregory, but Gregory wouldn't let him. Any slack Chris gave him, Gregory took back so that his arms were always tight.

Chris fumbled and was glad that Gregory's head was turned. He never realized how difficult it was to guide himself with only one shaking hand. Still, Gregory stiffened and let out a shuddering sigh. He relaxed into the pain, and Chris had to continue. He didn't let go of Gregory's hands. In fact, he tightened his grip. Gregory groaned and lifted his hips even higher off the cot. Sex in Chris's dreams was softer than this. "You have to relax," Chris whispered. "Tell me to stop. You can even shake your head if you don't want me to go on."

Gregory didn't respond. Chris relaxed some of the tension in his hand, and Gregory closed his eyes. Chris could almost feel him leaving and going to that other place; the place in the dreams. "No," Chris said. "Stay with me."

Chris tightened his hands, and conversely Gregory relaxed more, but he was entirely with Chris. Chris liked the way his muscles tensed and flexed. It took a second, but he spread his thighs, pushing Gregory's legs farther apart. Gregory cried out and that sound, at least, was familiar.

He used Gregory's hands to pull Gregory back onto his cock. He was surprised he had the upper body strength to do it. Gregory grabbed onto Chris's forearms. It must've hurt. There was no way it couldn't have, but Chris watched Gregory completely relax. "Yes, yes, yes," he whispered, under his breath. He was close enough to coming that Chris felt his muscles clenching.

And when Gregory did come, Chris dropped his hands. Gregory scrambled up, making the angle better for Chris without being asked. Chris climbed up with him. He braced himself and Gregory fucked back as hard as Chris fucked Gregory.

Gregory began writhing against Chris, and it was all Chris could do to just hold him. He needed the tension. He let go of Chris's arms, which was Chris's signal to let go. Gregory hugged the pillow, shaking. And Chris let him recover.

Though it didn't take long for Gregory to crawl around him. He stripped off Chris's condom and knotted it with practiced ease. Chris was still hard, and Gregory's hand, which had felt hot on Chris's arm, was practically cold against his cock. He held Chris with both his hands, and ran his cock over his lips and cheeks.

It was, perhaps, the most erotic thing that he had had done to him, but only until Gregory pressed Chris's cock against his forehead. He blew on Chris's testicles, and then licked his way up Chris's entire length. Being sprawled out on the cot, his hands up over his head, gripping onto the bar, gave him no freedom to move. Not that he dared to touch the back of Gregory's head. That would be wrong.

When Gregory parted his lips and took him, in that second Gregory could've asked for anything, and Chris would have given it to him. He didn't understand what that was, but in that heartbeat, no matter how small it would have seemed at the time, it would have been monumental.

"Please," Chris managed. The word came unbidden to his tongue. He wanted to say more, but Gregory pressed his finger against Chris's lips. Chris had broken his leg once on duty. It had been his own fault. He had been chasing a perp across a rotten roof and he'd stepped wrong. He'd fallen hard, and the sound of his bone snapping scared birds from their nests.

The doctors had him on a morphine drip as they fixed the bone. Chris had hated the lack of control and the floating sensation.

But with Gregory, the floating was in a wonderfully safe cocoon. He never lost the feeling of Gregory's lips around his cock, the warmth and softness as welcoming as any part of his dream.

Gregory put his hands flat on Chris's thighs, pushing his legs even farther apart. Chris let him, and Gregory let go of him, placing his mouth over Chris's cock.

Gregory took Chris into his mouth slowly, making Chris come half off the bed. Chris closed his eyes, letting Gregory just take him. Gregory's mouth was wickedly talented and Chris was coming, his body cresting in pleasure and warmth. He heard water, at first like a neighbor's shower, but the noise soon became deafening. He was standing on the edge of a raging river, deep inside a cave. Chris reached over and took Gregory's hand. There hadn't been any reason to think that Gregory was behind him, but Chris knew. His hand was warm. Their fingers intertwined, and they stood there in the dark listening to the water rushing past. He wanted to hold onto that moment forever.

# CHAPTER SIX

The sun in the window woke Chris. Even as early as it was, the heat was already excessive. It took Chris's talent to extricate himself from the tangle of limbs in which he found himself.

His clothes were still in the corner, his gun still in the holster. Chris felt different just strapping it on. When it had fallen to the ground he'd been just a cop, and Gregory had just been a witness. A witness at best, and at not…well, killing Heath had to be the definition of self-defense.

Gregory didn't wake, even as Chris kissed his forehead. That seemed monumentally forward on Chris's part, like fucking each other almost to the point of passing out was no excuse to take liberties. But Gregory only smiled. What he said had all the syllables of *I'll be right down*, but contained none of the right sounds.

Chris understood him nonetheless. The bathroom was done in some hideous shade of teal porcelain that had long since lost its shine. It was still spotless, right down to the smiling blue whales that benevolently watched Chris. He had to look away from them to finish urinating.

He washed his hands, and registered the fact that the sliding doors in the small yellow dining room were open. Chris's heart stopped. He put his hand on his holster before he was even aware of what he was doing. The hard galvanized rubber felt good in his hand. He unsnapped the safety strap and made his way carefully into the dining room.

The homeless man stopped eating his cereal mid-bite. He eyed Chris, as wary as a herd beast coming down to drink at a watering hole. Chris didn't move, thankful that he hadn't drawn his weapon, but they were both keenly aware of where his hand was. The man at the table eyed the sliding door, but his cereal obviously held too much draw. He opened his hand, obviously asking permission to continue, and Chris guiltily removed his hand from his gun.

"What are you still doing here?" Gregory said from behind. His voice was teasing as he came down the stairs. "I thought you'd long since finished your walk of shame." Gregory slung his arm over Chris's shoulder and kissed his cheek. He must've noticed the tension in Chris's shoulders, because he looked up.

"Oh," Gregory said under his breath, and separated himself from Chris. "David, what did I say about leaving the door open?" he asked, in a tone that most people are reserved small children and animals. "You know I hate flies."

David, if that was his name, dropped his spoon and hung his head. In the heat of the kitchen, there was no mistaking the smell of him, unwashed body combined with sweat and helplessness. But Gregory touched David's cheek.

David turned his face in Gregory's hands, and Gregory continued. "I'm not really mad. We'll get you washed up after breakfast."

David looked up accusingly Chris.

Gregory laughed. "I don't know if the good officer will be joining us. I tend to believe him when he says he has to leave early. But perhaps he could join us for a cup of coffee."

Two sets of eyes turned to Chris. They weren't related. Under the mat of hair that had once been curly, the blond was unmistakable. He'd been pretty. Probably still was, if it was possible to get past the slack-jawed look of bewilderment.

And there was nothing bewildered about Gregory. His green eyes shone with amusement as much as David's eyes were glassy.

Dark and light. But still, the same type. Jones's type, obviously. Gregory shook his head. "The officer gets it now, David. We are in luck. Still, he didn't answer my question."

"What question?" Chris asked.

"Coffee, Officer. Would you like a cup to go?"

Chris would only have to stop on his way anyway. He nodded, cautiously. Gregory smiled again, and busied himself manipulating appliances that once belonged to a dead woman. The thought was unbidden, but true enough. The place was a tomb. The family hadn't moved out, they…died. And that had let Gregory hide from Jones.

Gregory was staring at him, expectantly. "Did you ask me something?" Chris asked. When he last looked out, Gregory had just begun to peel one of the coffee filters free from its mates, but now the coffee was half up the carafe.

"I asked you if you wanted toast."

Chris nodded. What the hell. This mothering act Chris knew Gregory was giving off wasn't real, but it made Gregory feel in control.

"David doesn't like to chew toast. It hurts his teeth. But I like it."

"How did you find him?" Chris asked.

Gregory's smile faded, but only for a second. "It was hard not to," he said. He took David's hand in his. It wasn't like most street people that Chris had known. David's hands were still soft. Vulnerable. His long fingers were still elegant and beautiful despite how filthy his cheeks were.

"They're going to ask you where you'd been," Gregory said. "You know that, right?" He put the travel mug full of coffee and a plate of toast in front of him.

Chris nodded.

"Don't drink the water. Don't even hold the glass," Gregory said. "And don't let him touch you again, and you should be okay."

"Should be," Chris repeated.

Gregory opened his hands. "Should be," he agreed. "I'm fresh out of guarantees."

Chris took a bite of toast, and it was better than he remembered toast being. The butter melted perfectly into the crunchy exterior.

He wanted to ask Gregory to come with him, but knew it wasn't safe for him. He'd be exposed, and defenseless, so he kissed Gregory's cheek.

"One thing, and don't hate me," Gregory called as Chris was almost to the door.

"What?" Chris asked.

"Do you have cab fare?"

"Cab fare for what?" Chris asked.

"Anything," Gregory said. "Or you know, erosion."

And Chris wasn't kept in suspense for very long. He made it back to where he parked his car and thought for a second that his late-model Ford had been stolen. That was until he looked closer at one of the junkers parked where he swore he parked his unmarked car. The Ford looked as though it had been exposed to years of sandstorms. The deep forest green was the palest mint shade, and the middle had degraded to the point that he was afraid that it would crumble beneath his fingers if he touched it. But when he pushed the unlock button on his key fob, the car chirped to life and its headlights flickered like they always did. Donna, somehow, had done this when she passed it.

Erosion. Oh, ha ha. Chris didn't call a cab; he called a tow truck, and rode back to the station with the truck driver. He dropped the new junker at the carpool, signing over the damage sheet. That would be an interesting insurance claim. He showered in the change room, which was oddly empty. But then it wasn't quite six o'clock yet. The shift change didn't happen until seven.

He didn't like turning his back to the empty locker room, though he'd done it a thousand times before when he was a uniformed cop. He still kept a change of clothes in his locker, and was trying to remember which shirt it was when the feeling of being watched struck him like a two-by-four.

He froze and turned quickly. It felt like whoever was behind him was close enough that he should be able to feel their breath.

The empty aisle stretched out long and empty in front of him. He had to hold on to the wall to stop the vertigo from knocking him down. Shampoo stung his eyes and the sound of water dripping through the drain echoed in the empty room. He rinsed off the shampoo, not daring to turn his back to the empty room again. Even closing his eyes long enough to wash the suds off his face was almost too much to bear. The second he did, he knew he was being watched again. He wiped the water from his eyes, and reached blindly for the towel. It wasn't on the hook where he left it. He looked over to the right, knowing he had never put a towel on the wrong hook in his entire life, when he saw his familiar fluffy, yellow towel. It was folded neatly by his locker.

Chris's heart stopped. He didn't embarrass himself by asking who was there. Instead, he padded dripping wet across the change room. He felt completely exposed and couldn't snatch up the towel fast enough. He dried as fast as he could and got dressed. The creepy feeling didn't leave until he felt the locker room door close behind him. Still heebies jeebied all the way back to the bullpen.

Niles waited for him, sitting on his desk. He held two cups of coffee, and Chris was suddenly glad he had put his travel mug inside his locker so Niles couldn't tamper with it while he showered. He didn't really think Niles would try to poison or drug him, but he couldn't shake the eerie feeling from the shower.

Niles waved his own cup, sloshing the contents back and forth, and a brief, intense look of displeasure crossed his face. Niles put down the second cup he was holding and stood "Let's go."

"Go where?" Chris asked.

"To meet Reverend Jones. He says he has more information about Heath."

Chris's back bristled. But there was no way he could argue against going when he had told Jones to call if he had anything more to say.

"Isn't he getting ready for his television show right now?" Chris asked.

"He takes Tuesdays off," Niles said and smiled at Chris toothily. It was a pal smile, or a smile between co-conspirators. Chris's familiar urge to punch Niles was back. Still he managed a tight-lipped smile himself. "I'm driving."

"Do you have a vehicle?" Niles asked, false concern faked well enough for government work. He so obviously wanted Chris to ask how he could possibly know that, but Chris only shrugged.

"I will," he said simply.

He took sadistic glee in making Niles wait while he filled out the entire stack of requisition forms, though it took all morning to do so. By the time they did get onto the road, Niles was shaking with anger.

"Why me?" Chris asked as they were stopped at a red light. All around them, the city was awake. They were miles away from the big box stores. The tiny shops, smelling of coffee and flowers and baking bustled with shopkeepers and their clientele. The day was beautiful and still filled with promise. It wasn't fair that Chris had to be in a car with Niles.

"Turn here," Niles said, and he reached for Chris's hand. Chris, with Gregory's warning still in his head, snatched his hand back. Again, Chris felt rather than saw Niles's displeasure. "For heaven's sake," Niles snarled. "It's not like I was going to force myself on you."

"Don't touch me."

"You people are so sensitive," Niles said.

Chris refused to rise to the bait. "Just don't touch me."

They pulled up in front of Betty's Kitchen diner. Of course they did. It suddenly made more sense than anything else that happened before. And of course, even as they were still walking to the building, listening to the engine pinging, Jones would be sitting on the same stool where Chris had seen Gregory during their first meeting.

A cloth napkin, obviously not native to the diner, was protecting his very fine, powder blue suit. Jones was eating a plate full of eggs and bacon, toast and coffee. Just watching him shovel the food into his mouth disgusted Chris.

Niles nodded to him. Chris wasn't surprised how familiar the two seemed together. It was obvious, as Niles took the far stool, that Chris was expected to sit on the other side of Jones. He stayed standing. Jones wiped his mouth with his napkin and motioned Chris to take a seat in the booth across from them.

Chris sat and kept his face studiously blank as Niles tried to get him to shift over. It was subtle, but Brantley frowned and Niles skittered to the other side of the table. Alice herself came over, bringing them all mugs. Chris refused his. "This isn't a social call, Mr. Jones," he said. "You said you had some information."

Jones nodded. "You moved me, young man," he began, and Chris couldn't quite match the smug man in front of him to the screaming teenager. He narrowed his eyes and took a deep breath. Jones continued as though Chris was still paying rapt attention. "I spent the evening going through my personal records."

Chris nodded but didn't relax.

Jones smiled despite Chris's chill. "No need to thank me. I found his contact information as well as his release papers. We let him go after he threatened the life of his immediate supervisor. Do you think that's relevant?"

Chris nodded. "It certainly doesn't hurt," he said.

Jones's smile was a mile wide. "Thank goodness. I can't help but feel that we left things a little...unsettled after our last meeting."

Jones tried to take Chris's hand, and Chris yanked it back like Jones had waved a brand in his general direction. "You reek of him," Jones snarled. "He's in your pores," and Chris knew who he meant

*He should be. I sucked him off enough times*, Chris thought, but kept his face blank. "Who are you talking about?"

"Don't play stupid with me." The last semblance of niceness crumbled onto the table in front of them.

"If you feel I'm being inappropriate, you can take it up with my superiors," Chris said.

Niles and Jones exchanged obvious looks. "You're not hearing me," Jones said and frowned.

A tension headache struck Chris behind his eyes. The bands of pain tightened like drying leather. He didn't grab his skull, though he wanted to. His mouth twitched, once, and the sound of swarming flies filled his head. He stood up. "I'll let the two of you finish your meal," he said and left the diner, barely walking in a straight line.

It felt better being out in the hot sun. The air felt hotter on the pavement, so Chris moved to the cracks and baked dirt of the abandoned lot beside the diner. The grass was all dead, and it didn't look as though it had ever been healthy. Ice water trickled down his back, and, when he looked up again, he could tell he was being watched.

The limo along the road, parked blocking the driveway to the diner, hadn't been there before. The window was open, and even though Chris was over ten yards away, he swore he felt the air-conditioning on the backs of his hands.

The young man in the back seat was blonde, blonder than David, who had been the color of a light cream ale. This young man had the coloring of wave caps.

The shades he wore were mirrored, and yet still reflected nothing. Chris took a step forward just as the window rolled up. Chris could have walked over and rapped his badge on the door. And, in the real world, the young man would have had to roll down the window and answer his questions to the best of his ability or face legal consequences.

But the young man was still staring at him through the darkened window, and they both knew that this was far from what would ever be considered the real world. Chris was so far down the rabbit hole he'd be coughing up fur for weeks.

He got into his car and drove away, leaving Niles with the potentially dangerous witness. When he got back to the station, it was fairly obvious that something big had happened. Everyone spoke in urgent, hushed tones, and from the way the bullpen silenced as he entered it, he was fairly sure it had something to do with his case.

He checked his cell phone. The damn thing almost crumbled when he touched it. Corroded plastic had erupted from the battery. It hadn't happened the night before; he would have noticed it when he transferred it from his pocket to the new set of jeans in the change room. And yet he hadn't felt it explode in his pocket. Jones has destroyed it just by being near it.

Chris held the mangled remains in his hand, tight enough that the corroded bits from the battery should have caused serious damage to his skin. He felt the chemicals burn on his palm, but knew it wouldn't leave a mark. If anything, it tickled.

There had been another robbery. It had already happened, and Jamie was going to head up the investigation. It didn't feel as though anyone had died, but that was only because Jones must have been still recovering from backlash he felt when Hatch died from under him. Chris saw a snatch of it. The gray bun had been the most lasting image. Donna. His cop mind filled in the face, down to the details that would have made a sketch artist proud.

He saw earlier. Jones had called her into his office. Not the one in the bunker. The one in the grand house. Billy was there too, skulking in the shadows. He'd been called in as an afterthought, but Chris knew with sudden clarity that everything that Brantley could do, he had to do it through Billy. Brantley was thinking he could do it all himself because of what Gregory had done to him, but he was wrong. Brantley had just touched Donna's hand, which was still cool from holding the glass of spring water.

Two uniformed officers jostled Chris in the hall. For a moment, he was in both places at once, and tried to catch himself on the wall in Jones's office. Chris's nails caught on the treatment on the walls. The reason why Jones needed Billy in the room, even if he didn't know why, and how he…separated people from themselves, leaving their husks to be commanded like a pawn across a chessboard, it was right there in front of him.

But then Chris couldn't fight the separation, and he moved completely back to the side his body was on. The missing piece to the puzzle remained firmly on the other.

Chris stared down at the ruined cell phone. "Doesn't that hurt, sir?" one of the uniforms demanded.

Chris looked down to his slightly pink skin. "No. No, it doesn't."

Jamie caught his eye, motioning him to come over to her desk, but he shook his head. He hung out by the fringes and moved when he saw her going into the bathroom alone. She jumped when she saw him in the mirror, but nodded when he put his finger against his lips. He didn't know who Niles knew, and wasn't willing to risk Niles ever finding out. He took her shoulders, pulling her to him and dropped his lips to her ear. "Tell me nothing about the case."

"What case?" Jamie asked. "I haven't told you anything about what happened last night, and your cell phone wasn't on."

He shook his head. "Don't tell me. I don't want to know."

Her face was honestly amused. "You can't honestly expect me to believe you think Niles is going to have…spies do you?"

Chris was silent. So was Jamie, for over a minute. "I suppose that's not completely out of character," she allowed.

"You are going to be the head investigator on this," Chris said. "And you can't tell me anything, do you hear me? What's general knowledge we can't help, but anything privileged or any speculation on your side has to be kept completely away from me."

"Did you hit your head?" Jamie asked. "They are not going to make me lead investigator. Most of the guys out there have shoes with more seniority than I have."

Chris shook his head. "Trust me on this one," he said. "Please. For me."

Chris was sure Jamie was going to say something smart ass, but she was silent for once. "Yes, sir."

Chris heard the outer door of the ladies room creak open before Jamie did. He slipped into one of the stalls. Amy, one of the plainclothes from the day shift, poked her head into the washroom. "Jamie, the captain wants you," Amy called.

"What for?" Jamie asked.

"I didn't ask, but it sounded ASAP to me. Something about the robbery, I suppose."

Jeannie nodded and left the washroom. Chris waited until it was safe to leave before making his exit. He was still the lead on the Betty's Kitchen affair, and that meant dealing with Richard Heath's grieving mother. He wondered, briefly, if Niles knew that when he gave him the info on Heath's next-of-kin. That information had eluded them. No one had come forward despite the story running on all the local and some of the national channels. It felt good to be in the car alone.

Heath had lived with his mother. Or had at least until he had been fired from his security job. Chris had met the mothers, wives, and children of some really horrible people in his line of work, and Mrs. Heath proved to be no different from any of them. She was still sick with grief and overcome with confusion over what could have possibly gone that wrong.

Her bungalow had barely four rooms, and all around her were mementos and bygones of a much more rational time.

She welcomed Chris in without any questions. He even forced her to actually ask for his badge. She stared at it, confused about what she should do. He advised her to write down his badge number and full name before they spoke. She did so, putting the paper away once she had written on it. Chris was fairly certain it would never see the light of day again.

Still, sipping tea in bone china and nibbling on slightly stale lemon cookies across from the mother of the man his – his brain only balked at the word for an instant – lover had killed two days ago was perhaps the most serene part of his day so far.

She studied her cup as though she hadn't used a tea bag and she could divine the future with the loose dregs. Chris waited. He was good at it. When she finally looked up, he was ready for her. "You've probably heard this a thousand times," she said.

"If it helps you say it, then say it," Chris said

"He was a good man," she said staring at her bony, knotted hands. "He stayed with me because of my arthritis, you see. He had his own place, his own life, and I asked him to move back with me. He dropped everything to do it. He even worked nights so that he would be with me during the day. He was a good man. And I can't imagine…" She didn't finish. Chris didn't expect her to.

He shifted in his chair, the sound pulling her thoughts back to him. "Can you tell me anything about Brantley Jones?"

She turned her face away at the name. "That man." She spat out the words. "Richard started working for him about five years ago. Security guard, you see. Nights. The man offered Richard nearly triple what he was making…and put me on his health plan. I was going to need surgery, for my hands." She held her wrists out now. Two long scars, like those of a successful suicide victim, ran down the length of her forearms. "It would have crippled me and I was still a year from Medicare. If that man had asked Richard for his soul, Richard still would've signed on the dotted line."

"So he went to work for Brantley," Chris prompted.

"Yes. That man may have come across as humble, but there is nothing humble about his lifestyle. He would just jet to Africa, to help the poor, he says. But then he stays in lodges and hotel rooms so decadent even one night would pay for an entire village's medical treatment. He eats caviar for breakfast and makes the unchosen many who work for him toil for slave wages. He is not a good man, and…"

"And?" Chris asked.

She didn't flush, but her cheeks did turn faintly red. "He's a hypocrite. He rails on about the evils of homosexuality and then cavorts with young men. It's none of my business who or what he is or does, but then to condemn others for it? That's completely unacceptable."

Chris nodded. "So Richard didn't like Jones at all, yet he still stayed employed with him for four and a half years?"

"No." Mrs. Heath's voice went soft. "It wasn't like that at all. Three years ago, he just…stopped ranting about his job. And Mr. Jones started to take him places. He'd come back so exhausted. I begged him to quit; Medicare had started and he didn't really need all of that money, but he told me Mr. Jones needed him."

"As a security guard."

She frowned. "No. Not as a security guard. He just kept saying Mr. Jones needed him. He became Mr. Jones's right arm, and then…he was let go. For no apparent reason."

Mrs. Hatch put her cup down. "You could just be humoring me," she said and looked up at his face for the first time. "But thank you for listening to me."

Chris nodded. "Your son is accused of some pretty horrible crimes," he said. "But all we can prove he actually did was enter a diner and attempt to rob it. We'll probably never know why, but thank you for speaking with me today."

She nodded and sighed. "Can you see yourself out?"

"Of course," Chris said. They shook hands over the small table, hers as fragile as a baby bird in his, and he popped the lock on the door on the way out.

It was obvious to him that Heath was not operating under his own steam. But Chris didn't understand what power – and it had to be a power – could rob a man of his free will or reason. How, Chris didn't know, and it was maddening.

Chris thought of David and his soft hands, sitting in the sun drenched kitchen, and of a young man tending his mother and then murdering a diner full of people. He couldn't completely rely on what Gregory had said, and he made a note to check the compound for excessive energy use. If it was a drug, and they were stupid enough to grow it hydroponically, he might get lucky. More than likely, if Gregory were telling the truth about the call centers, one hydroponics lab wouldn't show up. He could also check shipping records but doubted Jones would get caught that way.

Chris was still using the logical part of his brain. The other part, the part that had already accepted Gregory's story and Jones as the cause of all the mechanical and electrical malfunctions, already knew that regardless of where he looked for reason he wasn't going to find it.

He was sitting on the curb, just thinking, when a marked car screeched to a halt in front of Mrs. Heath's little house. Niles got out of the passenger seat. He was fuming. His red face looked sunburned. The officer driving didn't wait for instruction but just put the car into gear and skedaddled.

"If you ever pull that kind of stunt again –" he began, but then took a breath and didn't finish.

And Chris really wanted to hear how the story would end. "You'll…?" he prompted.

Niles's lip curled. "I'll have you brought up on insubordination charges."

"Small issue," Chris said. "I'm not your subordinate."

"Do you think that really matters?" Niles asked, his voice suddenly like silk. "I'll have you on dereliction of duties, too."

Chris raised his eyebrow. "You knew where I was going to be, not why," he said.

Niles suddenly looked up. "Why are you here?"

Chris pointed to the house next to Mrs. Heath's, glad that he had chosen to park in a shady patch rather than park right outside. "Perp's mother's house," he said. "I thought I'd have my hand at actually trying some detective work." It was a risk; Niles could still verify the proper address if he had nefarious plans, but it just felt right to obfuscate.

"Was she there?" Niles asked. He was good when he wanted to be. The look of concern on his face came and went so quickly that, if Chris hadn't been watching for it, he never would have caught it.

"She all but chased me out with a broom," he said. "You know how those people are."

Niles's lip twisted again, for a completely different reason. "Yes," he said, then shook his head. "I can read your notes once we're back at the station."

"I'm off shift," Chris said and tossed the keys to his car. His entire arm ached to whip them at Niles's head, but he didn't – and Niles still missed his easy loft. The key ring struck him in the chest, and clattered to the sidewalk.

"We're not finished yet!" Niles yelled.

"Working lunch," Chris reminded him. "If you don't like it, take it up with the union. My hands are tied."

He left Niles standing by the car. His grandiose gesture left him sans transport, and Chris had to take a bus back to his apartment. Not that he minded. He was entering the city center late enough to avoid most of the daily commuters, which left a diverse group of people riding with him. They were young people and old, businessmen with briefcases between their legs and homeless people worse off than poor David. It was an eclectic group, and studying them kept Chris's mind off Jones for the first time in a while.

The homeless woman next to him began talking to an invisible companion about shoe shopping, and Chris wondered if that was any stranger than zombie receptionists searching for them the night before. It was only as he was getting off the bus and the bus was pulling away that he saw that the man dressed entirely in black had dust all over his suit. When Chris turned, the bad feeling in his gut getting worse, he must have been the only person who saw how blank the man's eyes were. He reached for Chris with dry, bony fingers. He opened his mouth but said nothing.

Chris tried running after the bus to get a better look, but he had to avoid a street light, and by the time he looked back up, the seat the man had been sitting on was empty. It was still a hot day in the city, but Chris couldn't stop the chill running down his back.

His apartment had only been abandoned for a day, but the air still smelled stale. For the first time in months, he didn't crank the air conditioning in the main room with his keys still in his hand. The apartment would have been out of his price range if it hadn't been for a lucky combination of a small inheritance and two co-workers needing to sell quickly in a slow housing market. He had been very lucky indeed. He loved the bright, airy room with its warm blue walls, soft wood floors, and huge bay windows with a panoramic view of the city. The wraparound balcony had sliding doors in both the living area and the bedroom. And, while he'd never used it, and probably never would, the fireplace offered a relaxing focal point in the room.

Only now, the plants on the mantle and counters had all but withered. He thought fondly of the beer in his fridge but watered the plants first.

Chris stopped in the bathroom to fill up his watering can again and spend extra time with the huge ivy in his bedroom. It was beautiful, but persnickety, and would drop its leaves at any real or imagined slight.

Like most of his past partners, he thought ruefully, and almost dropped his watering can as he heard the unmistakable sound of a beer cap twisting off behind him.

He turned.

Gregory leaned against the doorway, holding two bottles by their necks. Chris looked outside; the sun was now just starting to set over the city, turning everything a blood orange.

"I thought sunset was a dangerous time," he said, but took one of the offered bottles.

"It is. Which is why I'm here and not out there."

"I also thought I'd locked the door."

Gregory smiled, bringing the bottle to his lips, but didn't drink. "I can't help it if you're getting sloppy in your old age."

"Sloppy," Chris repeated but found himself smiling as well.

"Sloppy," Gregory repeated. The banter was now as familiar as the shadow of the ivy on his bedroom wall.

"Nice digs. Can I suck your cock?"

"Thanks," Chris said, not hearing the second part of Gregory statement until too late. "And, what —"

Gregory dropped to his knees before Chris could finish and after that there wasn't really much use for words.

Gregory worked quickly, unbuttoning Chris's jeans. He jerked them down over his thighs, and took Chris's cock. The beer in Gregory's mouth had only warmed slightly, and the effervescence to the bubbles stung for an instant.

Then Gregory slid his tongue over the head of Chris's cock, and everything was forgiven.

How Gregory did it, not letting a drop escape but still taking him all the way down his throat, escaped Chris. The beer, Gregory's mouth and his cock all slowly came to equilibrium in temperature. He didn't move, despite the urge to grab the back of Gregory's head and fuck him hard. He locked his knees and kept his hands behind his back.

Gregory placed his palms on Chris's bare thighs, coming off the back of his legs to do so. The sensations coming in waves perfectly timed with Gregory's ministrations. Chris could barely contain his breathing.

Chris didn't know exactly when Gregory swallowed the beer in his mouth, but it was good because it was becoming too hot. In its place, Gregory cupped Chris's testicles, holding them lovingly while wrapping his other hand around the base of Chris's cock. The tension was more than Chris was used to, but not uncomfortable. Not quite yet. It kept Chris on his toes, and Gregory obviously waited for him to say something. Chris kept his mouth shut.

Gregory pulled his mouth free, and it made a popping sound like a child with a lollipop. "Ready?" he asked, his devilish smile barely contained.

"Ready for what?"

He should have kept his mouth shut. Gregory went back to the task at hand with a ferociousness that Chris had never seen before. It was like his teeth, lips, hands, fingers were everywhere. His hands worked in unison, building the orgasm past the point where Chris ordinarily would have already come. His legs were weak, and the muscles of his stomach trembled. He couldn't make his hands release his wrists to grab onto

Gregory's head. "Please," he said, not knowing what else he could do. His entire body hummed in a frequency Chris had never felt before. He was as close to coming as he'd ever been, so close, so very close, and yet Gregory still kept building the sensations until Chris's entire body was burning.

Sweat broke out along Chris's shoulders, and Gregory pulled back. He trapped Chris's cock in his hands and began to jerk Chris off with his fist, harder than Chris usually liked. But then Gregory met his eyes, and the slight burn started to feel good.

"Come on," Gregory whispered, and Chris couldn't stop himself. The orgasm wracked him but Gregory was there, supporting his weight. His entire body wanted to shut down as the orgasm completely overtook him. When he came, he was flying, flying over desert dunes, the shadow and light so crisp they looked like a glossy painting. His head was filled with a buzzing sound again, but he'd never felt so free. The wind in his hair was felt real, and the breeze moved through his fingers.

And then he woke, in his own bed, with the shadow of the ivy stretched out over the wall. The moon was full and, without the curtains drawn, it was almost enough light to be able to read. He expected to be alone in his bed; he should have been alone. But, when he reached out, his mind already feeling the cold crisp sheets against his palm, instead he felt Gregory's warm shoulder.

Chris opened his eyes, swearing to himself that he had already opened them, but when he looked around the room was dark. There were no shadows on the wall. Gregory stared at him. "I stayed," he said. His fear of rejection was obvious, even under the jovial tone.

Chris stroked his shoulder. "I'm glad you did."

The tension Chris felt drained slightly, but didn't melt away. So he reached into his dresser and pulled out his bottle of massage oil.

Gregory rolled his eyes. "You have got to be kidding me."

"You have to trust me. I'm a professional." Chris used his best cop voice.

Gregory shook his head. "Tell me, does that actually work?"

"You'd be surprised how many people have cop fetishes."

Gregory made a disgusted sound in the back of his throat, but didn't protest again. Chris pulled down the sheets and spilled a little of the oil into his hand. "You don't like cops, I take it," Chris said.

Gregory flinched, even though Chris had warmed the oil before touching his back. "I don't like a lot of cops, no. I'm growing fond of you. "

"Why?" Chris asked. Gregory's muscles were tight again.

"Well, because you're rubbing my back right now. Unless you mean why I hate cops. I guess it's because I've been fucked by them one too many times. Have you ever thought of becoming, oh, I don't know, an air traffic controller instead?"

Chris straddled Gregory's lower back to get more leverage, and Gregory groaned.

"Well, on behalf of all my brothers and sisters in blue, I do apologize," Chris said. Gregory's muscles were still tense. Chris worked his thumbs into the worst of Gregory's knots.

"Dear God. Who taught you how to do that?" Gregory managed as Chris worked on his shoulder.

"I dated a guy named Hanz once," Chris said.

"And you broke up with him?" Gregory asked. "Pardon me, officer, but that was stupid."

"He worked nights," Chris said, "and when I started working days he met someone else."

Gregory buried his head into the pillow and muffled another groan. It was the most natural thing for Chris to do, once Gregory had relaxed completely, to slip his hand between Gregory and the mattress. The sound Gregory made was partly a growl. He began thrusting, hard enough that Chris had to press his hand against the small of Gregory's back so that Gregory wouldn't slip away.

Gregory turned frantic and fought as Chris turned him over. Gregory grabbed Chris's head, forcing him down his length, but even when Gregory was all the way into Chris's throat, it wasn't enough.

Gregory snarled a long string of particularly creative profanity and pushed Chris away. He got out of the bed and stalked away from him, as dangerous as a feral cat. Chris remained on the bed rather than follow him. "Are you okay?" he asked.

Gregory turned on him. His erection was still hot and tight, but he was shaking. "Forgive me, officer," he said. "I'm guess I'm not as low maintenance as you need."

Chris shook his head. "I never asked you to be low maintenance," he said. "What do you need?"

Gregory flushed. "You wouldn't give it to me anyway."

Chris tried not to take it personally. "We're a bit early in the relationship for you to tell me what I will and will not do."

Gregory shook his head, but the R word didn't scare him off. Chris got off the bed. Gregory stopped pacing long enough to let Chris take his shoulder. "Tell me."

Gregory spat at him. He supposed he was trying to scare him off, but Chris stood his ground. "You can let me fuck you, drag you across the floor and use you hard, and if I sink my teeth into your neck while I'm doing it you are just going to have to take it."

"So far not disagreeing," Chris said and somehow knew that any bite marks Gregory did leave on him would be gone the next day. But there was something wrong with Gregory. He didn't want that. Chris moved his hand of Gregory's shoulder. "Or?" He prompted.

Gregory swallowed and looked down. His face flushed with shame. Chris lifted his chin. "Tell me."

Chris offered his wrists to him. "You can tie me down," he said, voice thick. "Fuck me hard." He looked up at Chris, guardedly.

"Do you think I would say no?" Chris asked. Gregory waved his hand, taking in everything around them.

Chris put his hand over Gregory's other shoulder. "You don't trust me," he said.

"I do," Gregory said. "Or I want to."

"I have nothing to chain you to." The headboard was solid oak. Gregory's fists clenched. "But if you're sure you want this?"

Gregory nodded, too fast. Chris, still holding Gregory by the shoulders swept him off his feet. Gregory's eyes grew big, but he didn't fight.

"You can try," Chris told him. "But you're not breaking free."

As a plainclothes detective he hadn't had to use his restraining holds in years, but his muscles remembered. The more Gregory fought, the tighter Chris held him, but he didn't constrict his breathing. Chris had left the lube by the table, which was not smart. The more Gregory shifted, the more sexual his movement became. Gregory was begging him not to let go, to just keep him down and safe, just a little bit longer. Chris transferred both Gregory's wrists to the same hand – something he'd never do with a perp – and used the other to gather Gregory's cock up. It was dry, something else he wished he could change. But Gregory didn't seem to care. He thrust as hard as he could into Chris's hand, and the challenge became keeping the illusion of control from shattering out from under Gregory's need.

Finally, Gregory whimpered, arching his back. He came on the hardwood floor, his entire body shuddering as he did.

Chris got off him, but Gregory remained on the floor still curled up in a small ball. Chris helped him back to the bed and tucked him into his side. Gregory snuffled and buried himself into the pillows.

Chris wiped off the spot Chris had come on, and went into the main room. He wasn't sure what food he had, but found an apple that wasn't mealy and a jar of peanut butter. He took it out to his balcony. He sat in his swing, and curled his legs underneath himself.

He cut a section of apple and smeared it with peanut butter. It had seemed like too much work to hunt down some frozen bread, but found after the first bite that he didn't need it. A short time later, the bedroom door slid open. Gregory came out wrapped in a blanket despite the still latent heat of the evening.

"You are quite the gourmand," Gregory said, eyeing the apple.

"Don't knock it till you try it," Chris said.

Gregory rubbed his face. "Thank you, for that. I…ah…needed it."

Chris offered him the slice of apple he was going to eat, and Gregory took it, joining him on the swing.

"I locked the door behind me, Gregory," Chris said quietly. "I even drew the chain."

"I don't know what you want me to tell you," Gregory said.

"How about 'I used my mojo to break into your house, and although it is pretty cool, I promise to teach myself how to knock next time.'"

Gregory took a bite of apple, chewed, and swallowed. "Knock. Gotcha," he said.

Chris pulled him down to him, feeling the tension in his body as he practically manhandled Gregory 's head to rest on his shoulder. The moment it did, Gregory relaxed completely. "Where did he find you?" Chris asked.

"Ask me tomorrow," Gregory said.

It didn't seem like that large a request, and Chris could agree to it. He rested his head against the swing, and together they rocked it back and forth.

Phoenix wasn't a large city compared to New York, but it still pumped out enough light pollution to hide the stars most nights. But tonight with Gregory on his shoulder, the stars were out in multitudes. Gregory stole another slice, holding it out for peanut butter treatment. He shifted impatiently when Chris was perhaps slightly too miserly with the peanut butter.

"I thought apples were beneath you," Chris said.

"No. Just…it's not what I was used to." Gregory continued to munch away.

"Your days of caviar and champagne are long since over."

"Thank God for that," Gregory said with a slight peanut butter sigh.

"Are you going to spend the night or do you want to do your own walk of shame?" Chris asked. He wondered if he should still press Gregory about Jones, but decided that too could wait for a time when they weren't sitting under the stars together. Gregory even slipped his hands into Chris's.

"I'd like to stay, if that's all right."

"More than."

"And I want my own apple."

"That's pushing it."

"You didn't let me say the part about requiring my own knife and full possession of the peanut butter jar."

"We share the jar."

"Done," Gregory said and got off the swing.

□ □ □ □ □

Gregory threw the blanket over his shoulders. The room was slightly chilly, and he adjusted the thermostat before going to the fridge. It was a single man's fridge, with more bottles of condiments than actual food – not that there were many bottles of condiments. The bag of apples was visible in the crisper through the glass shelf atop it. He opened the drawer and knew before he even touched one of the fruits that he was being watched.

And not by Chris. Chris's gaze felt like a line of tiny bubbles, like something in a cola drink. This one was like cockroaches scurrying over his legs. He turned around, but already knew that Jones would be watching him.

And, of course, he was. Gregory was suddenly glad his back was to the very solid fridge.

"You had to know I would find you," Jones said, his voice oily. He reached to touch Gregory's shoulder, but Gregory ducked away.

"Always so sensitive," Jones said.

"You mistake sensitivity for despising your intestines," Gregory said. Through the glass, he could see Chris but knew from years of experience that Chris wouldn't hear him, even if he screamed. He was alone.

"Why did you leave me?" Jones said.

"Because I could," Gregory snapped. He didn't move from the fridge. Jones's smile creeped him out. "You're not welcome here," Gregory continued. He put steel in his voice that he did not necessarily feel, but it gave him the strength he needed.

Jones approached him, pinning him to the fridge. Its low hum was the only normal thing around them, but Gregory didn't move. Better to be pinned than have his back exposed; he'd learned that lesson the hard way. Jones smelled him, inhaling deeply right behind Gregory's ear. The old, too familiar desire to close his eyes, to give in to Jones, swept over Gregory like a drug-induced haze. He'd broken free once, but Jones was stronger now.

"But I'm not exactly here, am I?" Jones asked, whispering the words one by one, like a...like an insect laying its eggs, Gregory thought, sickened.

"Leave me alone," Gregory said. If Chris were to come in right now, Gregory had to wonder what he would see.

"Meet me tomorrow," Jones said.

It would be suicide. Gregory found himself nodding. "Just leave Chris out of this."

Jones laughed, but to Gregory's wrist. While Gregory felt his scaly hand over his own wrist, and Jones's too hot cock pressing up against some kind of foreign wool, he also felt nothing at all. "I'll take your officer, as well. You wouldn't be alone again."

"Over my dead body," Gregory whispered. Jones squeezed Gregory's hand over his own cock. It must've hurt, but Jones only squeezed harder.

"If that's what it takes," Jones whispered back.

"Gregory?" Chris asked, coming into the kitchen. "Did that apple do something to offend you?"

Gregory looked down to his hands. Apple juice had run down his fingers and pooled in his palm. His fingers were up to the first joint in the fruit. Chris took it from him and wiped his hands off as though he were a child.

"Come to bed," Chris said. "We can talk about this in the morning."

Gregory nodded. "I'm going to...shower first."

Chris nodded and wandered back into the bedroom. He hadn't told Gregory where the bathroom was, but Gregory found it after first discovering the laundry room and then the office. The shower was separate from the soaker tub, and Gregory reached in with cold fingers to turn on the hot water full blast. Then he shut the building's door behind him, not really aware of walking out of the apartment, down the hall, nor of summoning the elevator. He looked up once, to the balcony on the sixteenth floor. The streets were quiet, and they welcomed him back.

Jones had found him here, five years ago. It had seemed longer. He'd been just a kid, and David had seemed like the smoothest, most interesting person Gregory had ever known. He'd looked like a jewel on Brantley's arm. And if there had been a look of…panic when Brantley had touched him unexpectedly, Gregory convinced himself not to see it.

And the world had been amazing. Gregory had seen elephants crossing the road at dawn in Africa and had skied the finest slopes in Europe. And when Jones had crawled into his bed at night for the first time, well, that wasn't exactly new. He had the other place to go to, with the white sands and the blinding sun, and it was enough. Brantley had managed to taint a small corner of it, and even though it was growing, there were still plenty of good places to fly.

For a while it had just been him and David with Brantley. Their lives revolved around the great man. It had been the happiest time in Gregory's life, if he completely ignored what happened at night. He was good at ignoring that.

Then David had gotten sick. If sick was the right word for it. Jones kept them apart after that, and for a while he would see David around the compound. Then he didn't see David at all, and Jones stopped talking about him. Gregory had to get him drunk to find out what happened. But he knew…whatever Jones had done to David had made Brantley even more seductive to the masses and had stripped David's mind completely. Then Gregory had felt the same drain beginning on him.

He was tired. He should have been sprawled out beside Chris – or Jones, the dark side of his brain said. Instead, he found David sleeping in a cardboard box.

David poked his head out.

"I told you to always find a different spot."

David shrugged and climbed out of the box. The hair on the side of his head was flattened. Gregory ran his hands through it.

"Jones is too strong," Gregory said. "Why did we ever think we could get away from him?"

David stared at him. Sometimes, when the moon was full, Gregory could almost feel David so close to the surface that they could actually speak. This time he heard David in his head. There was no other alternative. They had to get away.

"He's not going to have the chance to take Chris."

David shook his head.

"It's not safe."

David reached out for him, but Gregory easily slipped away from him. He spent the night in the root cellar, away from everyone's prying eyes.

□ □ □ □ □

Billy felt Gregory do it. He'd been put in both David's and Gregory's place at least a year before he should have. While Brantley thought him the weakest of the three, Billy had taken his full weight and was still going strong.

Jones wasn't in the room with him, but still pulled from Billy like a generator. He was close, physically upstairs in his fancy rooms, but Billy didn't have to be with him to feel the man using him.

Billy took the stairs down to the room. The bedroom was a place of darkness for him. With his connections so strong, he could smell the layer upon layer of sweat on the bed – his, Jones's, Gregory's. Oh, Gregory'd been such a favorite. There was so much on the bed from the two of them. And, of course, from David. It was something that no change of sheets could alter. He left the room quickly and went to Jones's secret room. Here the smell was just of Jones. Of his sweat, of his semen, and of his blood. The room was pitch black, but Billy knew the wooden floor would be stained brown.

Billy sat down, where Brantley had, and closed his eyes. He could barely feel Brantley now; the pull was no more annoying than the distant buzzing from a fly. He waved something from his face, and felt the quiet sensation of wings on his skin. He closed his eyes.

Jones was being denied. Gregory had been cornered, miles away from his warren. And Jones had had him in his teeth. Then the contact had been broken, and Gregory had escaped.

And for that Billy was glad. Partly because he wasn't like David or Gregory. He wasn't ever going to be second chair to Gregory.

Something hissed and skittered in the corner of the room when Billy thought of Gregory, and the hatred came from everywhere. He heard water trickling all around him, and if he closed his eyes and concentrated, the babbling sounds almost formed words. The room was cold, but Billy no longer felt it. He was warm all over. It was the most natural thing for him just to lie back. The floor was so soft now. Warmer hands touched his thighs, spreading them. A mouth engulfed his cock. Fingers probed him. Billy lay still and let whatever or whoever was in the room with him just take him.

□ □ □ □ □

Chris knew something was wrong long before a normal shower would have been over. He opened the bathroom door and knew before the steam fully dissipated that Gregory was no longer with him. He dressed quickly and bolted from the apartment. He knew that in the same way that setting the car alarm was bad, calling Gregory's name would be worse. The streets were calm in either direction, and if Gregory had wanted to be found, he would have stuck around in the shower.

Chris shook his head. He stepped back into the lobby and let the door close in front of him. Every ounce of his being wanted to go find Gregory – and lead Jones right to him – but he couldn't.

It would have to wait until morning. He went back up to his room, but he didn't fool himself that he was going to sleep.

Morning came with a burst of color and someone banging on the door. Chris was up the next second. He all but yanked the door off its hinges. "Well, at least you learned how to knock –" he began, but then saw the pink cardigan. Donna's face was blank, but she reached for him with her fingers, still with their perfect French-tipped manicure. She caught him across the cheek with a single nail. He felt and heard his flesh ripping.

Blood dripped onto the hardwood floor. Pain blossomed on his face in a perfect line. He avoided the clumsy attempt at his eyes and pushed her aside. She ran into the small table he kept his keys on. It knocked her on her ass, but she launched herself up off the ground. This time she went for his groin. He knocked her down again, still trying not to hurt her. But each time he knocked her down she seemed to get faster and angrier. He finally pinned her down, stunning her long enough to get his cuffs from where they'd fallen off the table. She fought like a hellcat, snarling even as he pinned her. He made a phone call.

Her bag had spilled when she attacked him, and a thirteen-inch butcher knife had fallen from it. If she had come at him with that, it would have been a completely different story. But when he picked her up by the arm she began throwing her body at them. She was still mostly animalistic. He wondered if it had ever occurred to her to use a tool, even a destructive weapon like a knife. She began pulling at her handcuffs, scraping the skin off her hands. He threw her into the laundry room and waited for the patrol cars. When the uniforms did arrive at the door, however, they found a very frightened, confused older lady. She sat among the lint balls of Chris's utility room and shook.

"What am I doing here?" Donna asked, confused. She still had his blood on her hands. "Officers, thank God. This man…I believe this man kidnapped me."

"You have got to be kidding," Chris said.

Donna pulled herself off the ground. She lost her rhinestone glasses somewhere, and it made her cold eyes colder. But confusion seemed real. "Officers, aren't you going to arrest this man?"

The officers looked at Chris, confused.

"Take a scraping from her hand," he said. "And take her down to the station."

"On what charge?"

"Start with assaulting an officer," Chris said. "I'll meet you there."

"Yes, sir."

"Take a scraping as soon as possible, and definitely before you let her see her employer."

"Why would we call him?" one of them asked.

"I'm sure he'll be down as her emergency contact," Chris said. He touched his cheek and his finger came away bloody.

"You should get that cleaned, sir. It looks nasty."

"Worse than it actually is," Chris said.

"We'll have an ambulance come pick you up."

"Don't be ridiculous. I'll drive myself in," Chris said.

"Bad idea, sir," the second one said as the other read Donna her rights. They locked a new set of handcuffs over her wrists and gave Chris's back.

Donna walked away between the two, still accusing Chris of police brutality. It was morning. Gregory was still gone. His face ached, and he still had to go through an entire day with Niles. "Fuck," he said, and he called for a cab.

Chris didn't actually catch a glimpse of himself until the taxi pulled into the hospital parking lot. The cloth he had grabbed from the kitchen had managed to sop up most of the blood, but even he could tell it was a fairly deep cut. Donna had caught him with the edge of her nail, and she sliced rather than scratched. If he were lucky, he would just need stitches.

The nurse at the triage station told him to sit and wait, and it was there that Niles found him over an hour later.

Most people entering the aggressively air-conditioned interior from the outside gave a silent moment of thanks, but Niles didn't seem to notice. In mere seconds, he'd located Chris sitting amongst the sad occupants of the waiting room. A second later, and he was standing over Chris.

"What the hell did you do to that wonderful old woman?" he demanded loud enough that everyone in the room heard.

"I guess I caught myself on her nail. It was poor planning on my part; she had been going for my eyes at the time."

"You are having her…charged!"

"That's the SOP when someone attempts to kill you, or perhaps I just read that part of the manual wrong. She attacked me, Niles, and I had no choice."

Niles's lip curled back. "You will, of course, drop all charges."

"I will not," Chris said. Niles glared at him, but the droning of flies Chris was expecting along with a headache seemed like just a minor nuisance. No doubt because of his evening with Gregory. "Stop it. It's not working."

"Brantley won't allow this to go forward."

"I don't recall asking for Brantley's permission. And when I get back to the station, I fully intend on questioning her myself."

Niles smiled at him, but coldly like the air conditioner. "We'll see about that."

"Surely you're not threatening another officer, Niles," Chris said. "You have two employees of Jones going postal in two weeks, and yet you don't see a connection. Your pal is bad news, a danger to the community, and has terrible job-related perks."

Chris's name was called, far ahead of where it should have been. He looked around but no one seemed to notice. He followed the nurse into one of the curtained examination rooms. Chris was just glad that he was away from Niles. It still took over half an hour for the doctor. He closed his eyes, and didn't wake until he heard the curtain slide back.

The doctor didn't speak. Chris waited for him to say something, anything at all, but the man said nothing even as he began tapping out air bubbles from the syringe he held. "What is that?" Chris asked, unsure why he suddenly felt panicked.

"Novocain," the doctor grunted. He nodded to a nurse that Chris hadn't heard approach. She nodded back.

Chris couldn't take it anymore. Something was definitely off. He tried to get off the bed, but the nurse grabbed one of his arms and the doctor grabbed the other. Chris fought, kicking his legs out, but the nurse clamped her hand over his mouth just as someone else started to scream in the waiting room. It covered whatever muffled sounds he made, but he caught the doctor on the knee. The doctor crumpled. The nurse tried to scratch him, narrowly missing his already existing marks, but Chris caught her wrist and squeezed it hard enough that he started to feel the bones separate. She howled, trying to get at his eyes, but the moment he felt the bones shift, she collapsed to her knees as well. Chris bolted out of the curtained area.

"Officer Cunningham?" the doctor asked as he emerged, cautiously, rubbing his knee. He blinked at the bright light, and it was as though he'd just woken up. "Was there something wrong?"

"What the hell were you doing?" Chris demanded.

"If you don't want stitches, we can always do butterfly bandages."

"Do that," Chris said quietly. The doctor began to pull the curtain again, but Chris stopped him with his foot. "In the open."

"Honestly, officer, I–"

"In the open," Chris demanded.

"In the open," the doctor agreed, and if he truly didn't understand what was going on with Chris, he was a better actor that Chris gave him credit for.

# CHAPTER SEVEN

With nowhere else to go, Gregory went home. He knew he probably shouldn't, but it was his only safe place. The bad feeling he'd picked up from Chris came back the moment he put the key in the lock. The sliding door was opened, and the curtains blew in the slight wind.

"David?" Gregory called, closing the door behind him. Something told him not to lock it, so he didn't. There was no point. "David, I asked you to keep the door—"

A blond stood in the hall, but it wasn't David. He was fairer than David and darker at the same time. Gregory supposed lots of people had black eyes, but the man's irises and pupils swirled with an oily sheen set in the white eyes of a person who didn't drink, smoke, or stay up late at all. It made his almost albino-white hair seem like spider webs.

Gregory shivered, unable to stop himself. "Take what you want," he said, voice flat. "There's nothing here, but you're welcome to it."

"Anything I want, Gregory?" the man asked. He took a step forward. Physically, he didn't look much older than Gregory. In fact, he was probably younger. But just looking into those eyes made Gregory's stomach turn watery and his knees too weak to lock.

"How do you know my name?" Gregory asked weakly.

"I smelled your sweat off a mattress," the man said, and he smiled. "I tasted your hate."

"Brantley sent you. I told him I'd meet with him. What do you want?"

The man didn't answer, but put both his hands on the wall. "This was quite clever, I must say. Hiding away in the one place Brantley had forced himself to forget. That family never asked to be his first test subjects, but they were. They listened to every word he said. If you're quiet, you can still hear the radio playing his show. You were there, Gregory. You could have stopped him."

Gregory shook his head. "I was still a boy. I didn't know—"

"*Bullshit* is the phrase I think I'm looking for. This Billy's head is full of the most interesting phrases. All of this is so new. You showed him your world, Gregory. You showed him how to use the power of my water. Without you, none of this would have been possible. You must be very proud."

"Are you here just to congratulate me?" Gregory said. He took a step back, feeling for the door knob, but the man, Billy, if that was what he was anymore, was suddenly there, suddenly pinning him to the wall, and the position, all too familiar, made Gregory suddenly want to give into it.

"Do you think a parent has the right to avenge the death of a child?" Billy demanded. Gregory knew he should have felt the heat of Billy's breath, inches away from his ear, but instead he smelled of the same foul water that came from the spring behind the wall in the dark room. "Do you?"

"I—"

The thing inside the human skin howled, and it was the sound of an avalanche screaming down a narrow mountain pass. "Do I not have the right for revenge?"

"Yes," Gregory whispered, because there was no other way to answer the question. "But I haven't killed anything."

"You lie! You slew my children, my beautiful children with their sharp teeth and their sharp claws. You cut them down and slaughtered them by the hundreds."

"They would have killed me," Gregory said. He'd felt the beasts' claws and teeth catching him a hundred times. If the wounds hadn't disappeared before he woke up each night he would have been covered in scars. He would have given anything to have the knife in his hands again.

"I will enjoy this," Billy said, and when he opened his mouth, his human teeth were juxtaposed with a hundred thousand shark teeth, all in perfect rows, all ready to tear his throat out. Gregory couldn't stop himself from craning his neck back and offering himself up for the bite. Instead, Billy fell forward, his perfectly human teeth – sharp but not unnaturally so – grazing Gregory's skin.

Gregory found the door knob, but with Billy's weight on top of him he couldn't pull the door open. David stood behind Billy, but whatever inhuman thing that was in him was temporarily stunned. The kitchen chair David swung had splintered, but Gregory hadn't heard it.

Billy shook his head, for a moment as human as the rest of them, but then the blue part of his eye fogged over and went black. "Run," David said. It was his first word since Brantley had split him.

"I will feast on you," Billy said, and his teeth were back. But now David was in front of Gregory, and together they headed back to the opened screen.

"Gregory, run!"

"I can't —" Gregory said, but then the thing was over David, and the unmistakable smell of blood was back. Gregory ran, and kept running until he was far enough away that he didn't recognize the street he was on. His breath came in ragged gasps and the back of his throat tasted of blood, and it seemed to take hours again for him to find a phone and call Chris.

"David's dead," he said instead of a hello.

"What?" Chris asked.

"Something got him. He's at the old place. Can you…can you send someone?"

"Gregory, you have to come down, make a statement—"

"No!" Gregory said. "Please, Chris. I need you. Just…come get me, okay?" He gave the address as best he could and retreated to the shadows until Chris's taxi pulled up on the street. Gregory came out of the shadows and waited for him. Chris smiled. After a second, Gregory, despite everything, smiled back. "Hi."

"Hello."

"Officers have been by your old house, Gregory. The doors were open, but they didn't find anything."

"David's dead."

"They didn't —" Chris began, but then silenced. "I'm sorry, but I am glad to see you."

Gregory nodded. His shoulders slumped and he felt completely empty. He wanted to cry; he'd sure as hell cried enough when Brantley took David to begin with, but now he just felt freeze-dried and angry inside.

"What happened?" Chris asked.

Gregory told him, surprised he had the words to describe the creature's eyes.

"And David spoke to you?" Chris asked.

Gregory nodded. "He came back to himself, at the end."

Chris touched his cheek. "I am truly sorry."

Gregory thought then, for sure, the tears would come. But he had none left. "David died three years ago," he said, his voice breaking. "The rest was…it's over now. He's dead."

"I'm sorry," Chris said. He touched Gregory's shoulders, the only touch Gregory would have allowed, and Chris seemed to understand that. He shook his head. It wasn't safe to stay out on the street, and the thought of his old house was the mental equivalent of nails on a chalkboard. He had nowhere else to go, and couldn't make himself ask Chris for his sanctuary after Brantley had already violated it once.

"You don't have to ask," Chris said. "We're going back to my place."

The cab driver said nothing as they got into the back seat. Chris continued to hold him as the car pulled back into the street, and that was the only thing that mattered.

The night and the day passed, with Gregory on the balcony. He liked the way the cool evening breeze touched his skin so far in the sky, and Chris never once tried to get him to go in. He brought food out to him and sat with him a while on the swing, but didn't say anything. Gregory needed the time to smooth the edges of the idea that David was gone. When the sun set the second time, he took a final broken breath, and was adjusted to the idea that David would not be coming back.

He pulled open the door. Chris stopped working on his Sudoku puzzle. "Are you okay?"

"Getting there," Gregory said, and Chris nodded. He started to pick up the puzzle again, but there was a nervous twitch to his wrist. "You must be crawling the walls by now."

"Getting there," Chris said and smiled a bitter smile. "But you needed the time."

"And now I need to go out."

Chris dropped the pen. "Really?"

Gregory smiled as well. Chris had tried to make it sound like an *are you sure* type of *really*, but it came out way more on the side of *oh, thank God*. "Really," Gregory said.

"Come with me."

"Where are we going?"

"Someplace safe."

Gregory smile turned bitter. "The moon?"

"Not quite, but there are some places safer than others." Chris must have had a cab company on speed dial, and the lucky company must have had a cab ready just for him, because it took only five minutes for a cabbie to pick them up and drop them off in front of a bar on the outskirts of downtown. The cabbie stopped. Chris paid him with a twenty dollar bill and told him to keep the change, and Gregory realized the secret to Chris's success.

# CHAPTER EIGHT

Chris got out first and held the door for Gregory, who was still looking a little too fragile. Chris had lost friends in New York. It was hard to be part of the community and not know someone who was taken. He knew all too well the little sliver of relief that came with the pain when a sick person slipped away. Gregory didn't look like a person who took well to relief.

"An Irish pub," Gregory said. "What, buxom lasses and peat moss are supposed to keep me safe?" He was obviously distressed at the plain faced building.

Chris nodded. The old world door was ornately carved and the glass in the window was stained green but there wasn't any noticeable signage outside. "Go on, mock," Chris said and pulled the door by the brass handle.

"Oh," Gregory said. "You take me to a cop bar."

"Safest place outside the station," Chris said, then he wondered how Gregory knew. No one at O'Malley's was wearing a uniform. But then he supposed that it might have been a dead giveaway, the way the clientele all sat without a single back to the door or the way the room silenced the moment the door opened and then everyone went back to the quiet murmurs.

It was a Saturday and it was hard to believe that he'd found Gregory on Wednesday. The days between them seemed to have been weeks.

He led Gregory to one of the booths in the back and they sat across from each other. Beth, Chris's favorite waitress, came over with his beer, the head just barely contained in its glass. She eyed Gregory warily. "I'm going to need some ID," she said apologetically to Chris and ignored Gregory completely.

Gregory glanced over to him as though expecting Chris to say that it was okay, but Chris kept quiet, so he fished out his wallet and showed her his driver's license. Beth stared at it for a long time and put it down upside down. "Well, at least he's legal," Beth told Chris.

"How legal?" Chris asked, ignoring Gregory kicking him under the table.

"Legal enough in any state or protectorate," Beth said. "Anything else is for you to decide. Does he want anything?"

"Two?" Chris asked. It was the same brand as was in his fridge, and Gregory had no problem with that. Gregory nodded.

"And menus?" Beth continued.

"If you don't mind."

She nodded and went back to the bar. "What, she doesn't talk to civilians?"

"Not if she can help it," Chris said. He tapped the driver's license on the table. "That thing real?"

Gregory hesitated. "Real enough for the money it cost. It's got my age right, at least."

"It must be. Beth would have caught it if it was badly done."

"Brantley can afford the very best," Gregory said, and saying the name obviously hurt. He put the license away. "So, what's good?"

"Try the beef and kidney pie. Her dad makes them every morning."

Gregory made a face. "Do you know what kidneys do as a function in cows?"

"Try anyway. You'll be pleasantly surprised."

"Long walks in the park and roses are pleasantly surprising. Things that filter out urea for barn animals, not so much."

"I see." Chris shook his head sadly. "It's really too bad the waitress just won't talk to you."

"You're like...a stealth control freak," Gregory said, but he was smiling. "All that niceness you give off, it's all a ruse isn't it?"

Chris didn't answer before Beth returned with Gregory's drink. Gregory grinned at her, trying to beat her down with sheer force of will. Chris didn't have the heart to tell him that others had tried and failed miserably. "Thank you so much," he said.

And Beth ignored him. "Is he ready to order?" she asked.

Chris nodded. "I'll have my usual. He'll probably want to clog arteries with fish and chips."

Gregory nodded.

"Fish and chips it is then," Beth said and gathered the menus. She left them alone again.

"So how is it that a cop can believe that an evil spring is evil and a television evangelist is making zombies out of his labor pool?" Gregory asked. He kept his voice casual, but his eyes were as sharp as ever.

"I fell down a hole when I was a kid, out by where the compound is now. I've always known there was…something down there. And don't forget I've been fucking you in my dreams for years. When did you know? Was it something that—" Chris couldn't say the name.

"No," Gregory said. "I've been going over to the land of light for years, when my dad, when he…but Brantley showed me how to control it."

"So you're from here, originally?"

Gregory looked down. "Don't try to pump me, Chris. Please. I told you. I don't want to talk about it."

Chris wanted to tell him that if it was something minor he could help, but he didn't. If it wasn't, if it was something major, he would have to do something about that, too. He looked down to his beer.

"Have you ever thought about becoming a circus clown instead?" Gregory asked, voice heaping with bitterness.

"Can't say that I have," Chris said.

"Then let's talk about you. Where are you from?"

"What makes you think I'm not from around here?"

Gregory just looked at him. Chris sighed. "New York."

"And you came to this fair city because…"

"Officially, change of pace. The air good for the consumption, blah blah blah."

"Unofficially?" Gregory asked cautiously.

Chris shrugged. "I fucked my superior officer. If that wasn't bad enough, we began a relationship."

"And that was bad because…?"

"Because the divorce he said he had became a separation, then it was a trial separation, and then they were trying to work through their difficulties. I should have bailed when I noticed the wedding band line on his finger not tanning over. I was in love with him, and stupid. When I did break it off, well, he couldn't demote me, couldn't mess around with my schedule, so instead he –"

"Made your life a waking nightmare?"

"Worse. He promoted me. Made me the GLBT liaison. It's an important role, and I'm glad it's there, but I wanted to catch bad guys, not sound bites. So I bailed. It was masterfully played, I have to admit. Just not by me."

"I'm sorry."

"It's no one's fault. Things happen for a reason."

"I've always envied people who believe that. Sometimes they just happen, and there ain't nothing you can do about it."

Chris cleared his throat and raised his glass. "To absent assholes who made this meeting possible," he said.

"Here, here," Jones said and clapped his hands slowly.

Gregory jumped back, sliding as close to the wall as he could get. Chris carefully put down his glass. "It's okay. He can't do anything right here."

"Indeed I cannot. Nothing except talk. May I join you?"

"No," Chris said.

Jones smiled. "Come now, Mr. Cunningham. There's bad air between us, and I think a little head to head might clear it."

Chris looked at Gregory, who slowly nodded. He stood up.

"You have something that belongs to me," Jones said. "A piece of my property that lost itself."

"Gregory, could you please wait by the bar."

Gregory, for once, didn't argue. Chris waited for him to be out of range before speaking. "I am armed," Chris said. "And if I have to go through your parking tickets to find a reason to arrest you, I will. Are we absolutely clear?"

"My, but you do like to take control of the situation. We are perfectly clear."

Chris nodded, and Jones sat down.

"What do you want?" Chris demanded.

"A single malt from a dusty bottle in a private collection. So would Gregory, if he were to tell you the truth. The boy has very expensive tastes. Did he tell you that? Can you even begin to afford him?"

"I'm not renting him out by the hour," Chris said darkly. "I want you to leave him the hell alone."

"I really want that single malt. Life is disappointment. I will not be leaving Gregory alone until I can speak with him."

"And I'm telling you that's just not going to happen."

Jones bared his teeth. "So this is your protectorate mode. How charming. Misguided and misplaced, but charming. I hope Gregory has made it perfectly clear that he was a full adult when we began our...relationship; I suppose you can call it. He consented fully to everything we did together. In exchange for sexual favors that were willingly provided, I gave the young man practically anything and everything he asked for. It was mutually beneficial for everyone involved. When he left me, he left me in an awkward situation that could possibly cost me everything. I want us both to be clear that that may never happen, and I am willing to be generous to a fault to ensure that it doesn't. So I ask you again, may I speak with my former lover?"

Chris was silent for a long time. It was a plausible explanation for almost everything, but it still left a bad taste in his mouth. He leaned forward. "You practiced that, didn't you?"

"Give me Gregory," Jones snarled. "You have no right to him."

"Richard Heath," Chris said. "Did you just want to talk to him, too?"

"Heath was a loyal and kind employee. He has nothing to do with this."

"You sent him out to find Gregory. He was a good man, and you sent him out as a butcher. Do you know how many people he killed?"

"What Richard did outside of my employ was completely out of my control," Jones said coldly.

"And your assistant? Was she fired too when you sent her out in the middle of the night?"

Jones was silent for a moment, obviously trying to think of a plausible cover story, but drew a blank. Chris leaned back. "Don't worry. If all you are concerned with is protecting your reputation, I can assure you that Gregory is not going to the police. Your deep, dark secret that you are a filthy, hypocritical sodomite will remain that: a secret."

Jones did not look even slightly mollified. "And with that, I am supposed to leave the two of you alone?" he asked. He dropped his voice low enough that if Chris was wearing a wire it would not have picked up anything but ambient noise. "I need him. And you will not deny me."

"But I will," Chris said. "I'm going to have to. And Gregory may be terrified of you, but he's not just going to roll over."

Jones leaned into Chris's space. "Do you think Gregory can take care of himself?" he asked in a low whisper.

"Of course I do," Chris snapped.

"Then ask yourself why he is terrified of me," Jones whispered. "You do not want me as your enemy."

"It's a bit too late for that," Chris said. "I think we've already established quite firmly what we are to each other."

Jones spread his hands. "That we have. And you are such the hero. But you also have to realize that we are dealing with something ancient here."

"So?" Chris demanded.

"You know what they say about the only good hero, Chris."

"Leave Gregory alone. Leave me alone while you're at it, and this will be the end of it."

Jones smiled. "I am so looking forward to working with you. Give Gregory my love and tell him that he is always welcome to come back."

Chris told him to get intimate with the Costco sized bottle of Tabasco on the table. Jones didn't stay much past that.

# CHAPTER NINE

Billy waited for Brantley in the car. He was silent, and although Brantley preferred him that way, he'd been too quiet for too long. He'd wandered off during the day and was gone for most of it, and his security team had found him inside the compound at dusk, flat on his back. When he looked at Brantley, he'd smiled, and for the briefest second, all Brantley saw was teeth.

"What?" he demanded.

Billy blinked, once. "I didn't say anything, sir."

"You were about to."

"Was I?" Billy asked. His voice had a dream-like quality to it. "I wasn't aware of that."

"Billy," Brantley said, warning.

"He was there, wasn't he? He and the police officer."

"Yes. He was. You were right."

Billy nodded to himself. How Billy had known that, when Brantley had felt nothing, escaped him. Billy must have been doing more things better. When they coupled like beasts, Brantley felt himself get stronger. Controlling Donna hadn't taken his full attention as Richard had. It had taken him months to be able to control the fine motor skills he'd needed in order to trust him out there, seeking. Donna had taken moments before he felt comfortable in her skin.

Brantley sat back in the seat. All around him he felt his followers. It still wasn't a complete net, still only a very few number of people had heard him, but that was going to change.

Billy made a strangled sound. "Maybe."

"What was that?" Brantley felt a stab of annoyance. Billy was supposed to power this; he wasn't supposed to have any input. And yet Brantley wasn't willing to completely ignore him. Billy had found Gregory when no one else had.

"You need them both," Billy said. "In order to succeed, you need them both."

"I'm impressed. I thought you were dead set against bringing either one of them home."

"Things change," Billy said. He was back to speaking in that dream-like tone. "Wouldn't you agree, Brantley?"

Brantley nodded, taking immediate dislike to being talked to like an equal. *Subordinate*, the slinking voice in his head hissed. Billy wasn't even looking at him, where a week ago he'd have been terrified not to. "On your knees," he snarled.

Billy looked at him and smiled, but it was a tight-lipped thing full of Billy's own amusement. "If that's what you want," he said, and he slipped down to his knees. He took Brantley's cock out, because that was what Brantley wanted, too.

Even grabbing the back of Billy's head, lifting himself off the back of the seat to drive himself into Billy's throat wasn't enough for Brantley. He felt about as much tied to the sensation as though he were watching it on a screen.

He pushed Billy aside, who wiped his mouth like a cheap whore. "Do you really want to do this here?" Billy asked, his voice low.

"Station," Brantley growled through the speaker, and the car immediately switched lanes. Billy started to get up, but Brantley grabbed him by the shoulder and held him down on his knees. "Stay there."

ㅁ ㅁ ㅁ ㅁ ㅁ

Billy's head was down; all Brantley saw was the golden hair glowing silver in the oncoming lights of traffic, but he knew Billy was smiling. He'd won something that Brantley couldn't see, and even spread-eagled on the table, exposed and open for him, even when Brantley's hands held Billy's hips, crushing, pulling him back, over and over, impaling Billy on his achingly hard cock, he couldn't fuck that sense of victory from him.

Finally he collapsed bonelessly over Billy – the lights from the stage hot enough on his back that it felt like a brand.

Billy pushed him off, with the same disregard as a blanket that was too hot. He left Brantley on the desk, and made his way to the center of the stage. He found Brantley's mark, the place where only Brantley was allowed stand. Officially it was because it had the best light. But, in truth, it was also because standing there, with the cameras rolling and the adoring faces looking up at him from the audience and everyone's attention in the building focused solely on him, it always made him feel…

God-like.

Billy turned to him and grinned. "Now, you're getting it," he said, but Brantley didn't see his mouth moving.

The lights were really too bright. He was burning up, like an ant under a magnifying glass. He put his head down, no longer having the energy to follow Billy, and he rested.

□ □ □ □ □

Gregory joined Chris once Jones had left, but he was still shaking. "What did he tell you?" he asked, numbly. Beth brought the food, but they by and large ignored it.

"He wants to make a financial donation to ensure that your relationship remains under wraps."

"Is that all?"

Chris nodded.

Gregory's mouth twitched. He looked away, and the flush on his skin started to creep up his neck. "He didn't tell you anything else?"

"I already knew it started as a consensual relationship, Gregory."

"I suppose that's true. He did a lot of good, you know. In the beginning. Before it came down to donation per capita."

"I'm sure you saw something good in him," Chris said quietly.

Gregory's flush traveled the rest of the way up his cheeks. "You'd think wouldn't you? But I honestly can't remember now."

Chris reached across the table and took his hand. "Let me take you home," he said.

Gregory nodded and followed him out. They didn't make it halfway there when Chris's phone rang.

"Cunningham," Chris said.

Jamie's voice was crystal clear in his ear. "There's been another attack," she said.

Gregory hadn't opened his eyes since they'd gotten into the cab. "If you have to go —" He didn't finish, but he didn't have to. Chris had the cabbie drop him off at the corner. An unmarked car picked him up and drove him to the crime scene.

Betty's Kitchen, of course. Chris shook his head. Gregory hadn't been inside the building in three days, and it had lost what little luster that had remained. Now, with the yellow caution tape over the parking lot, it had become just another statistic against working the graveyard shift.

Jamie separated herself from the other officer and found him by the door. "I'm sorry, I couldn't not call you. It's still your case."

Chris nodded. "What happened?" he asked.

"It looks like another robbery attempt. They were after the personnel records."

"Did they find any?"

"No, sir. Off-site storage. Apparently the office has a bad history of flooding."

"In the desert?"

"That's what she said, sir."

Chris shrugged, if that was her story, who was he to argue. "How many hurt?" he asked.

"Three. The cook and the waitress. They've already gone to the hospital."

"And the third?"

"The assailant. She's in custody. She took a cast iron pan to the face and it still took two patrons to take her down."

"Good for them," Chris said. "Who is she?"

"A Donna Sanders. You may recognize her from her assault on you the day before yesterday."

"Let me talk to her."

"She hasn't asked for a lawyer yet, but we've read her her rights. You're welcome to her; she hasn't said much of anything."

Chris went down to the patrol car Donna was shut into. She was cuffed and belted into the vehicle. He slid into the passenger side. Donna was staring out the window as he opened the door, but the movement attracted her attention like a wild animal. She sat almost primly, but her lips had pulled back far enough that it exposed her pink gums.

She was hissing, like a snake continually warning. He heard her even before he slid the window open between the two sides.

She still wore the pink cardigan, though it was now gray with dust. Her perfect bun had gotten loose, and the curls that had escaped were wild around her face. Most of the make-up Chris had seen on her at the compound had worn off, but for the rivulets of blood red caught in the lines of her lips.

"Tell me, can you speak?" Chris asked.

Donna didn't stop hissing; they just went under her breath. It was like an angry mountain cat Chris had seen once when he was a kid. It had been trapped, too, and even though it was exhausted, it kept up its growls.

"Can you hear me?" Chris asked. "Do you know where you are?"

Still no response.

Chris tried a third time. "Brantley is going to be very disappointed that you failed," he said, and he kept his voice cross. "There is no excuse for failure."

"They were waiting for me," Donna said, although she struggled to form the words. "I didn't...they knew."

Chris nodded. He wondered if Gregory had warned them that someone was coming. Probably, Chris decided. "What did Jones promise you?"

Donna's face relaxed, slightly. She smiled, a beautiful thing, and relaxed against the seat. She didn't answer, regardless of how long Chris waited.

"You are going to jail for this," Chris said. "You know that, right?"

Jail was obviously the last concern that she had. She swayed back and forth, watching him for any weakness, and Chris was glad he'd left the door open in case he needed to beat a hasty retreat. "What did he do to you?"

She didn't answer. He didn't expect her to. He left her in the car and told the driver to take her straight to booking. Jamie drove with them. With nothing else to do, Chris went home.

# CHAPTER TEN

When Chris got home, there was Gregory, sitting on the stoop of his building. There was no reason behind how thrilled he was, just seeing him there. "Hello," Gregory said, but he didn't look up from hugging his knees.

"I thought you'd just let yourself in."

"You didn't give me a key."

"The building manager could have let you in." Chris waited. He wanted to say a half dozen things, all on the same theme of please-stay-the-night or please-stay-forever, but Gregory looked as though he still wanted to say something, so he waited. "It doesn't feel like home."

"I'm sorry," Chris said, unsure what else was proper to say.

Gregory looked up. "And Brantley's stronger. I don't know if I could hold the shield on the house. I have to be pretty angry to hold that much hatred for the guy, and really, if you think about it, it's all your fault that I'm just not that angry anymore."

"Clearly, it's entirely my fault."

"So the only thing you can do to make it up is invite me upstairs."

"Would you like to come upstairs with me?" Chris asked, dutifully.

Gregory pulled himself to his feet. "Yes. Please." Chris offered his hand. Gregory took it. "You look exhausted."

"It's been a very long day."

Gregory kissed him in the elevator and led the way to the bedroom. Chris remembered taking off his shoes, and Gregory filling the watering can for his plants, and then he was asleep.

□ □ □ □ □

Chris woke up in his own bed. For once, his dreams had been the simple dreams of having to get to an appointment that he kept becoming later and later for. It was a strange feeling, but he could rapidly become accustomed to it.

Gregory wasn't in bed. Chris lay still for a moment. The apartment wasn't that large despite how airy it looked, and he heard Gregory trying to be quiet in the kitchen. Chris sat up. His neck hurt slightly from sleeping one pillow short. He grabbed his robe, which had been untouched on the back of the en suite bathroom door for months. He hadn't used it for so long the terrycloth felt stiff.

Gregory was naked. And cooking bacon. Chris came up behind him and put his hands over Gregory's hips. "I love a man who lives dangerously," he whispered into Gregory's ear.

Gregory waved his hands over the splash guard on the frying pan. "And I love a man who has a well organized kitchen."

"Then unfortunately I'm not the man you're looking for. My grandmother probably put that there when she helped me unpack." Chris peered over Gregory shoulder. "Where did you find the bacon?"

"In the far reaches of your freezer."

"And the eggs and bread?"

"The corner store."

"How did you get past the security door in the lobby?"

"You keep your keys by the door, officer. And only three of them had _Do not copy_ stamped on them. I even had a backup plan. It involved full hands, a pathetic look, and a well-placed foot in the door. Plan C involved cloning the Mongol hordes, but that would have been messy."

Next to the stove, and completely unmentioned, Chris's handcuffs reflected the blue gas flame under the pan. Chris took them, and put them in his pocket. "Coffee?"

Gregory saw what he'd just done, but didn't mention it. Instead he motioned at the kitchen table. Small packets of sugar and creamer were stark indication of how early the relationship was. Chris took his black and brought it back to the kitchen. "You did get dressed, right?"

Gregory glared at him, but there was a hint of amusement around his eyes. "Yes, officer. I got dressed."

"And then decided to strip down again to cook me breakfast."

"I only have the one shirt, you see," Gregory said. He turned around and smiled. His face changed as he did so. The hard shell shifted and he was softer now, but he was still guarded as all hell.

Chris set his coffee down. He reached around Gregory and turned off the flame under the bacon. He took Gregory's hands. They kissed, a slow leisurely thing. The taste of Gregory; toothpaste and coffee and early morning sun was about the best wake-up Chris could ever hope for.

He led the way back to the bedroom. Gregory glanced to the bed, the first shadow of discomfort crossing his face, but Chris took the cuffs from his robe pocket. "Will these help?" he asked.

Gregory nodded, gratefully.

"Speak with me, Gregory. I don't want to do this alone."

"They'll help," Gregory said. His lips look swollen but were soft as rose petals when Chris ran his fingers over them. He looked down just for a second and then smiled again. "I think they'll help a lot, Chris."

*Chris*. Not *officer*. That was an improvement. "Then put your hands over your head."

Gregory exhaled, sharply. "Are you going to frisk me?"

"Do you want me to frisk you?" There was a catch in Gregory's breath that Chris hadn't expected. "I could, if you want me to," he finished.

Gregory didn't answer, and Chris let it go this once. Gregory put his hands over his head and turned around. His skin was tight against the muscles on his back. He trembled, which became a full shudder once Chris took out the cuffs. The metal was warm from his pocket, yet Gregory's skin broke out in goosebumps where Chris dragged the cuffs across it.

Compared to the rest of him, Gregory's wrists were dainty. Chris locked the first cuff. Gregory flinched. Still, he gave up his other wrist willingly. "If you need this, we will have to get you a proper pair of cuffs," Chris told him. "The metal can be hell on your wrists, so you have to promise me you're not going to struggle."

Gregory said nothing. Chris swatted his ass hard enough that Gregory had to brace himself. "Did you hear me?"

"Yes," Gregory hissed. "I hear you. And yes, I won't struggle."

"Good," Chris whispered. He still wasn't completely convinced, but put the key on the edge of the bed in easy reach, just in case. Gregory's legs were already spread, but not nearly far enough. Chris nudged him out far enough that it must have teetered on the edge of hurting.

Despite what he said, he didn't actually pat Gregory down. He didn't want to sexualize a ritual that had to save his life. Searching for weapons and for sharps and knowing each and every time that it could end horribly wrong was not the least bit erotic for him. So instead, he used his fingertips. He kissed the nape of Gregory's neck, and felt his throat work as Gregory struggled to swallow.

Chris introduced himself to a thousand places on Gregory's body. He ran his knuckles along the fine line of Gregory's clavicle. He skimmed his fingers along the ridge of the shoulder. He dragged his nails over Gregory's hip. Gregory hissed again and threw his head back, but he didn't fight the cuffs. The new sensations and the old memories melded together and it was good.

Chris closed his eyes. Gregory fit into him perfectly and for the first time so familiarly. He had an inch of height over Gregory, which nestled his cock firmly against Gregory's ass. "If you want, you can put your hands behind my neck," Chris whispered. Gregory didn't answer, but the cuffs clinked against each other when he moved.

"Fuck me," Gregory whispered. "Please, Chris."

"No," Chris said. "Not yet." He wasn't quite finished mapping out Gregory's body. He put his hands in the flat areas between Gregory's hipbones and his cock. He would never have Gregory's entire body plotted out, but it was a start. Gregory's breathing was so close to his ear Chris could hear how dry his throat was. Their heartbeats matched in a frantic tempo, and it was time.

Chris let Gregory go, if only to reach behind him to take the cuffs. Gregory had to take a step to keep his balance and Chris let him fall to the safety of the bed, but only after rescuing the key. He placed it on the bedside table and followed Chris down. Gregory was so ready for him. He had crawled to the middle of the bed, and Chris managed the lube and the condom with one hand while the other kept stroking Gregory's neck.

"Ready?"

"Yes, oh yes. Please."

Chris spread Gregory's legs and it left him completely exposed. He stroked the sensitive skin and debated whether he should stop what he was doing. He ran his tongue along the back side of Gregory's testicles. They were already so tight against his body that Chris decided more would be too painful. There was no reason to keep Gregory waiting.

The condom cut down on the initial rush and the overwhelming sensation of the heat and the tightness. The trust Gregory had in him was just bearable.

"Chris, please," Gregory whispered. "I want this."

Chris kissed the back of his neck. "You have it."

The urge to thrust was primal. He moved his hands to hold Gregory's head up. Gregory reached out, and his wrists were beautiful in their cuffs. Chris was mesmerized by Gregory's long fingers against the whiteness of the sheets. Even as he fucked Gregory as hard as he possibly could, Gregory still climbed up to his hands and knees and took the brunt of Chris's thrusts. He was smiling, too. Chris couldn't see him, but he felt it.

Gregory seemed to light up. He reared up even farther so that he was kneeling. Chris had to get up on one knee to make the thrusts longer. Gregory threw his head back and laughed. He reached behind him again and looped the cuffs behind Chris's neck. It tied them together, tighter than Chris would have wanted on Gregory's wrists, but they were both so close, so almost there, Chris couldn't stop. The metal touching his skin was as warm as Gregory's breath.

"This is…good," Gregory managed. "Please, just like that. That's so good."

Chris pressed one hand against Gregory's chest, pinning him to him, and wrapped the other around Gregory's cock. He loved the way it felt on his palm. He tightened his grip.

Nowhere else on the planet was something so vulnerable and so hard at the same time. He felt Gregory start to shatter from the inside like he'd felt no one else. Gregory sagged in Chris's arms before Chris was ready. But even as he felt himself come, bright, white light overtook his vision. He was flying again even as he felt himself orgasm. Gregory was there with him, his body the source of the light. "You're beautiful," he said. The words were like an anchor trying to pull him back to his body, but the flying sensation was too strong and the chain broke, freeing both of them.

The desert was endless, the two of them hand in hand. The whiteness looked as though it would last forever until they crested a final hill. The growing black spot below them looked cancerous. The cracked and bubbled surface of the mark made Chris's skin crawl, and he recoiled from it out of horror. "What is that?" Chris asked.

He felt himself falling, but before he could panic he was back beside Gregory in bed. His body ached pleasantly, and Gregory was asleep beside him. They'd managed to cover themselves with the blanket, no small feat, Chris knew, and Gregory was hugging the cuffs to his chest in his dream, cradling them like something precious. Chris fished the keys out from the nightstand and undid them.

Which woke Gregory up. Chris found himself wondering if he was dooming himself to a lifetime of feeling guilty because it might wake up Gregory every time he went to bed late or got up in the middle of the night. The fact that Gregory figured firmly in any long range plan that he made was both frightening and natural at the same time. Gregory rubbed his wrists. "What?"

"What, what?"

"You were looking at me."

"I was thinking."

"About the desert?"

"You saw it, too?"

"I always see it. It kept me sane when I couldn't find you."

"The…blemish," Chris said.

"Brantley. He found something in his dark room, where he goes to punish himself for fucking young men up the ass. Or something found him. And it's getting stronger."

"But the mark was so....small. It was tiny, really, compared to all the white."

"And Brantley's posed to go big any day now. He has branding, Chris. He's talking to network people. He's small now, but he has the makings to go huge, and that's exactly what's going to happen unless —"

"Unless...?" Chris said, but the sentence didn't need to be finished. Gregory looked away, and exhaled sharply.

Chris pulled Gregory to him, and Gregory only fought him for a second before giving in with what could only be described as a contented sigh. Chris just held him until their heartbeats synced, and then he caught a glimpse of his alarm clock.

"Fuck," he said and struggled to his feet.

"What do you think we just did?" Gregory asked, and sat up on his elbows. Again, the rightness of him in Chris's bed, rumpled sheets and the smell that remained of the two of them on the sheets, it was exactly the way it should have been.

"Something spectacularly amazing, but I'm late."

"You have the day off," Gregory said. "If you want me to go, just say so."

"I want you to stay," Chris said. He did, but he and his grandmother had a long-standing Sunday morning date, and, if he was late, she was not the woman to forget. Ever. As much as he loved her, and he did, she was a spry young seventy-year old who, despite the sunny disposition and cutting sense of humor, never let anything slide. "If it wasn't a dangerous practice, I'd be quite happy chaining you to the bed for the rest of the day. The rest of the week, actually. But if I'm late...well, I don't even want to think about it."

"Another hot date?" Gregory asked.

"You can say that," Chris said and then grinned. "Want to make it a threesome?"

"What?" Gregory asked, shock on his face clear. Chris put him out of his misery, quickly.

"My gran plays a mean game of euchre. Although don't play penny a point and don't fall for that distracted look she has. It's when she's at her most dangerous."

"Your…grandmother."

"Mother of my mother? Surely you've heard the concept before."

"You want me to visit your grandmother, with you."

"Well, you can go visit yourself, but honestly, I don't trust her alone with you."

Gregory sat back. "Yes," he decided, after Chris had dressed more than half way.

"Yes?"

"Yes, I'll come," Gregory smiled, shyly. "That would be lovely."

The level of formality was wrong, but the sentiment was appreciated. Dressed in one of Chris's old college sweaters and yesterday's jeans, Gregory was ready. Chris led the way down to the street, and the taxi dropped them off in front of the seniors complex. "You ready for this?" Chris asked.

"I think I can manage, yes."

# CHAPTER ELEVEN

The atrium in the complex was glassed in more to keep the moisture inside than to keep out the heat. Unlike the city, the glass room teemed with thick vegetation and life. The fountain had koi the length and breadth of Chris's thigh, and they swam unmolested, protected by a railing just under the surface of the water to keep the more rambunctious of the grandchildren and great-grandchildren from going fishing.

An old woman sat in a wheelchair by the pond. Despite the heat of the morning and the humidity that was already turning the back of Gregory's neck into pinpricks of sweat, her skin looked papery dry. She hugged the red fleece blanket to herself as though it were a lifeline.

Gregory looked at Chris, fairly certain the old woman wasn't the formidable dragon lady about whom Chris spoke, but Chris was already shaking his head.

"Don't be ridiculous," Chris said. The glass doors from the lobby slid open.

Chris's gran strode into the atrium. She wore a powder blue tracksuit with a white stripe down the side. Her hair was white and tightly curled to her face, but it was a face that set her apart from most other old people Gregory knew. She shared a lot of the physical features that made Chris prettier than most men, but with her, it made her look more handsome. The life in her bubbled through. And when she grinned, her entire face lit up. Chris went to her with open arms.

Gregory stood back. They were similar, but different. Chris's grandmother didn't have the vulnerability that Chris still had. It was the vulnerability that Gregory still found himself sometimes wanting to wrap around himself like a blanket, and at other times grind under his boot heel.

"Don't think like that."

It was a male voice, but it wasn't Chris's. Gregory turned, but only when he looked through the glass did he see David beside him, his face so pale he looked like a ghost for the first time since Brantley had hurt him. He was so weak. Gregory guessed that he could appear here only because this place was so tied to death that he wasn't the only shade in the atrium.

"You didn't have to do it," Gregory said quietly.

"I did." David said. His voice was so far away. Gregory touched the glass in front of him and felt nothing but cold. "You learned your lessons well, but don't forget that's not you." They'd both learned it on their knees in front of Brantley, and in the darkroom where it always seemed like something was on the other side of the wall, trying to get in. If it were possible for Gregory to strip that part of him off like an old sweater he would have, but he didn't know how many layers of skin and muscle it would take with it.

"I can't stay long," David said. "But thank you. I thought I was taking care of you, and you took care of me all these years."

Gregory nodded.

"Thank you," David said, and he slowly disappeared.

Chris's gran had a shrewdness to her that he knew Chris would take on eventually. When she looked at him, Gregory felt naked under her gaze. She cocked her head to one side.

For a moment, it seemed as though she had been looking at David, not him.

"And you are...?" she asked.

Gregory knew Chris must have introduced him while he was talking to David but he answered anyway. "I am Gregory."

"Gregory is but half a name." Her eyes, like Chris's, missed nothing. "Most people come with two at the least."

Gregory glanced to Chris. It was a cunning way to get the intel. He could have given his assumed name, but to be frank, the thought of lying to this woman scared him. "Gregory Osborne, ma'am."

"Osborne," she said and nodded to herself. "It is a pleasure to meet you. My name is Nan."

"Nan," Gregory repeated. He stuck his hand out, and she shook it firmly.

"I like him," Nan said to Chris. "He has a nice–"

Chris cut her off. "Gran, if the next word out of your mouth is *ass*, I'm leaving and taking him with me."

"I was going to say smile," Nan finished, smoothly.

"He hasn't smiled yet, Gran," Chris said between clenched teeth.

"No, but I can see it. It's in his eyes. You did well."

"I've barely kicked the tires," Chris said, but Gregory took his hand. Nan looked back and forth between them and nodded before offering them each one of her arms. "Shall we?"

Gregory started to take his, but a flash of red caught his eye. He turned to it out of instinct, and didn't entirely understand why the sight of the old woman's empty wheelchair caused his heart to beat erratically.

Chris felt it too, Gregory knew. It was like a storm front settling over the city a moment or so before the sky opened up. Chris had already taken Nan's arm, but used it to pull her behind him.

Gregory was already beside him. "Take Nan," he said. The old woman had cast her red blanket aside and stood beside her wheelchair. It shouldn't have been terrifying, but her legs were so spindly that it was obvious she hadn't stood by herself in years. They couldn't have supported her, but they did. When she moved, it was with the motion of a marionette whose puppeteer hadn't completely mastered his strings yet. The unnatural motion was the single thing that made this real. "Get her out of here," Chris said. He pushed Nan back to Gregory.

Gregory shook his head. The woman's face changed, the slackness was gone, and in its place was...Gregory stared, not quite willing to believe it yet. Her face was Brantley's, and Brantley in his cold rage got people hurt. "Gregory, this is your last chance," Brantley snarled through the old woman's voice. "Come back to me or I'll take everything from you until you do."

"Leave me alone!" he snapped. Chris was going to reach for his gun, Gregory knew it, but if he shot the old woman, there wouldn't be a tribunal in the world who'd let him off the wrongful death. He took Chris's arm. "You can't hurt her," Gregory said even as the woman stuck out her hands. Her nails were sharp in a neglected kind of way, and they would flay flesh to the bone if she was close enough.

So instead, Chris took another step back. The old woman's breath was labored and harsh, and as she walked closer to him there was another sound. A rattling.

Gregory hesitated. He'd heard it before, of course he had, kneeling in the dark room. When the darkness had stolen everything, the rattling sound had come and soothed him until the door opened again. He turned to Chris, but Chris's head was cocked; he was listening to it, too. Only it seemed to be talking to him, because he was nodding along to it.

"Take Nan into the lobby," Chris said, his voice calm. "I'll be right behind you."

"Are you —"

Chris looked at him, turning away from the danger of the old woman, but the woman seemed frozen in that moment. "Trust me," he said, and he smiled.

Gregory took Nan's arm. The puff of dry, conditioned air on his sweaty face was almost a relief. The door slid shut behind him, and they had to stand off to the side to keep the door closed. Gregory glanced at Nan, expecting an outburst, but she remained tight-lipped. "None of this surprises you?" Gregory asked.

Nan patted his shoulder. "Chris can take care of himself."

Chris walked up to the hissing and snarling old woman without a weapon. She went for his eyes, like Gregory thought she would, but Chris caught her wrists, the motion as gentle as a mother with a child, and pulled her down to the ground. The only danger the old woman posed was to herself; Chris held her hands to her chest and kept her in what looked like an embrace until the alarm sounded.

Orderlies were in the atrium in the next second, and why it hadn't occurred to Gregory to call their attention to the struggle in the first place escaped him. Gregory still felt David in the glass, but too weak to show. He put his hand on the glass, but not even that was enough.

"Do you see him often?" Nan asked, but didn't look away from the orderlies taking the old woman from Chris and helping her back into the chair. From the moment the others had entered the atrium, the old woman had gone back to her catatonic state, and the whole thing looked no more threatening than Chris holding up an old woman so she wouldn't fall until someone could fetch her chair.

"Chris?" Gregory asked, and knew his voice sounded a bit off.

Nan looked at him, her clear blue eyes telling him to cut the bullshit even if she wouldn't say such a vulgar thing. "No. Not Chris. The other one, who was just here."

"You saw him?" Gregory asked, weakly.

She said nothing. "Chris fell down a hole when he was a child. Since then...well, since then, things have been different. And living here, well, I suppose I got overexposed to death."

"His name was David," Gregory said. "But he's been dead for a while."

She held out a perfectly manicured hand to the old woman now sitting contently back by her pond, clutching her blanket again. "Martha hasn't been here for years. They park her in front of either the television or the pond for hours on end. Do you know how she could suddenly stand up and attack my grandson?"

"Poor viewing choices," Gregory said. "She's watching *Brantley Jones's Hour*, I can almost guarantee it."

"It's on every morning at ten."

"Tell them to put on *Maury* instead," Gregory said. "You'll notice a lot fewer zombies running about in the next little while."

"I wouldn't go that far," Nan said and then smiled as Chris came, winded, through the door. "Now, about that game of euchre."

# CHAPTER TWELVE

Chris and Gregory walked back to Chris's apartment. They'd been out with Nan all day and then had eaten at a tiny, local, Italian restaurant. They'd had the restaurant practically to themselves, an indication more of the lateness of the hour than the quality of the food. Chris slung his arm over Gregory's shoulder, only risking it since they'd managed to polish off a very nice bottle of Chianti, and Gregory let him.

He supposed that was a victory in and of itself. With Gregory so close he could feel the streetlight's circle of light on his shoulder like a blanket. Gregory stared at him, his mouth tight.

"Is this your way of asking me to kiss you?" Chris asked.

"Do you want to kiss me?" Gregory's voice was flat, like Chris's response wouldn't bother him either way.

"I do," Chris said. "I really, really do."

Gregory was silent but just for a minute. "So do I. I really, really do."

"Then look at me."

Gregory was sober, Chris knew, and he wouldn't have let his face become so open, so needful or wanting. When he looked up he was all of those things. Chris smiled. "That's better."

"This."

"What?"

Gregory took his face in his hands. "This is better."

"Gregory?"

"Yes, Chris?"

"Shut up and kiss me?"

"That's original."

"The word you're looking for is *heartfelt*."

Chris kissed him. Gregory tasted of garlic and wine. His lips were soft and his heartbeat was loud enough that Chris could hear it. He loved the way Gregory started to meet his tongue, and the way he shuddered under Chris when Chris broke away from the kiss long enough to kiss his chin, bite his earlobe, or run his thumbs along the ridge of Gregory's brow.

"We're going to do this so often that eventually you're just going to assume the position whenever the situation presents itself."

"Assume the position," Gregory repeated, but without an ounce of outrage. "And what position is that?"

Chris smiled. He tilted Gregory's head back, nudged his knees slightly apart and pulled down on his lips so that they were parted. "You can keep your eyes open or closed; it makes no difference to me."

"How did you get so demanding?" Gregory asked, but didn't move. He even clasped his hands behind his back.

"I told you. I dated a man named Hanz."

Gregory shook his head. "You are so weird. Can you please take me back to your place and fuck me senseless, Chris?"

"I think I could manage it."

Gregory took his hand and led him into the building.

Chris kicked the door closed, and latched it shut. Gregory had barely taken a step into the apartment before his shoes came off, then his shirt. The jeans made it to the hall, his shorts just beyond that, and by the time Chris made it to the bedroom, Gregory was naked, sprawled on the bedspread.

Chris leaned against the door frame. "Well?"

Gregory flipped over onto his back. "Well, what?"

"Are you just going to lie there?"

"Would you prefer me standing on my head?"

Chris pretended to think about it. Gregory shook his head. "Fine. Whatever. Perv. How's this?" Gregory asked. He licked his palm, which, to Chris was a very good start, but he didn't say anything. He kept his face stern. Gregory spread his legs, wide enough that it left him completely open. His cock was already hard, that Chris had felt against his thigh as they kissed. The muscles on Chris's thigh clenched involuntarily, but then he forced himself to relax. "Do you want me to do it fast or slow?"

"Do what?" Chris asked.

"You know what," Gregory said. His fingers held his cock, delicately, but even when his hips flexed involuntarily, he fought to keep as still as possible.

"I know what," Chris agreed. "But I want to hear you say it."

"If you want to watch me jerk off in your bed," Gregory began. He ran his fingers down the length of his cock, lazily, "You have to tell me if you want it fast of slow."

Chris swallowed. All control he had over the situation drained from him. He walked to the bed and sat down right beside Gregory's thigh. "Slow," he said, and the word stuck to the edge of his throat. "If you don't mind."

Gregory put his head onto the pillow. "Nope, don't mind at all," he said. He wrapped his hand around his cock, but rather than moving it, he moved his hips instead. True to his word, he kept the motion slow, which must have played hell on his body, but he kept to it. Chris reached out and touched his knee, surprised by how warm it was in the air-conditioned room. "May I –" he asked, and Gregory nodded quickly.

The muscles in his thighs were so hard. Chris kept his fingers light so that he only strummed the soft skin over the tight muscles. He ran his fingertips along the line of Gregory's inner thigh. Gregory stopped thrusting, trembling where he was. "Do you want me to stop?"

Chris was torn. Gregory was beautiful, and having him so open was perfect. But he wasn't, at heart, a voyeur, and not being involved in the activity was a thorn in his side. "I want you to fuck me, instead."

Gregory sank back into the bed, boneless for a second. "Oh, thank God for that," he said, but then he flipped over and up with a spryness that Chris could only envy. "Do you want to take off your clothes then? I think it would be easier."

Chris began unbuttoning his shirt, but Gregory finished it for him. His erection was hot and tight against his belly, and since Chris's hands were now free, he cupped Gregory's testicles lightly in his palm, and used the other to trap his cock between them. "That's unfair."

"Just keeping it warm."

"It's plenty warm enough," Gregory said, and he pulled off Chris's shirt. His pants were next, and there was a tangle of limbs as Gregory tried to yank the pants off over Chris's shoes, which, in hindsight, was something they should have probably attempted before the bottle of wine. Gregory finally sat on the back of his thighs, effectively pinning Chris down, and yanked the shoes off, then finished the job. He rolled off him, feigning exhaustion, and Chris took the opportunity to kiss him again.

Gregory immediately parted his lips, meeting him with his tongue. It wasn't a duel, something Chris hated getting involved in, but still a joyous exploration. Gregory moved his hands up and down Chris's shoulders like he was trying to restore circulation, and then broke free just to lick his way down Chris's neck.

Chris reached into the drawer for a condom. He tore the foil with his teeth, not trusting the little notch that failed him in the worst situations, and rolled the condom onto Gregory himself. "Turn over," Gregory said, and Chris wasn't one to argue.

"Do it," he said. He stretched his shoulders. "Send me flying, Gregory. Please."

"That I can do," Gregory said, and he did.

The wine in Chris's system helped him enter the proper headspace. He was there, on the bed, when Gregory touched him with the cold lube. Then, as it melted inside him, he wasn't there anymore. He could still feel Gregory entering him, knew Gregory's hands were on his hips, pulling him back to the thrusts. If he'd been stone cold sober and *there*, he might have even have protested the sharp hold. But he wasn't completely *there*. "Let it go," he heard Gregory say, but the voice came from so far away it was like a bad telephone conversation. "Trust me. You need something to anchor you."

"And that's you?" Chris asked.

He felt Gregory kiss him, felt the heat of his lips, the touch of his tongue and even the roughness to his teeth, but it was distant. "And that's me. There's something you need to see."

"I love you," Chris said. The words escaped him, but he had no desire to pull them back. Gregory just kissed him again.

Chris looked up. He was flying now. The sky was endless. If there wasn't the sharpness of discomfort on his hips, he could have flown up into the sun and been lost forever. If he was supposed to be strong enough to resist the urge himself, he wasn't. But Gregory had no problem keeping him held in place. If he was flying, he was doing so with a tether around him, but it was enough.

The rattling of bones was with him, audible over the sound of the wind through the dunes and desert grass. It wasn't just a rattle. There was a chant along with it, and the woman's voice was unearthly and seemed beyond what a human could make. He flew down to the earth, skimming the surface so closely he could reach down and disturb the sand as though it was the surface of water. Somewhere, far beyond where he was, he still felt the filthy mark that was disturbing the place, but here, in this section, there was only the chanting.

The native woman found him. She was dressed in snow white leathers – doeskin, his brain provided – and the beadwork over her chest and along the fringe of her skirt shimmered like mother of pearl. He watched to touch it, even though he knew it had been the clothes she had died in. "Who are you?" he asked, and shuddered. Gregory was still fucking him; without the connection he wouldn't be here, but he knew the moment either one of them went over the edge, this would be too much.

She didn't say anything. Couldn't, actually. She didn't speak any English. But she reached for his face. She'd been beautiful once, with flawless skin and black hair that had shone with the luster of polished ebony. But that had been so long ago, and she was as worn as the dunes and the grass. When she touched his skin he wasn't afraid, although it felt like being touched by a snake sliding past his face.

There were no words, but images. She'd been lured out to the desert, not through physical threat to herself, but to her family. And not just to any place. There had been a spring, but where the water emerged at the surface, no plants grew. The water was foul, and it poisoned the ground around it. The preacher had set up his ministry near it, claiming the water tasted just fine to him. Even as she took the deer path up to where the white man had put his permanent buildings, she could taste the foulness in the air. As he tried reasoning with her using nothing but the pleading sounds in his voice, she could barely contain her gagging. The spring emerged from the rocks, ran a dozen steps through the black-as-oil dirt around it, and then disappeared back into the ground, creating sinkholes as deadly as the pox or plague.

The preacher man, who wore all black despite the punishing heat of the sun, had tried to take away her rattle. It had been made from a gourd, a gift from her sweetheart, not anything sacred. But that hadn't mattered. He hadn't been a violent man, not until he'd set himself up next to the spring, and when she tried to protest, he had struck her.

She'd fought him, and lost. More than the rattle, apparently. She'd fallen into the black oily spring, and rather than help her up, he'd held her face into the water. Chris felt it, felt her urge to keep holding her breath until that alone killed her, rather than take a mouthful of the foul water, but some things were beyond her control. She died, gasping in a huge mouthful, and she felt herself split in two.

He dumped her body in one of the sinkholes. That had been the easy part. She'd watched as he'd done it and was comforted ever so slightly by the look of regret on his face. It hadn't lasted.

What followed were snapshots. She hadn't seen it all, but his mission had grown stronger and prospered. Natives and white men who'd already taken the desert as their home followed him. But his hold on them was tenuous. He stopped meditating in the wooden church he'd built, preferring the calming spring. When the last of his hold on the fragile minds of his followers weakened to the point of breaking, the spring told him how to get more.

And more.

And more.

There were a dozen sinkholes in the area, and over the years they'd become graves. It was her people who decided to stop it. They snuck into his now rich house and stuck him over the head with their sticks until he stopped moving. Then, they dumped him still alive into one of the sinkholes. The air trapped around him slowly became as foul as the water, and he died tasting how unclean the water had been all along. Her grand-nephew had been tried with the murder and they'd hung him just beyond the spring.

For a while that had ended it.

Until Chris and Brantley had fallen into the hole. Brantley had seen the preacher, the same way Chris had felt the woman. And Gregory. Gregory had felt her too, and that's how they'd found each other in this world.

She smiled, and he felt the hold on his hips pulling him back to Gregory. "Stop, stop it," Chris said, once again on his bed. Gregory broke off immediately, and Chris got off the bed.

"You saw," Gregory said.

"You could have told me. Warned me, at least."

"I couldn't. Brantley's power's too strong. I physically couldn't tell you anything, Chris, and I'm sorry. I wish I had been stronger."

"I felt her when I was a child. How did you?"

Gregory had been sweating, obviously from fighting with himself to keep the connection as open as possible. It left him cold. Chris grabbed the spare blanket – rarely used – from the closet and threw it over his shoulders. He was sweating too, he realized, but didn't feel the chill. "I felt her in Brantley's dark room. He'd built it special. You can hear the water running from behind the walls." Gregory stopped. His shoulders were tight, his head bowed. There was something else he had to say, but he wasn't going to say it unless he was prodded.

"What were you doing there?" Chris didn't want to ask the question, but the tension in Gregory lifted when he did. He sighed, then took a long, shuddering breath. "I was on my knees. Brantley thought I was praying, but of course I wasn't. I could feel them on the other side of the wall. It was so thin, Chris, so thin. I felt the preacher man, all the people he'd killed, all the men who drank from the spring. I felt their insanity. And I felt the beasts of the spring. They wanted to eat my flesh. It was all I could do to fight them off. I felt it, Chris. When she was there, she protected me, and when she wasn't –"

"You found the knife."

Gregory smiled. He looked down to his hands, and Chris saw as well as Gregory the rough calluses reappear, the calluses that had always been there in the dream. "I found the knife."

"What did you show Brantley, Gregory?"

"The preacher, he killed his victims. The…separation gave him power. There was so much more power in not killing the victims. Making them drink the water and holding them down, then letting the spring do the rest. I knew he was going to do it to me; I knew it was only a matter of time. And I couldn't not drink the water, he was right there, watching me. I could smell it. God, it was worse than sewer water, worse than sulphur, but I drank it. And when he held me down in the dark room, and I felt the walls break down around me, I was almost lost. But I found you, and you held me, and there was nothing in me for it to take. It was only a matter of time before Brantley let me go, like he let David go after he…after."

"And the family who used to live in your house?"

"Brantley used them to see if he could control them, like he did Richard. Like he did Donna."

"But he couldn't."

"Not then. But he can now, and I helped him do it."

"We will get him. You know that, right?" Chris said.

"Is that a promise, officer?"

"It is."

Gregory lay back on the bed. "Good. Now come finish what you started."

Chris knelt between his spread thighs. He stripped off the condom, tossing it into the waste basket, and licked at the head of Gregory's cock with the very tip of his tongue until Gregory was squirming. Chris pressed his fingers against the base, just hard enough that he could feel the vein beneath his fingers, and when he didn't think Gregory could take a second more attention on the tip, kissed his way down to the base.

Gregory groaned, and his fingers dug into the blanket. He was close before, and this teasing was torture. Chris kissed each testicle, tight against his body, and then stopped teasing.

"Holy fuck," Gregory said, and he all but sat up. Chris would have laughed, but with his mouth full of cock as it was, he was afraid he'd choke. Chris was all the way down him, the sparse pubic hair tickling his nose, and as long as he didn't breathe, he was fine. "Let me guess," Gregory continued when he could. "Hanz."

Chris bobbed his head up and down, stealing a lung full of air, then reached up and took Gregory's hands. He knew where they were, and he guided them back to the back of his head. Gregory was still, just for a second, but Chris trusted him completely. "Oh, God, Chris," Gregory whispered, and then slowly, ever so gently, began to fuck his throat.

Gregory never pushed too far down, but then Chris knew he wouldn't, and he guided Chris's head up enough times that breathing wasn't a problem. He was slow, as deliberate as he'd been when he'd sent Chris to their place alone, but this time he was only focused on his own pleasure. Chris loved it. He loved the way the precum tasted on his tongue, loved the little gasps that Gregory made in the back of his throat, and he loved the feeling of absolute trust. Gregory hesitated, his entire body humming with the need to come, and as carefully as he could, Chris nodded, giving over permission.

Gregory pulled him off, one more time, and Chris took a deep breath. He needed it. Gregory began fucking the back of his throat, taking long, deliberate strokes on which Chris would have choked if he hadn't been expecting them. "So close, so close," Gregory whispered. "Just one more second. Please. One more." Chris struggled to keep from fighting, his comfortable time without air just about to pass. But he kept as still as he could, trusting Gregory.

The dizzying sensation turned the world a light shade of purple. Gregory started to shiver just as Chris felt the cock in his mouth releasing, and Gregory pulled him off. He took another quick breath, then used his fist to finish Gregory off. Hot semen splashed on his cheek, caught him over the eye and up into his hair, but he couldn't have cared less. Gregory pushed his hand away; it was obviously too much for him, and Chris pulled himself back onto the bed. Only then did he realize how winded he actually was. He wiped off his face and licked his fingers clean.

They remained like that for a few minutes, Gregory needing all that time just to recover. When he opened his eyes, he smiled. "That's a good look for you," he said, and he used his thumb to gather up the splash Chris must have missed. He thought about what to do with it for a second or two, then held it out for Chris. Chris smiled and took the finger into his mouth, sucking it clean. Chris put his head down on Gregory's chest, content to listen to his heartbeat gradually slowing down, and he was almost asleep when Gregory spoke again.

"I love you, too."

Chris craned his neck back, kissed him on the line of his jaw, and pushed his head back into the pillows. There was no reason to wake all the way up for something that was so obviously obvious.

# CHAPTER THIRTEEN

Brantley was over Billy, pinning him down to the bed and using his body weight to hold him down. It wasn't enough. Billy wasn't afraid of him anymore, and there was nothing that Brantley could do to earn that fear back. Every attempt, from tying him spread-eagled on the bed to threatening him with the flogger only made Billy smile at him, and that smile destroyed Brantley on the inside. Every attempt he started to knock some respect into Billy's block head was met with the same derisive smile.

"Go ahead," Billy said from the bed. "Fuck me. Want me to stick my ass in the air and beg? Please, big man, show me just how big you are."

"Stop it," Brantley howled. There was a time he'd have brought his fist hard on the side of Billy's head, but now the thought of carrying through on the desire turned his insides into water. Billy stood up, knocking Brantley to the ground as though he weighed nothing at all, and stood over him. Brantley didn't move; Billy didn't want him to, and that was enough.

"Stop what?" Billy asked him, snapping his fingers. Brantley fought the desire; there was no way he was going to kneel down in front of Billy, but he couldn't stop himself. Billy smiled, and went to the table where a bottle of whiskey was waiting. He put two ice cubes in the crystal glass, then poured enough whiskey in the glass to cover them. He swirled them, and the perfect crystal let Brantley see the eddies and swirls of the alcohol mix with the ice cold tendrils of water. Water. Damn it. It was from the spring. He wondered how long Billy had been feeding it to him.

"For a while," Billy told him. "Little doses. But it's just better this way, don't you agree? I loved you, Brantley, but you're just not strong enough by yourself."

"What are you?" Brantley asked. He took the glass, for the first time smelling the foul melting water, but he was too weak. He wanted to taste it on his tongue, to savor it more than the single malt. When he held out his hands to take the glass, his hands shook. Billy smiled and gave him the glass. "Drink."

It sloshed down his chin onto his chest. The heady rush of alcohol, the burn and the need all came to him, leaving his head stuffed with cotton wool, and his cock hard and leaking precum.

"You made me lick it up. Go ahead."

Brantley dropped his hand, but couldn't quite force himself to gather up the drop on the tip of his cock. Billy crouched down beside him. "Do it," he whispered. "You won't like the consequences if you don't."

Brantley did. Now that he had the taste of the spring water on his lips, he could taste traces of it in the bitterness. "Good boy," Billy said. "Spread your legs."

"What? Why?"

"I'm going to fuck you."

Real panic flared, something no amount of water in his system could control. The thought of leaving himself open for this thing to just…take him was so wrong, but made him tremble at the thought at the same time. Wanting to be fucked was the darkest of all Brantley's desires, one that he had to beat out of himself with his flogger, and only when that didn't work anymore, when the demons inside him were too strong, he'd force Gregory or David to purify themselves in the dark room for hours in order to be untainted enough to actually put their dicks inside him. "You can't! I don't—"

"Bullshit. You made all your other boys ram it inside your tired ass. Are you going to say no to me?"

Brantley shook his head. Billy took his head into his hands, but Brantley looked away. He was backhanded for it, but gently. It was a slap that came from trying to get Brantley to behave better rather than from anger. He didn't understand why that made him grateful. He looked up into Billy's eyes and felt thankful that he was allowed. "No," he said finally.

"No, what, Brantley?"

"No. I'm not going to say *no* to you."

"You want your tired ass fucked. Say it."

"I want my tired ass fucked."

"And you want it fucked by me."

"I want it fucked by you," Brantley said. And the words felt so good to say. If he could close his eyes, he would have taken a long shuddering sigh, but Billy wouldn't let him look away. Brantley found himself smiling.

Billy stood back and backhanded him so hard it knocked him on his ass. Brantley touched the hot, suddenly inflamed skin, and looked up at Billy, shocked.

"Don't ask me why. You know you deserve it."

Brantley looked down. That was certainly true.

Billy's mouth turned down. "And I do want to fuck you. But first I want to turn your ass blazingly red. What would you prefer? Your flogger or the paddle?"

"Flogger," Brantley said too quickly.

Billy patted his head. "Paddle it is. Why don't you go get it."

Brantley hesitated. Billy knew as well as he did that the paddle was in the upstairs bedroom. There was no one else in the house, but that didn't mean there couldn't be. He had enough gardeners and housekeepers moving in and out of the grand house that he didn't know at any one time who could be where.

"Do I need to repeat myself? I can't tell you how disappointing that will be."

"No," Brantley said. "You don't. I'll get it."

"Now, Brantley."

"Now," Brantley agreed. It felt perfect and right to be naked down here in the bomb shelter, but in the cold passage way and the narrow staircase he felt ridiculous with his penis swinging in the breeze. Although it wasn't swinging, it was as hot and hard as it ever had been, and he would have put his hand over it and given it a squeeze if he didn't know it would annoy Billy. The large staircase felt a bit better, the carpeting easier on his bare feet. It was his house; if he wanted to walk naked in it, he would, damn it. But even as he thought that, he knew no one would look at him and see anything more than a punished school boy, because that was how he felt.

The paddle was under his bed. The housecleaning staff cleaned around it and said nothing about it. He'd bought it from a catalogue with a charge card under an assumed name, then destroyed all records linking him to it. It had been custom made to his exact specifications; thick water buffalo hide with the stitching on the inside. It was designed to hurt from the first blow and keep compounding the hurt until Brantley decided to stop swinging.

Billy, of course, knew it. He loved the welts the paddle had left on his ass, how white his skin was at the beginning, how red hot it was after. He'd be sore for days after, reluctant to sit and the grimace on his face when Brantley forced him to sit was poetry.

And now, that was going to be his ass. He ran the smooth leather up and over his cock, feeling it warm from touching his flesh, and he shivered. He would hate every stroke, but he would need it. And, most importantly, he would deserve it.

□ □ □ □ □

Chris woke up to the alarm. He'd been walking with Brantley to get the paddle a second before. The dream had been so vivid he knew it was real. His own cock was as hard as Brantley's was, but the shrieking alarm was quickly taking care of that. His arm was asleep, but he fought it free from behind Gregory's head and reached to turn off the alarm, but instead knocked the clock off his table. He groped for it, madly, and hit the snooze button with a triumphant growl. He lay back, suddenly exhausted. Gregory was hugging his pillow rather than resting on it – and in a position that Chris envied – but his eyes were open.

Gregory was hot from being under the blanket, and he flinched when Chris pulled it down over his shoulder. He slid in behind and kissed the back of Gregory's neck. Gregory pushed him back onto the bed and then draped himself over him.

"I have to get up," Chris told him.

Gregory didn't answer, but slowly began moving against him.

"Did you hear me?"

Gregory pressed his finger against Chris's lip. He began kissing his way down Chris's chest.

Chris groaned. "Look, it's not as though I'm not appreciative…" Chris began.

"Or observant, either," Gregory finished, kissing along Chris's thigh.

"What do you mean?"

"I set your alarm back fifteen minutes when you were asleep. I promise I'll be quick."

Chris actually looked at the clock and settled back into the pillows. "You're a devious, devious man, Gregory."

Gregory said nothing, just flashed him a smile that bared his teeth. "Now lie back. Keep your arms and legs inside the car, and please, enjoy your ride."

Chris touched his Gregory's forehead. "I want to stay with you, here," he said.

The evil smile was back. "You clearly mistake my meaning," Gregory said, and he drew his nail sharply on Chris's thigh. Chris jerked his legs apart, clearly as Gregory had planned all along. "Better."

He reached over Chris, but used his body to keep his legs apart. "Fair's fair," Gregory said.

"I don't know what you mean," Chris said. His body sparked with anticipation, and the low pitch to Gregory's voice sent flutters in Chris's stomach he hadn't felt for years. "Tell me what you want."

"You watched me jerk off. Do it for me."

Chris hesitated. Gregory grabbed the bottle of lube and put some on Chris's cock. "I like doing this. I want to do this a lot more. Do you think you can spring for something a little less industrial?"

"Name your brand," Chris said, although he realized in that moment he would have agreed to anything.

Gregory grinned. "I was hoping you'd say that. Jerk off, please, Chris."

The lube melted on his skin. Chris didn't think he could thrust himself into his fist like Gregory could, which was okay because he really was a two-handed kind of guy. Despite him asking for Gregory to perform, it took a heartbeat for him to be ready. It was hard, taking something that had been, well, not shameful, but private and do it in the open, with Gregory not only watching but making encouraging sounds.

"It works better if you actually move your hands," Gregory said helpfully. He finished with the condom, throwing the foil over his shoulder with a grandiose gesture. "Want me to do it for you?"

"Wouldn't that defeat the purpose?"

"Then just do it. I want to see what works for you."

"You work for me."

"Nice try. Jerk that cock, Chris. Go on. You're going to be late."

"Do the words *performance anxiety* mean anything to you?"

Gregory sucked on his fingers, slowly pulling them into and out of his mouth in such an obvious movement that Chris felt his body respond. Gregory smiled, slowly, then ran his fingers down his throat and his body, and then sucked on them and gathered up some of the excess lube on his fingers. "I dunno. Do they mean something to you?"

Chris began moving his hand, loose at the base, tight against the head of his cock. "Not anymore."

Gregory pushed Chris's legs farther apart. "Good."

And then Gregory was inside him, but didn't look away. On his back wasn't Chris's favorite position, but being able to see Gregory thrusting inside him, holding onto his hips? The look of concentration on Gregory's face was something beautiful. "Don't look away. Look at me."

Chris wanted to tell him he talked too much, but he couldn't. His hands automatically synced their rhythms, hard when Gregory pushed inside him, looser as he rocked his hips to give Chris that extra little bit before pulling back out again.

"You're very good at this," he said instead.

"I know," Gregory said. "Ready?"

He hadn't been, but with Gregory looking at him, he was now. "Are you going to come for me, Chris?"

Chris nodded. His lungs couldn't take a full breath of air, he was sweating, and God, his cock was suddenly very, very ready. "Don't look away."

"I'm here. I'm really, really here."

"Good," Gregory repeated. He straightened, pulling Chris back a foot or so, and began thrusting so hard Chris had to fight for the next breath. Gregory's eyes were dark. "I love you. I do. I love you."

Chris couldn't stop himself. He twisted, but Gregory didn't let him go, even as he came. And Chris was coming too. Touching his cock was suddenly too much stimulation, and he broke off. Gregory grabbed his free hand, entwining his fingers in Chris's, and then didn't move until the rich and heady waves reduced to a trickle, then left them.

Gregory collapsed back to the bed. "Wow."

Chris was going to agree when his alarm went off again. He reached again to hit the snooze bar, when Gregory used his considerable lower body strength to kick him off the bed. "Don't even think about it. You'll be late."

"Sadist," Chris growled, but pulled himself up to his feet.

"Apparently not until you get me a proper set of cuffs," Gregory called back. If there was anything else, it didn't carry over the water pressure.

Chris returned to the bedroom to dress. Gregory knelt on the bed and helped Chris with his tie. "I don't think Brantley's entirely in charge anymore," Chris said.

"What do you mean?"

"I had a dream. It felt real. The young man…Billy is his name?"

"Billy, yes."

"I had a dream that Billy was in charge. And Brantley, well, he liked it that way."

"I doubt that very much," Gregory said. "I want you to play nice with the other kids."

The other kids included Niles. The warm feeling Chris had in his chest dropped by about seven degrees.

# CHAPTER FOURTEEN

Niles didn't disappoint. He had his eye obviously on the clock, and when Chris sat down at his desk, precisely at eight, he spoke. "Did you have a nice weekend, Chris?"

"It was lovely."

"Brantley wants to see you."

"I'm sure he does. Do you want to tell him to go stuff himself, or are you going to give me the pleasure?"

"Don't get smart with me."

The entire bullpen was oddly silent. People worked around them, but didn't look up from what they were doing. Even Jamie had the look of concentration people only got when they are still mostly asleep.

"What did you do?"

"I didn't do anything, Chris, and I resent the implication."

"What did your master do?" Chris said, just rewording the same question.

Niles smiled. "You can ask him yourself."

"I told you, he should go stuff himself. I'm not meeting him."

There was another pause. Niles smiled at him, the smile an adult would give to a stupid child, and motioned to Jamie. She worked diligently, but at nothing more difficult then collating pages. She wasn't at her desk, but in the photocopier area, and the paper cutter shone by her right hand.

"Do you want to repeat that?" Niles asked.

"Jamie's not under your power."

"Do you want to put that to the test?"

Jamie stopped what she was doing, like someone had cut her strings, and she was waiting, listening. "Jamie!" he called. She began to turn her head, but the muscles in her neck didn't seem to let her. "How are you doing this?"

Chris stood up and went to Jamie. The smell was back, the foul smell from the compound was back, just a whiff, and he followed the smell to the water cooler. "You filled the bottle with the water from the spring."

"Yes," Niles said. "It's temporary, but she will cut off her own hand if I tell her to. Or, you can just meet Brantley. It's entirely your call."

"She's an officer, just like you are. Or were. You wouldn't do that to her."

"Brantley Jones is the new way," Niles said. "This job is nothing compared to him. He is great, and what he wants right now is you."

"Niles, you're crossing a line here. It's a step that you're not going to be able to take back. Be very careful."

"You need to come with me. And if you speak again, I'll tell Brantley that you were not cooperating. You're not going to like that at all, I assure you."

Chris didn't argue, though it choked him.

Niles waited until they were out of the building before pulling out his set of handcuffs. Chris opened his mouth to complain, but got a finger waggle as though he were a misbehaving puppy. Chris glared, the only thing he could do, and crossed his arms over his chest. There was no way in hell he was going to voluntarily slap cuffs on himself. Niles grabbed him by the shoulder and pushed his back to the wall, into the building. He fought, but Niles had his center of gravity pinned to the dirty gray stone wall, and he held Chris there. At least Niles had to let go to lock the cuffs in front of him, then hid the metal cuffs with his jacket so that none of the other officers walking into the building would see. Not that most of them would, the Monday morning haze was almost as strong as the water. The metal burned his skin. "Any more tricks like that and I'll shoot you in the leg," Niles snarled.

Chris bowed his head. Niles was an awful shot; he was afraid Niles would miss and hit something vital. He hated walking with his hands cuffed. His center of gravity was off, and he was all too aware of Niles behind him as well. There were a dozen squad cars, but Niles took an unmarked one. "Get in."

Chris just stared at him. Niles grinned and unlocked the door for him. Chris waited, and Niles opened the door all the way almost begrudgingly. He reached across Chris's lap with a sneer, and locked the seatbelt in place. He yanked it tight, too tight, and snorted at Chris's grunt of discomfort.

He walked around the hood of the car and got in his side. They were on the street a moment later. "I suppose I should let you talk when we get to Brantley."

Chris leaned back against the head rest. His fists behind him ached to strangle the life from Niles in such slow degrees that the eventual death would be a blessing. Niles was watching him when he wasn't keeping his eyes on the road, and Chris knew he knew exactly what he was thinking.

"So, are you going to tell us where Brantley's boy is? Or are we just going to assume he's at your place?"

The leather in the seat cracked. Chris felt his nails digging into it, hard enough that it hurt, but the pain felt good. "You hurt him—"

"Ah-ah," Niles said. "You are just that stupid, aren't you? Brantley won't hurt your boy, not more than the boy likes it, at least. He was a whore, Cunningham. Always had been. He bent over for Brantley the very first time Brantley asked. He'd spend hours on his knees and greet Brantley with a smile the size of Kansas for the privilege to suck his cock."

"Doesn't that mean Jones is going to burn in hell with the rest of us sodomites?" Chris asked. "And you follow every word he says. How does it feel, as a straight man, to bow down to a fucking fag?"

Niles punched him in the stomach. If he hadn't been driving, he could have done a lot more damage than he had; Chris hadn't expected the blow at all. His breath escaped him, and it took what seemed like forever to find it again. "It's different for him," Niles hissed. "And don't you ever forget it."

"How is it different? Does it not count if you only suck cock with the left side of your mouth? If you turn around twice and spit, does it cover the fact that your great leader likes ramming his cock up the ass of some kid? Or getting his own ass reamed, if what Gregory told me is right."

Niles slammed on the brakes. The seatbelt against Chris's throat was already too tight, and when the brakes locked, the belt locked as well. He was thrown against it, and swore he could feel the crush against his throat. They were stopped dead in a merge lane, but Chris didn't think Niles cared.

"I told you. Shut up about that shit. It's different for him. You bastards make him. It's not his fault. His one human weakness and you all exploit it. I hope he breaks every bone you have before cutting your throat."

Chris coughed. His first breath felt like it had been sprayed with pepper, but the second one slid inside him smoothly. "Is that how you get through the night?" he managed.

"Shut up," Niles screamed. "Shut up, shut up, shut up! He wants you, he can have you. Disgusting filth! You don't deserve him! None of you do!"

The car behind them honked, and the one behind it. Niles pushed the gas just as the light was turning amber and trapped the rest of the cars behind him in the red. That was probably a good thing. "You belong to him, now. And when we drop you off, I'll be in charge of bringing the boy. That's what Brantley wants, that's what he will get. Your kind has no comprehension of what real love is. Brantley will show you."

"Before or after he cuts my throat?" Chris asked, voice still rough.

"Which would you prefer?"

Chris snorted, but didn't answer. He looked up, wishing he could at least touch his throat. "When you go for Gregory, if you can find him, can you do me a favor?"

"You're hardly in the position to ask for favors right about now," Niles snarled. He pulled onto the interstate, heading out of the city, and Chris knew they were on their way back to the compound.

"I beg to differ. You would think I was in the perfect position to ask."

"Well then, ask."

"Brantley will send his goons with you, won't he? Big guys? Tell Gregory that I said it was okay and not to fight."

"That's it? And he is just supposed to believe me?"

"He can believe whatever he wants. But remember that Brantley wants him alive and unhurt. You send goons after

Gregory, he won't go quietly. And if he gets hurt, or worse, disfigured, you're going to have to deal with the consequences."

"His goons, as you put it, know the consequences of displeasing Brantley."

"I'm sure they do. But what about displeasing Billy?"

"Billy? Billy fetches coffee."

"Billy fetches more than that. Please, Niles, I never beg, but please. Just this once. If you go, don't let them harm Gregory. Please."

Niles shook a long finger at him. "Stop this. I want you to stop talking now. You're Brantley's problem now."

"The first time he makes me suck him off, I'm sure he'll be thinking of you the whole time."

That did it. Niles began striking Chris, but, because of the angle, each was just a glancing blow. Chris's throat still hurt, but he forced himself to laugh. "This is all you got?"

"I'll kill you!" Niles howled.

"How, by floundering me to death?" Chris demanded.

Niles got out of the car. He jumped across the hood, in what should have been a smooth, practiced motion, but instead got himself twisted. Chris took the opportunity to unlock his seat belt. It retracted across his throat like a snake, but Chris remained perfectly still. Niles had to push himself across the rest of the way, and took a moment to straighten his clothing. He yanked open Chris's door, but didn't haul him out like Chris had hoped he would. He was too much of a coward for that. Instead, he began punching Chris where he sat, and these blows had his full weight to them. The third one caught him on the temple, harder than the others, and Chris had to swim against the current to keep his eyes open. Niles saw him swoon and smiled. "Fucking faggot can't take a punch," he mocked, holding his fist up, threatening. He leaned in, head close enough to the car door, and Chris smiled, even as Niles went to punch him again.

"Fucking fag doesn't want to," Chris corrected him. He grabbed the fist, twisting the cuffs around it tight, which Niles had locked his arm to give it maximum weight behind, and pulled Niles toward him with all his strength. When Chris yanked him, the hood of the car caught Niles on the side of the head. The crack was loud enough to set Chris's teeth on edge. He unbuckled the belt himself and pushed Niles who was still dazed, out of the way. With both hands and the metal cuff around them, he only needed one blow. He caught Niles in the jaw, and the blood flew. There was even the sick, unmistakable sound of a human tooth meeting something harder, and Niles crumpled to the pavement at Chris's feet.

"Stupid fuck," Chris howled. "You cuff a man, you always cuff him his back." Chris's urge was to kick and keep kicking until something inside Niles broke irreparably, but that wasn't really him. The drivers in the cars now backed up to the main lanes of the intersection were all on their phones, no doubt all calling this in, so Chris picked up Niles's dead-weight body and threw it into the sage brush beside the road. "I hope someone steals your shoes," he called, and ran back to the driver's side.

He gunned it. It was just the start of rush hour, but even from the dead stop he had no problem merging into the outside lane. He was less than a mile to the next overpass, where he could turn around and be back at the station in fifteen minutes.

He saw the maroon SUV pulling into the merge lane too fast. _Never a cop around when you need one_, he had time to think. He didn't have his turn signals on, but since Chris wanted his spot in the exit lane, he slowed and waved him over regardless. Rather than speeding up, the SUV slowed. Chris slowed even more, flashing the lights in the dash and waving him to merge. Then the SUV's window and his came abreast. The driver had a beautiful smile. He locked eyes with Chris, nodded his head, and turned the SUV into Niles's unmarked car.

# CHAPTER FIFTEEN

Gregory knew.

He knew the first time Chris felt the metal against his skin. Chris had felt it as a burning sensation, but for Gregory, it was cold and needling. Not even Chris's bed could protect him from it. He struggled to stand. It was difficult when he felt his entire body shutting down, but it wasn't his pain. If Brantley had just taken up millimeter of slack in a choke chain around Gregory's throat, Gregory couldn't have gotten the message any clearer.

The question was: what could he do? The daylight wasn't safe, not without Chris beside him. Together, they made a complete person, he knew. Without him the exposed part of him that needed Chris was a huge neon light for Brantley. The moment he stepped out into the daylight, Brantley would be able to feel him. He supposed with Chris in Brantley's grasp that Brantley *might* be too busy to look, but Gregory somehow doubted it. And they would come straight to Chris's apartment.

He wasn't wrong. Even as he was struggling to dress, he could feel Brantley's henchman at the gate. They waved badges in front of the super, and the super had no choice but to let them in. And there was already an elevator waiting for them in the lobby. The super's keys locked off the second car, and they smart enough to leave a man at the door to the stairs.

Gregory was fucked.

"Or not," he told himself. It was too soon to hear them pounding down the hall. He didn't barricade the door; they'd only knock it down. So instead he unlocked it and left it open. It wasn't fair to Chris to let them damage his place for something Gregory had brought down on him.

He went to the balcony. The sun was up and the wind from the desert smelled of faraway places. He'd flown on it a hundred thousand times, but never on this side of the curtain. He climbed on top of the barrier and the wind touched his bare shoulders as though begging him to come and play. It wasn't a simple matter of falling asleep and going over, or in the middle of an orgasm when his brain was otherwise mostly occupied. He could go over when he was awake, but it only worked half the time, and it was the other half he was worried about.

They were at the door. Gregory took baby steps to turn around and face the apartment. "Jumpers always fall forward," he told himself. He'd seen it on TV, or maybe in a movie, so it had to be true. Chris would know he'd never willingly jump, and he supposed that was enough.

"There he is!" one of them shouted. Gregory didn't get a great look at his face, but he looked familiar. Toward the end, Brantley had tired of his followers being the weak, lost, and forlorn, so he made Richard hire a security force. Richard hadn't seen the point and wanted to argue it, but had given in. Everyone gave into Brantley, eventually.

"Stay back," he called, but his threats were meaningless. He saw that the instant that the first one stepped onto the balcony. They weren't here to bring him back; their faces were too set for that. They were here to kill him. Gregory knew it, and the moment after he knew it, they knew he knew it, too. Brantley would never send someone to kill him. That would have been too easy.

"Tell your master, whoever it is now, to go fuck himself. Tell him I said that," Gregory said, and when the next gust of wind tugged at him, he let himself go. One of them lunged at him, faster than he should have been able to move, but his hand only caught on Gregory's jeans, and just for a second. Gregory shot him the bird, then let his arms open.

He didn't let himself think of how little ground there was between him and the pavement. It was an apartment building, not a high rise, and he could already hear the screams below him. He couldn't think of that. He could only force his mind blank. When he opened his eyes, and he would, any second, he would see nothing but white and be flying. There was no time to think of what would happen if it didn't work, and when he released that thought, he felt another gust of wind pick him up. He wasn't quite willing to risk opening his eyes, not until the sensation of falling became the sensation of flying, and he could actually feel force of gravity relent in trying to pull him down.

Like that. He was flying, faster than he ever had, and so close to the ground he could smell the sand. He opened his eyes, now facing the earth rather than the sky, and he hit the ground with his shoulder first. Tuck and roll, the instinct was automatic, so he did. If this was real sand, rather than the remembrance of sand, each time he hit and rolled it would have torn bits of him off, but instead the sand was soft and billowy, like a resort's beach. When he came to rest, he did so on a patch of sand that was no less comfortable than Chris's bed had been what seemed like hours ago.

He took a long breath and stood up. His shoulder hurt, just a little, from the initial landing, but the rest of him was practically untouched. He dusted himself off, but before he could straighten, the heavy sensation of being watched came from right behind him. He didn't want to turn, didn't think that he was brave enough, but he had to turn. It was how this story ended.

So he did. The man dressed all in black and a roman collar was inches behind him, close enough that Gregory should have felt it in the roots of his hair, but he hadn't. He wasn't a corpse, or at least his face didn't show any obvious sign of not being alive. The only signs of something wrong were the granules of sand in the corner of his mouth and at the base of his nose. He'd suffocated, then. Gregory bet that information hadn't been introduced at the native man's trial for his murder.

The preacher touched his throat and opened his mouth to suck in breath. But he couldn't. Not without Gregory's permission, at least. Gregory knew he could have walked away, leaving the preacher in his own kind of hell, but there was a sadness to his eye, a heaviness that Gregory didn't want to see in anyone. He nodded. "Go ahead."

The first intake of breath sucked the air past Gregory's arm, and the hair on his forearm stood in alarm. It was a breath that had been denied for centuries and it seemed to go on for hours. "Thank you," the man said finally.

Gregory nodded. "I know who you are," he said. "I know what you did. You caused all of this."

"Gregory," the man said, and the fact that he knew Gregory's name should have been terrifying, but it wasn't. It was cold, like the touch of metal he'd felt with Chris. "You know that's not true."

"I know I felt you. I know I felt you with Brantley. You killed people. You made Brantley kill."

"I didn't make Brantley kill. That wasn't me. And I didn't kill people."

His face was so earnest. Of course he wouldn't have thought that killing natives was wrong, but not truly wrong, not like killing a white person. He was a product of his age. Gregory wanted to shake him, but that would have involved touching him, and Gregory didn't want to infect himself. "I'm glad you're dead," he said instead. Men like him drove homosexuals into the peat moss and burned old women at the stake, all because it wasn't wrong at the time. Gregory wanted to spit.

"The other one, your Brantley. He's in danger."

"From what?" Gregory asked. "And how can I help them?"

The preacher's face fell. "We heard you, Gregory Osborne. We heard you praying to be free, on the dark side of the wall. On this side. You fought the others. You felt them coming for you in the dark room, and you fought them off. Do you think everyone is as strong as you?"

"That was just…" Gregory couldn't finish. There were times in the dark room, where Brantley put him until he was pure enough to stop tempting him, or pure enough to fuck him up the ass, or for whatever deranged reason was in Brantley's head at the time, he had heard them. And without his knife, they would have eaten his flesh. He shook his head again. "That was just in my dreams."

"You don't believe that."

Gregory had touched his belly. One of the things had cornered him, a small creature like a toad but with coarse hair all over its body and with row after row of teeth.

"What do you want?" Gregory said, voice cold.

"You need to end this," the preacher said. From nowhere, Chris's knife appeared. He'd lost it, here, when they'd forced him to drink the water and he forgot who he was. The blade was darker than it should have been, not exactly rust, exactly, but metal when exposed to the ages. The edge still shone from its edge; it had either been recently sharpened or it had never lost its edge. Gregory took it and ran his finger down it. Red blood welled in the thread of open skin, but the pain that should have followed was muted. "What do I do with it?"

"You know," the preacher said. He pointed behind him, and Gregory could see the stain against the desert again. The purple bruise had gotten worse; it stained the sky. "Take it and hide it."

Gregory nodded. He started to walk past the preacher, but the man grabbed his arm, holding him in his place. "Please."

"Please what," Gregory demanded, and tried to pull his arm back, but it might as well have been caught in stone.

"Please. Release me."

Gregory looked at him. "You may be innocent according to your laws, but you're not according to mine. I can't."

"You must! I can't stay here in limbo. My soul—"

Gregory shook his head. "I can't. But that doesn't mean I won't. I just can't, not now. That woman you killed had a sweetheart. The men you killed had families. You don't think they didn't feel their loss?"

"They were godless savages," the preacher said, but his voice wavered. "I was saving them."

Gregory looked at him. He couldn't move, not unless the preacher released him, but he still had the control. "Dear God," the preacher said finally. He let Gregory go. "Forgive me."

"Sorry, Father," Gregory said. "I can't do that, either. Not yet."

The man nodded, then turned to sand and fell where he stood. Gregory stared at the spot, just for a second, and then walked around it to the dark spring.

Ordinarily, he'd be able to gather himself up and soar, like a dream, but the closer he got to the stain, the less he had that ability. He forced himself to continue, and the beasts and things that fed from it surrounded him. They were too afraid of the blade to attack. He remembered them being ravenously hungry, throwing themselves at him when there was nothing else to feed on for miles. But that had all changed. They were bloated and fat, contented and still cruel. If he let them catch him, they'd fight over his choice pieces and leave the rest of him out here, exposed but never able to rot away. He shivered and waved the blade again.

He skirted the spring because he could. That wasn't his goal, not on this side. Sometimes the dark room had felt like a coffin, and the rotten wood was inches away from his hand. Sometimes it felt as though it were cavernous and if he didn't stick to the walls he could run for years and never reach the door. In reality, on the real side, it was no more than ten feet by ten feet. Brantley had made it real on this side; the sand was stained with his blood in almost a perfect square. Gregory walked on sand, but felt the cold earth beneath his feet. The sky here was dark, a shade of purple rarely seen in nature. But there was still enough light to see, and to plant the blade in the corner of where the wall should have been. He didn't have much margin for error. Too close to the wall and it might get trapped inside, too far away and it might be discovered. Still, when he buried the blade a good foot into the sand, he knew it would be exactly where he needed it on the other side.

The beasts came for him, but he was already gone. Nothing tied him to the earth anymore, and he could fly. It wasn't safe to travel on the other side, not when Brantley had more men out there.

# CHAPTER SIXTEEN

Chris had had a partner. Gregory couldn't think of her name, not for a full minute, and then the word emerged, like a bubble moving slowly through oil. When it broke surface, the name came to him: *Jamie.*

He said the name. And with it, Gregory could find her. He'd never been to the station, but he needed to be there now. Whether the walls were industrial gray or institutional green, it didn't matter. All he needed was an abandoned part of it, a hall, or an empty, unused room.

When he opened his eyes, he was in some sort of storage room. The lurch was enough to make him sick, but it passed. At least when he'd gone into Chris's apartment he'd taken the time to get his bearings watching Chris fuss with his plants. Here, he had nothing but the old files and dusty air to comfort him.

Most doors were only locked from one side, and this one was no exception. He unlocked it and made it down the hall, holding himself up with the wall. It didn't take long for someone to find him. "Where's your visitor badge?" the uniformed officer asked. Gregory couldn't see his face. His eyes couldn't quite focus on that amount of detail yet, but at least the guy didn't sound angry. Not yet.

"I need to speak to an officer named Jamie," Gregory said.

"You shouldn't be back here without at least a badge," the man said, but he didn't try to take his arm. Gregory didn't think he could have handled that.

"Please. Let me speak with Officer Jamie," Gregory said, and he sat down. Well, his legs gave out, and he slid down the wall. Someone helped him up, and led him into a gray room with a metal table and chair. The table at least felt real. Someone else brought him a cup of coffee, and although it tasted more of sugar and of the waxy paper cup than actual coffee, it was exactly what he needed. Coming back normally wasn't this bad, but coming back to a strange place was.

And then Jamie was there. And she still smelled of Chris, however faintly. "Gregory," she said from the doorway. "What are you doing here?"

"He has Chris."

Jamie came into the room. "Officer Cunningham is with his partner. I can assure you—"

Gregory shook his head. "Don't, please. Just listen to me. He's not…safe. He's in danger, and you have to do something."

Jamie turned around, looking at the door, but Gregory didn't look away from her face. She had to believe him. "Where is he?" she asked, quietly.

"Niles just checked in. He said there was some sort of incident on the side of the freeway, but they're both fine," someone from the doorway told her.

"When?"

Gregory didn't believe it, not for a second. "He's not there. Get him on the phone. You can't. I swear to you won't be able to. He's in so much trouble—"

Then he felt the SUV hit. The unmarked car Chris was in at least had an adequate crumple zone. Gregory felt the metal give way but stop just short of being fatal. Chris had been thrown forward, and the breaking glass from the side had cut his face. There had been real terror, but also bitterness; Gregory saw the smile on the driver's face as much as Chris had.

And then, nothing. Even with his seatbelt on, he'd been knocked out from the impact to the side of the car, but at least there hadn't been any secondary crashes. And Brantley had been waiting; that little detail couldn't have been from whatever was driving him now; it required too much fine motor control. That was all Brantley. The driver of the ambulance, the EMTs all worked silently. They pulled Chris from the car, and if anyone noticed that they failed to completely immobilize his head, no one called it in. One more accident on the city's deadly interstates. It was a bad collision location, however. And of course Niles had called it in. He'd probably pretended to talk to Chris over the radio. It would come to light, too late to do any good, that he'd actually only called one ambulance, and that was for the SUV driver, who wouldn't remember slowing down to plough into Chris's car.

Gregory put his head down and groaned. When Chris woke up, he was going to feel the pounding headache that Gregory had. Gregory's fists clenched. He'd kill Brantley. His hands, soft on this side of the world but finally remembering the calluses that had built up over the years, ached to be the ones holding the blade.

"Are you all right?" Jamie asked him.

"Headache," Gregory said. "Can you reach Chris?"

Jamie's mouth twitched. "We'll see, okay?"

She stood and talked to someone in the hall. She looked tired. The smell of the foul spring water was in the halls, but without Niles to guide them, they'd all shuffled off the control. Someone answered her, speaking just a little too thickly, though Gregory couldn't hear the actual words. "Well, get him on the phone. Would you stay here, Gregory? This should only take a second."

Gregory nodded, but didn't lift his head off the table to do it. He doubted it. Jamie left him.

Chris was asleep, Gregory knew. But it was drug induced, over and above the blow to the head, and Gregory couldn't penetrate it. At least Chris wasn't afraid. After the ambulance had left the accident scene, the driver had turned off the sirens, so they ebbed and flowed with the traffic around them. They'd given him too much of whatever it was, and Chris was in gross danger of not breathing. But Gregory was there, whispering in Chris's ear not to give up, to take that next breath, and it worked. Chris's breathing became more regular, and Gregory held his hand for as long as he could. He was still aware of Jamie just outside the door talking on a cell phone, and like all cell phone users, had raised her voice to be heard.

"He is? You sure about that? Officer Niles, please, you can interrupt them. Just put Chris on the phone, it's urgent," she said with suitable pauses between. "All right then. Thank you, sir," she said, and she covered the speaker with her hand.

"Officer Cunningham's partner says that he is still interviewing witnesses and can't be interrupted. "

Gregory lifted his head, and her face slowly came back into focus. "You talked to his partner?" Gregory asked.

She nodded.

Gregory's mouth twitched. "Tell him to tell Chris that I need to speak to him. Tell him it's urgent. Tell him that I don't care about police procedure. I need him, and I need him now."

Jamie stared at him. "Are you sure about this?" she asked.

"He's not there. I'm telling you. He's not there, and Niles is hosing you."

Jamie repeated what Gregory had just said. There was a long pause. "I see. He said that?" Jamie said carefully and clearly. "Thank you, sir. Yes, I'll tell him."

Jamie frowned. She was going to lie to him, to tell him not to worry, that everything was fine, but then she shook her head. "He said Chris said that it wasn't the place for personal matters, Gregory."

"Niles is in on it."

"You're accusing an officer of the law of, what, kidnapping his fellow officer?" Jamie asked. Her voice was incredulous, but she wasn't fooling him. She was beginning to think at the same moment that Gregory just possibly might be telling the truth.

"He's in on it," Gregory repeated. "Please. You need to get him. You need to find him. Chris is in serious danger."

"Stay here," Jamie said, holding her hand out for the cell phone again, but Gregory knew before she even hit the redial button, that there would be no answer. "Send someone to the scene," she said. "Now, Johnson."

Someone yes ma'am'ed her, and Jamie followed him out. Gregory paced, until he couldn't, and then sat back down again. Chris had wakened again, but his panic was short spikes pushing into Gregory's spine. Gregory shouldered it, hoping that it might help Chris cope, and then felt him pass out again. Gregory banged his fist against the table. He stood, went to the door. While it wasn't locked, there was another officer posted outside the door. "Where are you going?" he asked, voice like gravel.

"I have to go," Gregory said. The officer had the skin tone of sunbaked honey, and Gregory was so mostly outside of himself that he fought the urge to lick it. "Please. Let me go."

"Officer Wilson wanted you to stay. I'd really appreciate it if you turned around and sat right back down," the man said.

Gregory looked past him, down the hall. "She's not going to find him. She needs me."

"Look, kid, can I get you something to eat? Something to drink? This might be a long day."

"I'm not a kid," Gregory said, but he began pacing again. "Let me out, please?"

"No one is stopping you," the officer said. "But we would appreciate it if you would stay and allow us to use your expertise."

"You can't keep me here."

"And we won't. Now, if there's nothing I can get you, maybe you should just sit down for the next little bit."

"Leave the door open?" Gregory asked, and hated how weak that made him sound.

"Of course, sir," the officer said, and then he stepped back off to the side. Gregory moved to the corner, slid down the wall, and waited.

Three o'clock came, along with a dry sandwich and a room-temperature lemonade. Gregory ate it because he was starving, and then the officer took him to the washroom so that he could use the facilities. Gregory thought about bolting for the door, but the officer's hand came heavily down on his shoulder, and the idea was pretty much kiboshed.

Jamie was back at the room when Gregory got back. He was relieved to see her, because, if nothing else, Chris had trusted her. Gregory's the smile died when he saw that she wasn't alone. There was a man with her, and he stank, positively stank, of Brantley.

Gregory threw himself back against the door. The officer behind him stopped him, again, hands on the shoulder, but rather than feeling relieved, it just trapped him. "What are you doing with him?" Gregory demanded.

"Gregory, this is Officer Niles. He just spoke with Chris, and he said he dropped him off at his house. So, it looks like everything is okay."

"Call him," Gregory said.

"That's really not necessary. He was fairly tired – " Niles began, false smile firm on his lips, but Gregory cut him off.

"You can't listen to a thing he says, he's in on it. He...he offered Chris up. He's in on it!"

"Gregory, Niles is an officer of the law, I don't think..." Jamie had changed. She'd drunk the water, and although she'd sloughed off the control, it was back, ever so slightly.

"If Chris is at home, fine. Call him. Go ahead. Please, call him. But he's not at home, and this man knows where he is. He knows where he is and he's not telling you. Please, you have to believe me!"

"I believe you," Jamie said, but Gregory knew he was just being humored. "We'll call him."

"That won't be necessary," Niles said, but now there was steel in his voice.

Gregory shook his head. "Please. If he's home, I want to speak with him."

Jamie dialed the phone herself. It rang and rang, and then Chris's answering machine picked up. It was just his voice, reciting the number Jamie had dialed and requesting that the person leave a message.

Niles stood up, loudly scraping his chair back. "I'm not going to be accused of anything by a deranged young man. Officer Cunningham could be asleep. Or not picking up. I dropped him off at home, and that's the end of it."

"We'll send a car," Jamie said, and stood. "This is just going to take a little longer. May I ask you to continue waiting?"

Gregory backed away as Niles approached the door. He looked coiled, but held himself back until Jamie was gone.

"Let me come with you, please," Gregory said, trying not to beg.

Jamie began to nod, but her face froze. "You need to stay here," she said distantly. Then shook her head and smiled again. "It will be an hour. No more. I'm going to his house myself."

Nile's eyes were frigid, but he smiled too, as dark as a drop of ink.

"I don't think that's a good idea," Gregory said, but he knew he was wasting his breath. Jamie was gone.

"Are you telling Officer Wilson how to do her job?" Niles asked, voice mild. He had a huge bruise on his jaw. Chris had given it to him, and he was still furious about it. No one questioned him about it, and the officers around him were all nodding to music that Gregory couldn't hear. Fear was back, as hard and cold as a block of ice in his chest.

"Of course he's not," Jamie said. She patted them both on the cheek. "I'll go to Chris's apartment, pick him up, and bring him here. I think that's for the best, don't you?"

"Don't leave me here!" Gregory said. "Please! I came here for help!"

"And you'll get it," Jamie said. She exited the room, drifting like seaweed, and Gregory watched her go with horror. Niles motioned the guard. "Don't take your eyes off him," he said. "Keep him here for me."

The officer nodded. He was even more glassy-eyed than Jamie was. This was going to be very bad. Gregory tried to go back, but it was too soon; sometimes there were days when he had to wait twelve hours before he could push through again. He tried, and tried and tried again, each time with less ability, and it left him exhausted on the table.

The door closed, and Gregory went back to his corner. A moment later, the door opened and closed again. It didn't feel like Jamie, and it definitely wasn't Chris, so Gregory had no incentive at all to open his eyes. But he had to. Brantley wanted it that way.

"You took a big chance coming here," the officer said.

This officer was bald, which made his black eyebrows seem even blacker. And his voice was flat, like a man who was asleep, and yet still having a conversation. He was tall, taller than most, but walked with stooped shoulders, even beating his nightstick in his palm like he was.

"Did you think he wouldn't find you eventually, alone?" the officer asked, in his same flat voice.

Gregory pulled himself up to his feet. "Brantley?" he asked, again, glad for the wall behind him.

"No," the man said. Then he smiled, a beautiful, calm smile, as he smacked the nightstick again. Gregory, despite himself, looked down to the shiny club. "Not yet. He's…occupied. But he'll be with us, shortly."

"Brantley won't like it if you harm me," Gregory said too quickly. That didn't stop it from being true. Brantley hated the look of bruises on any skin other than his own.

The grin turned sickly. "Brantley only specified that you be returned in one piece."

"That's a lie," Gregory said, but he didn't even believe that denial himself. Brantley would want him punished; the other thing wanted him dead. This had to be Brantley.

The officer just smiled at him, and continued to smack his nightstick.

"Tell him to let Chris go." Gregory tried again, because he had to. "Please. Tell him...tell him I'll do anything. Just let him go."

"You will do anything, Gregory, because you're a sad, pathetic little whore who slipped his chain once, and now that's never going to happen again."

Gregory hated the way he forced himself to nod, as though he were eager to do it. "Never again. I promise. "

"Lying whore," the cop said, only it wasn't the officer with his sloped shoulders, but Brantley himself. Gregory would have recognized the twist to his lips from anywhere. "Do you really think I'm going to believe you?"

"How can I prove myself?"

Another swing of the nightstick, only this time the officer caressed it, running his hand up and down its shiny length until the oil from his hands muddied the finish. It was soon dull and dirty, and Gregory didn't want to be touched by it. Not that he wanted to be touched by it to begin with, but now it was...unclean. "Put your beautiful hands on the table, Gregory. Flat out, fingers extended."

Gregory shook his head, unable to speak.

"Do it, darling boy, or do you know what will happen to your cop friend? Do you know what I'll do to his hands?"

"No," Gregory said although he did know. And it disgusted him. His hands shook, but he placed them carefully over the cold metal finish of the table. "Okay? Please, don't do this. Brantley...please."

"Look at me," Brantley said, and even the muscles of his meat puppet's face began to look like him. "Look away, even for a second, and your friend will pay." He raised his stick. Gregory braced himself, knowing that regardless of how prepared he was, the actual pain would be worse, but didn't dare look away from the gleeful look in Brantley's face.

"Do it," Gregory told him, not looking away. If Brantley wanted to drink in Gregory's pain, he wasn't going to stop it. "Do whatever you want to me, but leave Chris alone. Please."

Gregory splayed his hands even farther. He even went so far as to kick the chair out behind him so that he was kneeling in front of Brantley. "Please."

Brantley raised the stick even farther with a gleeful smile, but instead of bringing it down, he turned his head aside as though he were speaking to someone. A look of panic crossed the officer's face, and Brantley was suddenly afraid. The stick fell from his hands, bouncing on the table with a clamor, completely missing Gregory. The officer's body sagged.

Gregory bolted away, unable to stop himself, but then grabbed the man's shirt. "I would have done it!" he said, shaking the officer like a rag doll. "I swear. You leave him alone. I swear to you, I will kill you. You leave him alone!"

"What are you–" the officer said, his voice thick. He was just himself. Brantley was gone. Gregory dropped him, and he fell the rest of the way to the table, where he remained.

He ran past the officer to the empty hall. The smell was back; and most of the people in the room were under someone else's control. He saw them look at him. Then, they all abandoned their tasks and started toward him. "Fuck," Gregory said.

Whoever was controlling them didn't have the fine muscle control. It wasn't Brantley, then. He bolted for the stairs, hoping they couldn't manage them as well. The parking garage was the bottom three levels. Jamie wasn't in the first or second one – or at least from the stairs he couldn't see her on either of the half levels the staircase spanned. He found her on the third, staring dumbly at her key.

She was the farthest away; maybe the control over her wasn't complete. She saw him, and something went off in her brain, but she didn't take more than a step toward him. Gregory slapped her, hard, throwing her against the hood of the car, and when she straightened, the glassy-eyed look was still there. Stronger. He closed his eyes and backhanded her again.

"Ow! Damn it! Stop that!" Jamie howled at him, and the look in her eye was just one of anger. "Where the hell am I?"

"In the parking garage. They sent you on a wild goose chase. The water in the cooler, it's not good."

It was a lousy explanation of what was happening, but Chris must have told her something was wrong, because she only nodded.

"Can you drive?" Jamie asked.

Gregory nodded. She gave over her keys. "You have to come," he said.

She shook her head. "I drank that water. If he…" She didn't have the words for being put back under Brantley's control, but she must have known what it was like. "The control won't last forever," Gregory said. "Just get out of here. You couldn't have drunk that much."

She nodded, but not at his words. It made her shake her head violently enough that spittle flew, and she stood back. "Just go. But dump the car; they'll be looking for it."

"Grab him," someone from the railing cried. "Don't just stand there!"

Gregory slid into the driver's seat just as the elevator doors opened and Chris's colleagues spilled out. They yelled for the attendant at the parking lot to lower the barrier. But the attendant hadn't had any water at all, and wasn't in the control of anyone. Chris drove past her, and pulled onto the eastbound traffic lane without even looking to see if anyone was coming. No one was, which was good; it would have made his Great Escape rather short-lived.

Gregory wondered if Brantley could control his people to drive a car. He wasn't followed at any rate.

Gregory abandoned Jamie's car at a bus stop, but not before memorizing her house address from the registration papers. He felt Brantley's presence in over half the people he saw on the street. He would have needed an enormous power to be everywhere at once. Just as Gregory felt cornered, he crawled into a sewer entrance pipe. There were bars, but not until a foot or so into the pipe. It gave him enough space to hide from the dying day.

He felt nothing more from Chris, it was like the door between them had slammed shut. *He couldn't be dead.* But the door didn't budge, and he couldn't escape the fear that it might feel exactly that way if one of them were gone. He shook his head, not letting himself follow the line of thought. He'd wait out the day, then he'd go get Jamie. If she could help, he'd take her with him. If she couldn't help, he'd go by himself. Whichever option it was, it was going to end, and end by morning.

He closed his eyes. Sleep escaped him, but at least he managed to avoid overthinking any more until the sun set. Once the sun set, the only light in the sky was reflection from the eastern clouds, Gregory crawled out. This pipe overlooked a flood plain and the ground was dry and cracked. As the harsh light died, however, the first signs of life – rodents and insects – crept out. The little remaining light revealed everything in shades of amber and indigo, and Gregory still saw the light reflecting from their eyes, even the cold black ones of the bugs.

Brantley was getting stronger – but then again, so was Gregory.

Jamie didn't look surprised to see him, even after he approached her backyard in darkness. He scratched his nails against the glass rather than knocking properly and she didn't turn on the porch light. She opened the door and he slid into her house.

"Where's Chris?" Jamie demanded. She had changed into sweats and had pulled her hair back into a ponytail with a scrunchy that was twenty years out of fashion. But her face was hard. Not that she was angry with him, but it was obvious that she was worried and wanted to hide it. "I know you know. Where is he?"

"Jones has him."

"The evangelist?"

Gregory nodded.

"How do you know Jones?"

"Biblically," Gregory said, and he laughed. It was barely this side of hysterical so he clapped his hands over his mouth. "I'm sorry. I was his toy for years. He has Chris. You have to do something."

"There's really nothing I can do," Jamie said, and the party line she was toeing was obviously heavy. She shook her head. "What would a famous man like Jones want with someone like Chris?" she asked.

"I don't know. He has a great ass? I wanted him first? Mercury in retrograde? He has him, and no one is doing anything about it."

"Would you like us to storm the Bastille?" she asked.

Gregory didn't smile. She threw up her hands. "I need to bring the captain in on this."

"You can't," Gregory said.

"I don't have the authority…"

"Your captain paired the two of them together," Gregory said patiently. "Didn't it strike you as a bit strange? Chris knew it. He tried to tell you."

"I can't just knock on the door and ask them to just give him over."

Gregory crossed his arms over his chest. "You have to do something."

"I'll try," Jamie said. "But honestly, my hands are tied."

Gregory looked back down to his own wrists and remembered the feeling of metal on them. "Mine, too," he said, "but that's never stopped me before."

# CHAPTER SEVENTEEN

Chris woke, strapped down to a table. For a heartbeat, he could explain everything away. He'd fallen asleep; his face had been bitten by an insect. But then he felt the needle digging into his flesh again. He opened his eyes. Someone was working on a cut on his cheek. Jones was watching him, from the doorway of the room. Even though he couldn't see Niles, Chris felt him watching, too.

"Do a good job. I don't want any scars," Jones said and came over to the bed. "Do we understand each other?"

"Yes, sir," the doctor said. He irrigated the wounds more. "That shouldn't be a problem."

"What are you doing?" Chris demanded. "You can't possibly expect that you can just keep me here."

"But I do," Jones said. "And you're not exactly in a position to argue the point."

Jones stroked Chris's hair. Each touch of his flesh made Chris flinch. Brantley must have known how much the contact hurt, because he kept his thumb firmly pressed against Chris's forehead. "Look away," Jones whispered. "Look away and I'll stop."

The pain amplified second by second. Chris's eyes watered and his fists balled up. If Brantley had dropped liquid fire onto his forehead, it would have hurt less. It seemed such a simple thing, to just look away. His nails dug farther into the balls of his hands, but he refused to look away from Brantley's gray eyes.

"Look away," Brantley snarled. "It's such a little thing. Look away."

"Fuck yourself," Chris said. He made himself not flinch. It seemed Jones was burning a hole through his skull, and he started to feel himself slip back under. He would've welcomed the dark, thick blanket, but Jones snarled in disgust and let go. Chris laughed, suddenly finding the whole thing uproariously funny. Then the dark blanket found him, regardless. Sleep was good.

Chris came back again in a dark room. His hands were up over his head and the shackles were fleece lined. A strap of some sort pinned him down across the chest. It was too tight, and it constricted his breathing. His legs were shackled spread eagle and he was naked, of course. The room was dark and warm enough that it wasn't uncomfortable, but he still felt exposed.

The room didn't seem to have a door; there were no light spots on the ground, no air moving, and no sound. He finished looking around and put his head back down again, hard, against the plush bed he was on.

The light came on, banishing the darkness and flooding the room with pure white. Chris's eyes felt as though they'd just been stabbed.

Of course it was Jones, and Niles followed like a well-trained pup right behind him. The young man, Billy, was behind Niles, with an uncomfortable look on his face. He scoped out the room from wall to wall, floor to ceiling before taking his place by the door. Brantley moved as though the young man had a tether around his throat, but Niles was oblivious to the changing of the guard. Jones smiled and looked down Chris's body, obviously lingering on his cock. Chris knew he was supposed to feel ashamed for being naked, but he ignored Jones's gaze.

"Is there any point in me telling you how many laws you are breaking right now?" Chris asked.

"Not really," Jones said. "Is there any point in telling you there are a dozen places within a mile of the compound that make an excellent – what do you call it – body dump?"

"You're not going to kill me," Chris said.

"You're sure of that?" Jones asked.

"You would have programmed your puppet to use the knife if you'd wanted me simply dead." Chris opened his mouth, testing the stitches on his cheek. "And you wouldn't have bothered to stitch me up so pretty."

Jones smiled. "I suppose that's true enough." He put his hand over Chris's left ankle. The contact didn't hurt.

Chris closed his eyes. "Don't —" he said, but he swallowed rather than continue.

"Don't what?" Jones asked mockingly. He moved his hand up, to the inside of Chris's calf. If Chris could have slammed his legs shut, he would have.

Chris opened his eyes again. "I will kill you," he said, voice flat. "Do this, and I will kill you."

Jones stopped his hand just shy of Chris's knee. He was about to say something else, when Niles interrupted him. "Brantley, stop this. You don't need to…sully yourself with him."

Chris fought with every ounce of control he had not to give Jones the satisfaction of feeling him flinch.

"This isn't about sullying," Jones said, and he smiled down at Chris. He looked back up to Niles. "Come here. I want to show you something."

"At least cover up his nudity," Niles said, but he stepped into the room.

Chris, for the first time, flushed and looked away. Jones tsked. "There is nothing shameful about looking down at the nude body of your inferior."

Niles still wouldn't look at Chris. And Chris couldn't look away from his face. He willed Niles just to turn around and go. Niles was a hateful little man, but he wasn't a rapist. Niles stopped himself and went to the table instead. "Niles," Chris began, but realized using Niles's last name wasn't going to make a dent here. "Jack, please," he tried again. Niles's hand came down, just at the lowest point of Chris's thigh.

Chris twisted away as much as he could with the strap across his chest. "Jack," Chris said again, the words twisting free from him. He squeezed his eyes shut and refused to open them again. The moment he said the words, something changed. Chris felt it. He could convince himself that he was not afraid of Jones and would have believed it; but the moment he begged, something had changed. He'd given power over to Jones, and Jones knew it. There was no more need for false bravado or even emptier threats.

And Jones knew it, too. "That wasn't so hard, was it?" He asked.

"Is this how it begins?" Chris asked. His eyes were still closed, and he preferred it to the light.

"For some," Jones said, and Chris could feel him smile. "What are you afraid of? I am not going to take what you are not willing to offer. Not yet. But rest assured, you will offer it to me."

"I would rather die," Chris said, and he hoped that was still true.

"Let's just see about that." Jones stroked the length of his arm, from his shoulder to his wrists, and Chris expected the stinging bite that even the fleece-lined cuffs couldn't protect him from, but somehow Brantley and undid the cuffs without pinching. Chris didn't think that was possible.

Brantley still watched him, with the same amused look on his face, but didn't stop Chris from undoing the strap over his chest. He sat up, still tied to the bed but unwilling to untie his feet while Brantley looked at him. He couldn't help the fact he was asking permission to undo them, but he was, and Brantley nodded and Chris found himself bending over, exposing his neck and back to Brantley while he struggled with numb fingers to release his feet.

"Did Gregory tell you what he is, or what I am, or what this place does to us?" Brantley asked, walking around the bed. He had done something to Chris, something Chris did not understand entirely. He felt as though he were twelve feet underwater and no longer knew which way was up. He was in better condition than both of them and could easily have taken them on together or separately – and yet for some reason he was actually…afraid…of getting off the bed in front of Jones.

"He didn't tell me anything," Chris said. "I didn't even think he understood it, himself."

"Oh, he understood it." Jones's smile died. Chris heard it in his words. "Our little toy understood everything. And I need him back. You are going to bring him back for me."

Chris felt himself shake his head. "He won't come. He's smarter than that."

Brantley scratched a long fingernail over Chris's chest, down his stomach, and just barely through the light hair on Chris's lower belly. "You don't think he won't charge in here on a white horse to rescue his Prince Charming?"

"You are deranged."

Brantley smacked Chris's flank, as though he were disobedient puppy then leaned in close, close enough that Chris felt his lips just barely touch in his earlobe. "Listen to me well, because I'm only going to say this once. I find you attractive, and would not mind if you made the right choice and joined me. You are correct in assuming I find your face pleasing. But if you speak to me like that again, I will slice off everything there is of you to slice off. Do we have an understanding?"

The worst part was that Brantley's voice was so calm, so soothing throughout the entire threat. Chris believed him, and suddenly was more afraid at that moment than he ever was spread eagle on the bed. Not letting that show on his face was the hardest thing he'd ever had to do. He didn't trust his voice to be there when he opened his mouth so instead he nodded and drew his knees up to his chin.

Brantley patted him on the head, and motioned Niles to follow him out.

□ □ □ □ □

They didn't abandon Chris forever, though to Chris it sure felt as though they had. He couldn't bear to still be on the bed, but rather took up a position in a corner as far away from the far wall as he could, though it made him closer to the bed. It was different on this side of the dream, but he didn't have to be told that the spring was here, just on the other side of the wall, and he could feel the things Gregory had fought against moving behind the wall.

When the door opened again, Chris was almost glad. But it wasn't Jones or Niles. Instead it was the other one.

"Who are you?" Chris asked.

"I suppose that depends," the blond said with a smile. "I'm not who I once was, but for the sake of a name, you can still call me Billy."

He put the tray he was carrying onto the bed and turned to Chris. "I'll see if I can get you a blanket if it gets much colder."

"You know, this makes you an accessory." Chris didn't move from his corner. The white light was all around, and even through the wall he felt the things retreat. That made it better. He felt safer. Even though he knew it was a false sense of security, he still needed it.

The young man laughed. "Do you truly believe that being an accessory even registers for me?"

"It should," Chris said. "Think about the future."

"And you think with that I'm going to let you walk out of here?"

"If you were smart," Chris said, and he pulled himself to his feet. The young man looked him over again, but Chris pretended not to see.

"This isn't a movie, officer. When Brantley comes for you, you will go with him. Maybe not the first time, maybe not the second. But you will crave his touch. I've already decided that I am going to allow it. You are going to be his final test."

Chris walked to the door. "There is no way that is going to happen." He rattled the door. "Do you hear me?"

The young man came up behind him and touched his shoulder. It was such a light touch Chris almost didn't feel it, yet it still calmed him. Still, he laughed at Chris, and although Chris barely heard it, he felt it as a puff of expelled air on his shoulder.

"Test for what?" he asked, finally. "I think it's pretty clear he could fuck me if he wanted to."

Billy smiled. "Of course. I want to see if he could fuck you and then kill you, officer. He's been using the gift that I gave him and squandering it solely on his personal gain. That, to me, is unacceptable. He has to serve me, as well."

"And what are you?" Chris asked, his voice flat.

"Do you really want to know?"

Chris didn't. And he was already mostly sure. Billy was the spring, the thing that made the preacher kill in the first place.

"It didn't start there," Billy said. "Brothers have been murdering brothers, children parents, lovers each other on that spot for centuries. It didn't take much to open the rift between the white world and the dark, and I'm the dark."

"What do you want with me? With Gregory?"

"You, nothing," Billy said. He ran his nails along Chris's legs. "If Brantley can't kill you, of course. Gregory will die. I've promised it to all my followers. Your lover boy has slain more than a couple of their brethren, and they demand his blood. But if you're still alive, you'll be free to go."

Chris swallowed. "No."

"No?" Billy asked, amused. "What do you mean, no."

"Take me instead. Gregory loves me. You kill him, it's over for him. Kill me instead, and he'll have to live with the loss. Gregory's not afraid to die, his death will mean nothing to him. Mine will torture him. And that's what you want, right?"

"Do you usually assume you're going to get your own way, officer?"

"I'm offering alternatives. Gregory only acted in self-defense. Please."

"For a man who had never begged before, it sure comes quickly to your lips."

"No, it doesn't. But I'll do it, regardless."

Billy's hand moved up to the inside of Chris's thigh. "When you both fell into the cave, I thought I'd picked the stronger of the two. I see now I'd made the wrong decision."

Chris shuddered, remembering Brantley's screams.

"Yes," Billy hissed. "I'm sure you would have had no problem crossing the line between serving me and serving yourself."

Chris closed his eyes. "Let Gregory go," he said, and in the darkness the words came easily to him. "Let him go, and I will serve you. You want a final test? I'll cut Brantley's throat myself. Do you think I'd hesitate for a second? It's not too late to switch horses."

Billy said nothing. His hand was too hot on Chris's thigh. Hating himself, Chris spread his legs, offering himself to this thing who wore Billy like a suit. "You want me, you take me. But leave him alone."

"I don't think for a second that you would give yourself over willingly," Billy said, but his voice was thick.

"What does it matter? It serves your purpose either way."

Billy had him flat on his back, pinning his hands to the cold floor. "You'd let me fuck you right now, right here."

"Yes," Chris whispered.

Billy licked his way down Chris's cheek. "Tempting."

"Let go of my hands," Chris said. "I'll show you tempting."

Billy got off him, pulling himself up like someone had drawn his strings. "I will take it under advisement."

"The moment Gregory is hurt in any way, the deal's off the table," Chris said. "I swear to you. I'll kill you myself."

"Such strength," Billy said, and left Chris alone with his meal.

The food was unappealing. Chris ignored it and went back to his corner, where he tried to sleep. It wasn't a real sleep. He still felt the cold hard floor hurting his hips and shoulders, but he relaxed and, soon, a dream found him.

# CHAPTER EIGHTEEN

It wasn't like before. There was no rain, no sun. He was in a gray haze, thick enough that when he moved his hands the fog shifted. But it wasn't cold. It wasn't damp. It wasn't heavy. He could see it but felt nothing. That left him more freaked out than it should have.

"Don't be," Gregory said and stepped out of the grayness. He was real and solid and warm, and Chris found himself clinging to him when he didn't remember moving. "The fog will put you back together if you need it. But if you ever do need it, I will kill him."

There was so much Chris had to say, but he wasn't willing to pull away. Not yet at least. He didn't let go, not once Gregory felt so real right next to him. Nor did Gregory let him go. He held on just as tightly until the overwhelming need that focused Chris's world around Gregory finally started to crack.

When Chris could stand on his own again, Gregory looked him over and actually felt his arms and legs as though he were a horse. "Are you okay? Has he hurt you?"

Chris shook his head. "If anything, he provided excellent medical care," he tried to say, but the words didn't come.

It wasn't right, but Gregory pressed his fingers against Chris's lips. "You have to learn to talk again. I did it. You can too. Just be with me right now."

Chris realized he was shivering, though he didn't actually feel cold. It must have been release. Gregory brushed the hair from his forehead. "You should know he won't try to force you," he said and walked to the bed. So they were still in the room despite the grayness around them. Chris joined him. "No matter what his threats he can't force you. If the sex isn't willing, with anyone, what he wants to do with you will not work."

He found a sensitive part behind Chris's ear and began stroking it with his long, elegant fingers. "You just have to stay strong."

"How long did you last?" Chris asked. It was getting easier.

The fingers hesitated, but only for a second. "Oh, I rolled over the first time he asked," Gregory whispered. "But you're not like me. You can do this."

Chris shook his head. "Don't come, Gregory. Please."

"What are you saying?"

"I can do this. I can get to Brantley and take care of him. If you come, they'll kill you."

"If I don't, they'll kill you."

"Maybe not. But I'm not letting you risk it."

"You're not letting me risk it?" Gregory repeated. "For fuck sake, Chris, do you think I'm going to roll over and let them just…have you? You're mine, damn it, you gave yourself to me, and there is no way in hell that I'm going to just let someone else, anyone else, take you."

"Brantley's not in charge here. Billy is, and believe me when I say you can tell things have changed."

"I know. He tried to kill me. Brantley would never have tried to kill me. Not before I had the chance to beg for my life, at least. But you have to trust me. Please, Chris. You have to trust me."

Chris could do that. He closed his eyes and relaxed. "I can do that."

"But?" Gregory asked.

"How did you know there was a but?"

"There's always a but."

"You have to trust me too."

"Well, that's settled," Gregory said, but there was an unspoken promise in his voice too. Chris's mouth twitched.

□ □ □ □ □

He woke in the bedroom, but didn't think he was alone, not for a second. Brantley was with him, sitting on the foot of the bed. Chris didn't move from his corner. "What do you want?" he asked.

"Did you dream of him? Of my Gregory?"

"He's not yours."

"He was," Brantley sounded a lot farther away than just the bed. "Once."

"He hates you."

"Well, he should. But I still want him back."

Chris stood. He still didn't approach the back wall; he wasn't that brave. But there was still plenty of room to pace. "And how will you make him stay? You want him to want you, but he hates you."

"People like Gregory do a lot of things they don't want to do," Brantley said. "The trick is finding the right bargaining chip."

"Be smart, for once in your fucking life, you moron. Do you think that thing inside of Billy will let you have anyone or anything besides itself? When it demands your complete loyalty, that's it. You might as well get used to the fact you're going to be its cocksucker for as long as it chooses to have you."

"That's your opinion."

"Yes, that's my opinion. It's not too late for you, Brantley. Open your eyes. You have a multimillion dollar industry here. Walk away. Keep what you have. You don't want to invite that…thing into your life."

"You don't understand."

"What is there not to understand? It's evil, and you're just greedy. That leaves you in a pretty poor bargaining position."

"You left me down there."

"Where?" Chris demanded. "The hole? The hole that you dragged me into?"

"The preacher man was waiting for one us. It could just have easily been you. When he came for me, you weren't there."

"You can't possibly blame me for not waiting to stay around the teenager who wanted to hurt me. You wanted to hurt me, Brantley. I felt it from you in waves. You couldn't wait to get your hands around my throat." He leaned forward. "Is that how you got off, back then? You couldn't fuck the boys, so you beat them up instead?"

"Shut up about that."

"You started it. I left you there? You deserved everything that you got. How long have you been Billy's bitch? Did you even notice the rug being pulled out from under your knees?"

The self-pity died, leaving nothing but a weak, undirected anger. If Chris's plan was going to work, he needed Brantley a hell of a lot stronger than he was. "He'll give me everything I ask for," Brantley whispered. "If I follow him."

Chris went to the bed and backhanded Brantley has hard as he could. The room was still dark, but he could hear the wet sounds of his breathing. He aimed for the noise, knowing exactly when he made contact, and the follow-through was a beautiful thing. His body, here, liked hurting people. The room made him stronger, he felt the power crackle the same time he heard something in Brantley snap, and he fell. "You really are that stupid! Do you know what you have to do to win him over?"

"Anything," Brantley whispered. Chris pulled Brantley back to him and backhanded him again.

"You have to kill me," Chris said, uncaring that he was tipping Billy's hand. A man like Brantley was the kind of man who could talk himself into almost anything, but doubted he could cross that line. "Did you hear me?"

There was another sniffling sound. "I could," he said. "If I wanted to."

"Bullshit," Chris snarled. "Maybe you could, if it was a matter of giving the order. Or even pushing a button from a different room. But that isn't going to be enough, and we both knew it. He'll want your hands around my throat. He'll want to feel you feel the life choking out of me. Do you know how much strength you're going to need to crush my trachea? Do you know how long you'll have to keep squeezing? Your hands will get tired. And I'm not going to make it easy for you."

"Why are you doing this? I didn't do anything to you!"

"You brought me here!" Chris said. "You demanded it." Brantley hadn't gotten up from the second slap, so Chris knelt over him. It took a second for him to find Brantley's hands. "So do it. Goddamn you, lazy bastard. You want something? You work for it. It'll even be easier in the dark. You won't see the eyes bulge or the tongue sticking out. Come on!"

"Leave me alone!" Brantley howled, pushing Chris away, just as the door opened and the light switched on. Chris had to cover his eyes, it hurt that badly, and Brantley started to sob. "This, this is your champion?" Chris demanded, getting off the bed. "Let me tell you how proud I am to be considered for his position."

"Shut up!" Brantley howled.

"Silence," Billy said. "You're trying to push me, Chris. I don't like being pushed."

With Billy in the same room, Brantley straightened. "Give me another chance," he said. Chris looked back to Billy, then to Brantley, and he saw much the same need he had for Gregory. But, his need for Gregory made Chris a whole person, Billy's and Brantley's mutual need detracted from them both, made them less. "He could have all the chances in the world, and you know he'll never be as strong as you need him to be," Chris said, and he wiped his forehead with the back of his hand. He knew he should be feeling tightness from his stitches. But his face had already healed, and the lines that had been open wounds were now no worse than insect bites. "You do what you have to do," Chris said. He took a long, shuddering breath. "You know my price."

Billy stiffened. "Visitors," he said, and Chris's face suddenly ached. Billy was summoning…things to him, and although he couldn't see them, they all came from the other side of the wall. "The only problem, Chris, is this. You're tying strings onto your unconditional loyalty, and that defeats the purpose. Brantley would never try to control this thing that we are. But don't worry, this will all be over soon."

Chris grabbed Billy's arm. "Let him go," he tried one more time. "No more strings. Just this one thing, and I'll be yours forever."

Chris heard a crash from the other side of the wall. Billy's creatures swarmed over Billy, ready for blood and the taste of meat. Chris only saw them out of the corner of his eyes, but that didn't stop Billy from scratching one under the chin or rubbing another's ears. There were no words – Chris doubted the beasts spoke in words – but the love was there. Billy took his shoulders, and although he hadn't seemed that much taller than Chris was, he now loomed over him by at least a foot. "You're already mine," Billy said, and he kissed Chris on the forehead. "I promise you that."

Chris remained still, just for a second. He swallowed. "May I…please see him?"

"Is that all you're asking for now?"

Chris swallowed. He couldn't believe he was about to say the words, but it was the only way. "I'm not asking."

Billy smiled a smile of pure victory. "Put him into the dark room. I'm sure his lover will be joining him soon." He turned to go but stopped, just as Brantley grabbed his arm. "I want you to know, as a favor to you from me, Gregory is not alone. There is a woman with him. I gift you with this: she will live."

Chris took Billy's wrist and almost dropped it. He was cold, as cold as spring water got on the coldest January night, and rather than feeling a pulse, he only felt the current running just under Billy's skin. Unlike Donna or poor David, there was nothing left inside Billy at all.

"Thank you," Chris said. Words weren't strong enough to express the sudden overwhelming gratitude he felt, but they would have to do. Billy nodded distractedly, and went back up the stairs.

"When it's time, I'll do it," Brantley told him.

"I'm glad," Chris said. He felt dead inside, and he wondered if it was how Richard felt. Or David. He could honestly say that if Billy offered the glass of water to him right now, he'd gulp it down if it meant ending the pain he was in. There were beasts all around him, horribly fanged and toothed, but they ignored him. He was meant for someone else, and they seemed to know that.

# CHAPTER NINETEEN

Gregory thought he was being so sneaky, when in fact even Chris could feel him approach, and he wasn't nearly as tied to the spring and its tendrils as Billy was. It was almost a letdown. Maybe on the other side, when Gregory had his knife, he would have had a chance.

Jamie's service revolver cracked half a dozen times, but there was nothing to shoot at. Not really. The black beasts wouldn't be real until their teeth were about to sink their teeth into the fleshy part of one of her thighs. She wouldn't reload in time. He expected…something. A snarl, or the smell of fresh blood, something to indicate that Billy hadn't kept his word, but no blood was spilled in the desert. Chris would have felt that. Instead, came the sound of a struggle.

Gregory fought where Chris couldn't, and it was only a matter of minutes after Billy had left the lower level that Gregory was thrust inside the room. It was pitch black. Chris couldn't have seen Gregory if he wanted to, but he wouldn't have traded the ability to touch him, to hold him, and to hear his heartbeat, as frantic as it was, against his chest.

"I told you to stay away," Chris said.

"And I told you there wasn't a chance of that ever happening," Gregory shot back.

"He's going to kill you, you know that." Chris didn't pause. "And that's entirely my fault."

Gregory was on the move. He prowled the edge of the wall. "Well, you're just going to have to live with that, aren't you?"

"Are you even going to kiss me?" Chris asked.

"Later for that," Gregory said, too shortly. He was sounding cross. The creatures avoided him, too, furious at being made to wait. But wait they did. Chris heard something, a sound that if he didn't know better he would have said was the sound of a large knife being pulled from a dirt floor. Gregory let out a relieved sigh, and the skin on the back of Chris's shoulders prickled. The sound was exactly what it seemed.

He opened his mouth, but Chris covered it with his own. "Later for that," Gregory repeated, and Chris followed Gregory's arm with his own hand and felt the blade. There were so many questions he had, but none of them mattered. "Chris?"

"Yes?"

"You're naked."

"Yeah. I am."

"Been naked long?"

"You could say that."

"Hm."

"Hm? That's all you have to say about your lover being molested by your crazy insane ex-master?"

"Okay, hm, and we'll have to use my pants. I hope they'll be long enough."

Even by touch, Chris knew nothing looked more like a wrapped up giant knife than a wrapped up giant knife. Chris brought Gregory back to him. "This is the room he put you in."

Gregory nodded, carefully. Chris couldn't see it, but he could feel it. All joking was finished, the time for it had come and gone. He felt Gregory shiver, and kissing him didn't take away the bite of fear he tasted in Gregory's lips. "Don't blame yourself, Chris."

"How can I possibly not?" Chris whispered.

"I had to come. I had to be here. How could I possibly have gotten the knife if I hadn't? I'm supposed to be here."

"He's not kidding. He will kill you. Think those beasts are…his children."

"Then I'm only sad I didn't kill more of them," Gregory said.

"I may be able to get you out, still."

Gregory snorted. Chris wanted to say something, argue the point, but his points of logic fell at his feet, and it left him with nothing. "When are you going to realize that we're in this together?" Gregory asked. "The room is soundproof, courtesy of our friend Brantley. But I'm sure he's waiting for the two of us to have sex."

"You're kidding, right?"

Gregory was looking at him intently. Chris felt it strong enough that the hair on the back of his neck stood up. "It's the only language something as ancient and elemental truly understands. He let Jamie go, brought me here, so we know he likes you. We'll have sex where you'll fuck me as the dominant one, then he'll haul us out and try to make one of us kill the other. Then he'll probably have to kill the victor, because I don't think Brantley could kill you bare-handed."

"And that doesn't bother you? Not at all?"

Gregory kissed him. "I'm sure we'll try to put a monkey in his works," Gregory said. "But you forget, I was brought here for the purpose. I know that now."

"And that's it?"

Gregory kissed him. "He's not human," Chris said. "He knows nothing of equality. Nothing about trust, or how much I love you, or how much I trust that you are severely going to fuck him over. Now, have sex with me. He'll think it will only weaken you, but we both know that's not true."

Chris didn't think he physically could, but there was so much adrenaline in his system when Gregory dropped to his knees in front of him, his erection was almost psychosomatic. Gregory, with his mouth full, could only growl his approval. Gregory put him down flat on his back. He'd already stripped off, and the feeling of his naked skin on Chris's was almost worth everything that had led up to that second.

Chris reached out, glad that he'd taken the time to map out Gregory's body. He only had to touch the pectoral muscle and know where his sensitive nipples were. He couldn't kiss them, not with Gregory holding him down, but it let him caress them before moving down. He got to the sensitive spot between Gregory's hip bone and his cock when reality set in. "I don't have a condom," he said.

Gregory's shoulders slumped. Chris knew it without seeing it. "Brantley always kept his toys' health impeccable," he said. "And there's really been no one else, since."

Chris closed his eyes, even in the dark. He could see it; they would have been inconsequential back alley meetings where not even names were exchanged over layers of clothes and silence.

Chris didn't think Gregory would have trusted anyone naked, being pushed down.

"And you?" Gregory asked. He was less than an inch away from Chris's cock, and when he shifted his hips, it pulled a groan from Chris's lips.

"No one," he said. Not unprotected, at least. It had always been his philosophy to assume every partner could possibly be infected and he'd always acted accordingly. "And bi-annual check-ups to back it up."

"Chris?"

"Yes?" Chris asked. The mood had shifted again, the slice of their other reality, as unreal as the beasts were in the waking world, was enormously sobering.

"Will you fuck me, Chris? Please?"

"I can do that." The words were heavy, even without Gregory's hands on his chest.

Gregory got off him. "But will you?"

Chris found him again in the dark and they kissed again. Parted lips, hot tongue, Gregory's breath whistling past his ear when he broke away. "I will."

"Slowly," Gregory whispered. He kissed Chris's clavicle, just above his left nipple, his flat stomach. He lingered there, just for a second, then continued his way down. The dark room was unnaturally warm, but he hadn't realized how cold his cock was until Gregory engulfed it.

Spit was a lousy lube, but Chris took his time. He sucked on his fingers, found Gregory, and traced the line of his back to his tailbone, then below. The ring of muscle was tight, but Gregory relaxed and gave way to just his finger. Chris's entire body shuddered as Gregory found the perfect angle. "Careful," he warned.

Gregory stopped. Chris slipped his second finger inside, slowly, just like Gregory had wanted. He worked his fingers in and out, reducing Gregory to needy sounds from the back of his throat. "Careful yourself, Chris," he whispered.

"I guess that means we're ready," Chris said.

"I guess it does. You've never not used a condom? Not even your first time?"

"My first time I used two," Chris said. Something told him not to ask Gregory about his first time. If he saw Gregory in an alley, Chris also saw him in his bed, posters of favorite sport teams on the wall, and a huge, heavy hand that covered half Gregory's face to muffle the sounds he was going to make.

"Come on, Chris. Evaporation's your enemy." His voice was too forced to be light. He knew what Chris was thinking about. "I'm here, now. Please."

Chris pushed inside. Gregory gasped, hiding his face in his arms, and involuntarily he clamped down. Chris worked the muscles on the small of Gregory's back with his thumbs, relaxing him as best he could. "Say the word, I'll stop."

"No," Gregory said. "No. Go on. I need this."

Chris used more saliva and didn't stop until he was all the way inside. Gregory's legs trembled. He didn't move from where his head was still against the floor, but he took a long, shuddering sigh. "Better," he said finally. "Yes. Better. Please."

Chris didn't say anything, just withdrew enough to thrust again. It was different without a condom. He felt Gregory around him in a way he'd never felt anyone before. Gregory laughed, a rich, earthy sound, and moved against him. "You're afraid."

"I don't want to hurt you," Chris said.

Another laugh. "You can't. Not here. Not anymore. I promise."

Chris braced himself, pulling Gregory back toward him, and he was right. What had been tight and burning was now slick. A minor miracle, turning spit into proper lubrication, but one that Chris was willing and able to accept. Gregory shivered and put his head down. "At least someone is looking after us," Chris said.

Gregory twitched. "We're looking after ourselves," he said. "We have every bit as much of a right to be here as they do."

It was an odd thing to say. Chris grabbed onto Gregory again, feeling the amazing thrill of being inside Gregory, of being here, of the primal act of thrusting, feeling Gregory giving him the gift of receiving. It was a beautiful thing in any environment. The darkness stopped being threatening and allowed him to react purely to Gregory's instinct with his own.

This was their spring, too. Gregory started with his sounds again, softly at first, then louder until the dirt walls couldn't absorb the sound any more.

Chris couldn't thrust fast enough to keep up with the need that rode him. Gregory took it and begged for more. They were running out of time; Billy would want to finish this, but rather than that thought killing the mood, it heightened Chris's desire. Billy thought it would weaken him; instead, it strengthened his resolve. Before the best he could have hoped for was that his offer be taken and that Gregory go free. Now, he wanted it all.

"Yes," Gregory hissed. "Now."

And Chris was flying. The orgasm ripped through him, shattering him into a thousand sharp pieces, then put him back together again, more complete. Gregory was inside him, he was inside Gregory, and there was nothing that could possibly stop them.

The darkness returned, slowly as they came back to themselves. Chris felt the restrictions inside his skin again, but at any time he could reach out and touch Gregory, and Gregory responded. He was sore; Chris felt the burning muscles as though they were his own, but it was a welcomed strumming of nerves. It left him open, and as long as he concentrated on the low grade muscle ache, he could hear pulse all around them. It wasn't theirs, that he knew. Theirs were in matching staccato beats that he still felt in the roof of his mouth. This one was slower, older, but just as pleased with himself.

"Leave the blade here," Chris whispered, and then climbed to his feet. "We're going to get through this."

"Promise me," Gregory said.

"I promise. We're going to get through this."

Gregory nodded, and joined him standing. Chris walked to where the door was. He knew where it was like he would know where the holes in a skull would go. He banged on the door with his fist, twice, and the door swung open.

There was light. Just dull candles that smelled of burning tallow. Chris had never smelled it before, but he recognized it here. Brantley was the one who had opened the door for them, but his face was blank. Billy was naked like they were, and he was taller still. His head almost touched the top of the door frame, and his enormous penis looked like part of a fertility statue. It was engorged, and he stroked it not for arousal's sake, but from boredom. This build up was nothing to him.

Chris almost missed Niles in the corner. He was still alive, or at least he blinked his eyes regularly and he breathed. But Niles was gone. Something had to have fueled Billy's quick growth, and Chris suddenly knew why they'd been afforded all the time they had. "Why not just kill the body?" he asked. "I thought you were good at that."

"The energy lasts longer," Brantley said, but he spoke flatly, like he'd been compelled.

"This is what is going to happen," Billy said. "I find you intriguing, Chris. I would like to taste your insides. If not tonight, then eventually. I'm giving you that chance to be my eventual meal."

He snapped his fingers. The beasts emerged from the shadow, fangs and teeth visible, and they drove Chris away from Gregory. Gregory didn't move, even as the things climbed his legs, leaving violent red scratches on his pale skin, but he wasn't going to show Billy how much he was afraid.

Billy approached Gregory and smiled. "I've been waiting for you," he said. Chris had to relax his hands out of their fists. "Your boyfriend would do anything to save you. You know that, correct?"

Gregory nodded, but didn't move. One of the furry creatures scurried around his throat. At first Chris thought it was snake-like, then he felt the thousand little feet and the claws digging into Gregory's skin. "How many of my darlings did you kill?"

"I don't know," Gregory said. "A lot, I suppose."

"A lot. That is all you have to say?"

Chris wanted to step in to take the heat off, but Gregory shook his head, minutely. Chris respected his decision but didn't like it.

"They were trying to eat me." Gregory had to crane his neck back to look at Billy, but he did. He was doing the same thing Chris had done, trying to get Billy angry enough to act, but Billy wasn't falling for it.

"You are meat," Billy whispered. "You deserve nothing more."

Chris couldn't stop the sound he made, and suddenly all Billy's attention was on him. "And you," he said. He smelled Chris's hair. "You I do not know what to do with. I should kill you, but that would be too easy.

A beast scurried over Chris's foot, its claws sharper than lancets. "If I take you as mine, you know you will change, correct? You will hunger for what I hunger for, and consume what I wish."

Chris nodded.

"I am generous to my slaves, however, and give them what they desire. Weak ones like Jones make that too much work. But for you, for you I know exactly what you desire."

Billy looked at Gregory. "It is perfect. You will take him as my gift, and with my teeth in you he will hate your newfound tastes. And when you tire of his meager talents, you will willingly give him to my darlings." Billy learned in so close to Chris's ear he could smell the odor of rotten meat on his breath. "And when they feast on him, body and soul, you will fuck the new toy I give you to his screams."

Chris fought the revulsion. There was no way in hell that was going to ever happen. Still, he forced himself to smile. "If that is what it takes."

"Kill Brantley. When he is dead, you will invite me in, or I will tear the both of you apart. Do we understand each other completely?"

Chris nodded. Brantley tried to protest, but it was no longer about him or his will. He backed away, straight into the dark room as though he'd been party to their plan all along.

"What are you hoping for now?" Chris called, following him to the dark room. Gregory followed as well, and Billy didn't try to stop them. They were nothing but ants to him. Chris smiled, but only because he knew it would make his voice sound different. "Running isn't going to save you. I can smell you now, Jones."

And he could. The sour smell of fear might as well have colored the air around them a putrid yellow.

"Look, Chris, we can talk about this," Brantley began.

"We can," Chris agreed. "But you are going to find it difficult to keep up your half of the conversation as I'm choking the life from you."

"Officer Cunningham!" Jones managed. Chris had been sneaking up on him, slowly, and Brantley had no idea where Chris was until he felt Chris's hands on his throat. "There are several different ways to properly choke a man," Chris whispered. "Don't fight me on this."

"Please," Brantley managed.

"It feels different the first time you beg," Chris snarled, then leaned in close to his ear. "If you want any chance to survive this, Mr. Jones, stop fighting me."

Brantley squeaked like a mouse, but was rapidly running out of air. Chris resisted the urge to slack his fingers and help a man even as odious as Brantley Jones, but everything depended on his death. Chris turned his head away, glad for the total darkness so that he didn't have to see the frantic look in Brantley's eyes. His heartbeat was as frantic as that of a wounded sparrow, and Chris hated the fact he had to keep enough slack so that Brantley would stop breathing but not do any damage. It seemed like it took hours. Brantley finally stopped kicking, and he felt the single heartbeat in the room. It was stronger now.

"Now," Chris whispered. Gregory moved, in the darkness tilting Brantley's head back and pinching his nose. If Gregory couldn't bring him back…Chris stopped himself from thinking about it. The pulse from the wall was more localized now than it ever was before, but Chris knew Gregory would get time for only one stab.

Chris stepped back into the main room and cleared his mind. His eyes were as well adjusted to the darkness as any desert beast.

The furry creatures around Billy welcomed Chris, making a purring sound from throats that had only known how to growl, and it suddenly seemed right that Billy should give Gregory to him; he'd taken him away from his ex-master with his bare hands. "That's just the start," Billy said to him, though he wasn't using English. The words were the sound of water, and the foulness was welcoming. "Go, claim your prize."

Gregory was his prize. He would bite down on the back of Gregory's neck and force him to take his cock. That was only right. He deserved it. He–

Billy's howl shook the room. Chris felt Brantley take his first shuddering breath without Gregory's help the same time Billy did, and Chris bolted to find Gregory. The lack of light meant nothing to him, Gregory had found the blade and Chris found Gregory. They picked up the knife together. There was only one place in the wall that the sound of the heartbeat came from, and together they stabbed the blade all the way through the wall so that only the handle remained in this world. The flash of light was blinding, but Chris saw the blood spurting out of the wall before the darkness descended.

Billy's body fell over in the other room, and Brantley coughed. Together, they carried Brantley into the other room.

The alarm had been tripped by more than a dozen squad cars. Jamie hadn't taken that long at all to bring backup. Whatever Billy was, it was obviously too old to know of things like pulmonary resuscitation or cell phones.

# CHAPTER TWENTY

Niles blinked. "What the –" he began, then swore when he saw Chris and Gregory naked. Chris had forgotten all about his clothes. He found them neatly folded and stacked at the foot of the bed and told Gregory to get dressed.

"Mr. Jones, how are you feeling?" he asked.

"You tried to strangle me," he managed, with a voice that sounded like he had tried to swallow a cheese grater.

"I didn't try, sir. I strangled you. And you have every right to press charges, but I will tell the truth when they ask me what happened here."

"You wouldn't."

"I would. In a heartbeat," Chris whispered

"Let me speak with Gregory."

"I am telling you right now that that is just not going to happen."

Brantley spread his hands. "Believe me when I tell you that he is in no danger from me. Not anymore. You have won, I've lost, and I would still very much like it if he were to sign a nondisclosure agreement with me. I would be happy to pay him a settlement for his trouble."

Gregory looked up to where Chris was standing, as though he could hear what they were saying. Chris asked him if that would be all right, and Gregory gave a half-hearted shrug.

"Go ahead," Chris said. "But you hurt him, and I will kill you. Again. This time a hell of a lot more permanently."

Brantley touched his throat, where the ring of bruises was just now starting to bloom under his skin. He cleared his throat, a very painful sound, and Chris found himself wincing. "I mean this not as an admission of guilt, but I am sorry for what we did. It was always our intention to bring you back."

"I understand," Brantley said, and Chris saw in that instant that he did. "The two of you have nothing more to fear from me."

Chris nodded, though saw nothing in Brantley's future that brought him happiness. Sex would never be a joyous thing for him, and any relationship he might have would be a sham. It was a sad, sad life and one that Chris wouldn't have wished on anyone. Except for, perhaps, Niles.

Speaking of Niles, he was still crouched where Billy had put him. He was confused, but obviously not confused enough to forget how to glare. "What did you do?" Niles asked.

"We stopped an insane stalker from attacking a famous evangelist. I was quite brave, and you weren't so bad yourself, but it made you consider what was important in your life, and now you want to move to Wisconsin."

There must have been residual amounts of elemental magic about, because Niles only nodded. "I don't like cheese," he said in a small voice.

"Even better," Chris said.

He finally looked back to where Brantley and Gregory were talking, though they both didn't appear to be saying much at all. Gregory had his eyes down, but his shoulders were knotted, and when he shook his head, he did so furiously.

Chris went to them. Brantley was at the desk in the room, signing something, and he sealed it into an envelope. "There is a pretty airtight nondisclosure agreement included, contingent on you cashing the check. I hope you do cash it, Gregory. It was why I originally wanted to contact you before…before all this. I really did appreciate all your services as they were rendered."

"Fuck off," Gregory snarled.

"I won't ask for a handshake from either of you, and hope, for all our sakes that we never see each other again," Brantley said. "If you will excuse me, I have most of your coworkers on my lawn."

Chris and Gregory followed him up the stairs. Jamie ran up to Chris, throwing herself at him, and he barely stopped her momentum before they both came crashing down. "I thought we had lost you," she said.

"You had," Chris said. "But Gregory looked between the couch cushions, and there I was."

"Sorry the backup took so long; that thing touched me and I lost track as to why I was here."

"The deranged stalker had you separated from the civilian," Chris repeated. "I'm sure that was what you meant. We'll bring the time you arrived closer to make up for any lost."

Jamie shuddered. "That thing," she began, then hesitated. "It wasn't a stalker."

"No," Chris agreed. "But it's going to have to be on paper."

He glanced over to Gregory, who was holding onto the envelope and a leather paddle. "I'm going to take Gregory home. It will make sense now, but I'm sure there are going to be questions later. Can you hold this down?"

Jamie nodded. She even gave him her keys, something that she exchanged rueful looks with Gregory about, and he made a note to ask what had happened when he had been out of it.

"Where to?" Gregory asked.

"I thought we might go back to our place," Chris said guardedly. Now that he had Gregory he didn't want to let go. The sudden thought that perhaps Gregory wouldn't appreciate another long-term thing so soon scared him worse than anything that had happened in the dark room.

"You know, I'm not this great catch," Gregory said. "A guy like you can do much better than me."

"I have a father who has alcoholic dementia in a home somewhere. My mother won't tell me where, and most of the time when I'm speaking to her, I can't be arsed to ask. She spends most of her time throwing money at bubble-butt pool boys who break her heart, and I've got color-matched baggage in one of my closets over that. I'm out, I'm proud, and I've pretty much been in love with you since the first time you emerged from the fog. And if you try to interfere with my happily-ever-after, I think we're going to have to have words, because I – for one – think I deserve it." Chris had run out of air during the last sentence, but had pushed on regardless.

Gregory had said nothing throughout it all, and when he spoke, it was with carefully guarded words. "I see," he said.

"Damn right, you see," Chris put Jamie's car into gear.

"You might want to add the fact that you are a control freak and you don't have a reliable method of transportation if you're ever going to list your faults as you're pouring your heart out again," Gregory said mildly.

"Will I ever need to?" Chris asked.

"Not if I have anything to say in the matter, ever again."

Chris relaxed. "Well then."

"I think we settled that."

"Indeed."

If Chris was caught in any speed traps on the mad rush home, Jamie never told him.


The apartment looked different. The door wasn't locked, but in a secured building, that wasn't too much of a concern. But when Chris crossed the threshold, he did see that the home had been violated by angry men. He turned to look at the door frame, expecting to see splinters of wood from where they must have kicked down the door, but it was intact.

"I left it open," Gregory said. "One of them must have shut it behind them, because they sure didn't leave how I did."

"You jumped."

"Yes," Gregory led the way back out to the balcony. "I kinda had to. I had a very bad feeling."

Chris closed his eyes, trying to imagine what it must have felt standing on the railing, but he couldn't. His head swooned just past the point where Gregory had let go of the railing to stand up. "You don't have to imagine it, Chris, really."

"You didn't know it was going to work," Chris said instead.

"I knew you would believe that I wouldn't jump unless I thought it would work. And at that point, that was all I needed."

Chris looked over the city. There was another storm coming; this one would puzzle meteorologists for decades, but the city needed to wash away the last of the foul spring. The air crackled with static electricity, and the coming storm pulled the moisture from seemingly nowhere. But Chris felt the connection with the other world. "Can we go back?" he asked.

"I can't see why not," Gregory said. "Why wouldn't we?"

"I don't know," Chris said, but he just didn't know how to put it into words. In the books, when things like this happened, there was almost always a way that closed things between the worlds. He shrugged.

"Well, as the only expert here in stabbing evil springs with a huge honking knife that can cross dimensions, I assure you, we can still go back."

"Good to hear it," Chris said. Gregory came up behind him, putting his hands on Chris's hips.

"Can I fuck you out here?" Gregory whispered.

A wall of rain had fallen, covering half the city in darkness, but here, the evening light seemed brighter in the path of the storm. They still were touched by the spring, and Chris knew, even out in the open, even with any other of the other building occupants looking right at them, they still would not be able to see. "Yes," Chris said. "You can."

"Good," Gregory said. "I'll be right back. You can take off all your clothes if you want."

Chris wanted. Gregory returned with the bottle of lube, but no little foil package. "If that's all right," he said.

The wind touching Chris's bare shoulders should have been cold, but it was as warm as bath water. "It's all right," he said.

Gregory nodded, and took Chris's hand. The rocker felt strange on the back of his legs, but Chris completely forgot about it once Gregory knelt between his thighs. He put both his hands on Chris's knees, and waited. "You know I love you," Chris said.

Gregory nodded. "My name is Gregory Osborne," he said. "You don't have to go behind my back to do a search on it, I'm letting you do it without feeling guilty."

"What did you do?" Chris asked, with a sinking feeling inside him that was suddenly large enough to swallow the entire building.

"I stole my step-dad's truck and totaled it. There's a warrant out for me. I think there's a flag on my file that says to call him first if I'm ever picked up."

"That sounds like the very tail end of the story, Gregory."

Gregory looked up at him, his eyes suddenly dark. The ghosts of the bruises he'd carried were suddenly visible to Chris, and it was all he could do to remain sitting. Gregory needed him here just now. "You don't need me to tell you the beginning and middle, Chris. I'm sure you've heard it a thousand and nine times by now."

"It's just a warrant? Not a conviction?"

Gregory nodded.

"I'll take care of it."

"You don't—"

"I do. I'll take care of it. Now come here."

Chris's gran hadn't bought the swing for the care and ease of two adult men engaging in anal sex, but with some adjustments, they made it work. Chris had to slide down farther in the seat for Gregory to be able to crouch over him, and actually getting Chris's cock in resulted in both of them having to wipe the tears of laughter away, but that was good, too. The feeling of Gregory against his chest, helplessly caught in an unmanly giggle fit was as good for Chris as the feeling of warmth against his cock. Gregory reached behind him, bracing himself on Chris's thigh, and the look of absolute concentration on his face didn't slacken until Chris was all the way inside him.

"Good," Gregory decided, as though Chris had actually managed to ask a question. He opened his eyes, locking them with Chris's, and he bared his teeth. "You can put your hands on my hips, if you want."

"That's all the involvement I'm needed for?" Chris asked, but ran his hands down Gregory's sides before finding a good place for them on Gregory's hips.

"I'll tell you when you can come," Gregory said, and he moved up. His erection was against his belly, and Chris could feel the heat from it on his own stomach.

"You sure I couldn't take care of that for you?" Chris asked, raising an eyebrow.

Chris braced himself on the back of the seat, his body coiled like a spring. "I don't think you could," he said. "Stop bracing the swing with your feet."

Chris almost couldn't do it; he liked his legs braced when they were flat on an unmoving bed. It was hard, giving up control to the swing or to Gregory. The first time the swing moved he slammed his feet down, locking it in place. Gregory made a sound in the back his throat, but that was his only sign of disapproval. "You don't want to do this, say the word," Gregory said, and he began slowly fucking himself up and down over Chris's cock, the muscles in his thigh as hard as stone. "But you have to trust me."

Chris sighed, but lifted his feet up again. Gregory purred in his ear, then licked his way over the lobe. "Good boy," he said. "Close your eyes if you think it will help. I'll find something else to amuse myself."

Chris did, and the darkness did help. Gregory began moving the swing with the power of his legs alone. It only took a moment to build up the momentum needed, then the natural motion of Chris riding him was all the swing needed to maintain the rock for Chris to fuck him. "You're a genius," Chris whispered, eyes still closed.

"I've been called worse," Gregory said. Chris felt the strain in Gregory's arms as he used them to pull himself up and down, bucking against Chris's body in a tempo that Chris didn't think he could maintain, but he did. Without his feet down, Chris couldn't force himself up and inside Gregory, though he desperately wanted to. He was being used, in the best possible way, and it was an odd feeling, to just be able to selfishly worry about only his own pleasure. He held Gregory's hips, pulling him down just a quarter inch more, and then back off, but even that met with an angry hip twist. "Just let me, Chris."

"Sorry," Chris managed.

"Good. I'd hate to have to get you to put your hands over your head."

Chris shuddered at the thought. "Bastard," he hissed.

"Yes," Gregory agreed. He slid into the next gear, pumping him and the poor swing more than either was really meant to, and the frictionless fuck on all sides was almost too much for Chris. He had to let go or dig his fingers into the skin. Gregory's skin had become too slippery to hold, regardless.

And it wasn't just the sweat. The rain had come, washing away the evening's horrors. For how dark the clouds were the rain should have been needles against their flesh. It wasn't. Buckets of warm water fell on them. Gregory threw his head back and howled.

"Now," he managed, letting go of the back of the seat to grab Chris's head. "Do it now. Please!"

There was no way Chris could have stopped himself. He had to put his feet down, unable to come elsewise, and that froze the moment as much as it did the swing. Gregory suddenly needed him to hold him up, and he did, glad to take over. After all that he'd done, Gregory was as boneless as a rag doll, and Chris felt him come against both their bellies, without either of them touching him.

It took a few minutes for them to catch their breath. Chris stood, lifting both of them for that instant, then Gregory found his feet again. They slipped inside while the rain still obscured them because the last of the magic had slid off them with the rain. They showered together, and no matter how hot Chris could make the water, it still wasn't as warm as the rain had been.

They gave a great deal of gravity to the decision about who slept on which side of the bed, and then Chris was asleep with Gregory in his arms.

When Chris woke, Gregory was still dead asleep beside him. He turned off his alarm, kissed Gregory's bare shoulder, and got dressed silently. He took Jamie's car back, driving in the near dark. The streets had been blasted clean from the rain, and there was a green, living smell from the desert, though it was still months away from the rainy season. He let himself into the station, empty but for the skeleton crew on early mornings, and dropped Jamie's keys off at her desk.

IT must have done a mandatory reboot of all their computers during the night, because his took an extra long time to start up. He opened their Identichek program, and the hourglass told him to wait. When the search menu came up, he typed in Gregory's age, first and last name, and, a moment later, typed in Phoenix as home town. The hour glass came back up, turning slowly.

The record of the warrant was still active. Chris read the charges. It was clearly a domestic situation, and one that should have been handled through an insurance agency rather than through any legal channels. But Gregory's step-father was a cop. He wondered why Gregory hadn't mentioned it.

It was just a charge of reckless driving, and after seven years the statue of limitations would have nullified it regardless, but Chris knew that the fear Gregory had for going back had nothing to do with the charges and everything to do with being released back into his step-father's custody. He didn't think Gregory knew that once he became a legal adult, he could refuse to be released, but logic and fear never made good bedfellows.

He copied down the address, grabbed Jamie's keys again, and drove out as the sun crested over the desert.

There were lights on in the single story bungalow with its water saving landscaped lawn. He slammed the door and went up the walk. Someone must have been watching from the inside, because the door opened the second after Chris knocked. A young boy answered, as solemn as Gregory had been when Chris first met him in person, and the bad feeling inside Chris grew worse. The boy looked up, his huge green eyes already too wise, but he didn't let go of the safety of the doorknob. "Is your father home?" Chris asked.

The boy nodded.

"Tell him there's a police officer here to see him."

"My daddy's a police officer, too," the boy said, but he almost sounded glum about it.

"I know."

"Peter?" a man's voice called. Roger Gall looked older than he should have. He was a big man, with a big gut and salt and pepper hair. He was a sergeant, but still a beat cop. All that walking hadn't done him a bit of good, apparently. "What is it?"

"My name is Chris Cunningham," Chris said. No rank. This was a private matter. "I know your step-son."

A look of panic crossed his face so quickly that if Chris hadn't been waiting for it, he never would have seen it. "You found him," he said. "Tell that no-good—"

"No."

Roger jerked back, so unaccustomed to the sound of that word it temporarily left him speechless.

"No. I won't tell him anything from you. You are going to drop all charges, Mr. Gall. I'm telling you that right now. You're going to let Gregory go. Now."

"My truck was completely written off. He crashed it into a brick wall."

Chris grabbed Roger by the undershirt he wore and threw him against the door frame. "They didn't find any brake marks, you bastard. It was in broad daylight, and Gregory didn't even attempt to slow down. He wasn't trying to total your vehicle. He was trying to total himself, and it would have been entirely your fault. You will drop charges, and if there is even a whiff of you abusing any children in the house, I will make it my personal mission to destroy you."

"I would never–" Roger began, but he was already broken. Part of him seemed relieved, Chris felt, and that disgusted him even more. He dropped Roger where he stood, and wiped his hands off on his slacks. "Not my own kids," Roger finished, weakly.

"You better pray that's true," Chris said. "Or that Gregory doesn't want to involve himself in any trial, because that's still an option on the table."

"Tell him…" Roger looked down. "Would you tell him that I'm…sorry."

Chris was going to spit, but his cell phone rang. The display was unlisted, so he flipped open his phone. "Cunningham," he said.

"It's me," Gregory said. Of course Chris's own phone was unlisted. The darkness inside Chris lifted immediately.

"So it is," he said. Gregory's voice sounded thin. "Is something wrong?"

"I think you should come home," Gregory said.

"Gregory?"

"Just come home," Gregory said. Then, as an afterthought, "Please."

"Of course." He flipped the phone shut. "Are we clear here?" he said, but the dark need to hurt the man in front of him was gone. He felt only pity for Roger.

"Crystal," Roger said, but he didn't look up.

"Good," Chris said, and he went back to his car.

He was still driving against traffic on the way back to the condo, but he knew he'd be caught in the snarl on the return. He parked the car in his spot that he never used, and then took the elevator from the parking level. The door was still locked, there was no immediate sign of struggle in the main room, but Gregory was pacing back and forth around the small kitchen table as though he was tethered to it.

"What's wrong?" Chris asked.

Gregory looked up and the relief on his face was immediate. "You're here."

"Yes," Chris said. "What is it?"

Gregory pointed to the check that Brantley had signed over to him. Chris stared, unbelieving that that many zeroes fit in the small area meant for the dollar amount. "Ten million dollars," he said.

"Ten million," Gregory repeated. "Ten million dollars! Just…sitting there."

Chris picked up the letter accompanying the check. The fine print on the back seemed pretty airtight. If Gregory told anyone anything by any method known or not yet invented, the money had to be returned. Other than that, Brantley had made no demands on him. It was dated over six months ago, so maybe, in the beginning, before the madness had started, Brantley had tried to do the right thing.

"Do you…want it?" Chris asked.

"I…don't know," Gregory started pacing again.

"Do you want to sleep on it?" Chris asked.

"If by *sleep*, do you mean fuck like bunnies?" Gregory asked.

"I'm flexible about terminology."

"And I'm just flexible," Gregory said, and he smiled. "Okay."

"Okay?"

"Okay." Gregory said, and he kissed Chris on the cheek. "Bring the check. I'm feeling literal today."

# ABOUT THE AUTHOR

ANGELA FIDDLER lives with her wife in southern Alberta. She has four previous gay erotica vampire novels released through Loose Id, a novella in the Blood Claim anthology, and is working on several other pieces. She is always surprised her stories contain as little kneeling as they do.

Stimulate yourself.
READ.
www.manloveromance.com
THE HOTTEST M/M EROTIC AUTHORS & WEBSITES ON THE NET